The Moving Finger

An Ethel Thomas Detective Story

By Cortland FitzSimmons

Originally published in 1937

The Moving Finger

Published by Resurrected Press

This classic book was handcrafted by Resurrected Press. Resurrected Press is dedicated to bringing high quality classic books back to the readers who enjoy them. These are not scanned versions of the originals, but, rather, quality checked and edited books meant to be enjoyed!

Please visit ResurrectedPress.com to view our entire catalogue, and like us on Facebook at Facebook.com/ResurrectedPress to stay updated!

ISBN 13: 978-1-937022-93-8

Printed in the United States of America

Other Resurrected Press Books in *The Chief Inspector Pointer Mystery Series*

RESURRECTED PRESS CLASSIC MYSTERY CATALOGUE

Journeys into Mystery
Travel and Mystery in a More Elegant Time

The Edwardian Detectives
Literary Sleuths of the Edwardian Era

Gems of Mystery
Lost Jewels from a More Elegant Age

Anne Austin
One Drop of Blood
The Black Pigeon
Murder at Bridge

E. C. Bentley
Trent's Last Case: The Woman in Black

Ernest Bramah
Max Carrados Resurrected:
The Detective Stories of Max Carrados

Agatha Christie
The Secret Adversary
The Mysterious Affair at Styles

Octavus Roy Cohen
Midnight

Freeman Wills Croft
The Ponson Case
The Pit Prop Syndicate

The Uttermost Farthing: A Savant's Vendetta

Arthur Griffiths
The Passenger From Calais
The Rome Express

Fergus Hume
The Mystery of a Hansom Cab
The Green Mummy
The Silent House
The Secret Passage

Edgar Jepson
The Loudwater Mystery

A. E. W. Mason
At the Villa Rose

A. A. Milne
The Red House Mystery

Baroness Emma Orczy
The Old Man in the Corner

Edgar Allan Poe
The Detective Stories of Edgar Allan Poe

Arthur J. Rees
The Hampstead Mystery
The Shrieking Pit
The Hand In The Dark
The Moon Rock
The Mystery of the Downs

Mary Roberts Rinehart
Sight Unseen and The Confession

Dorothy L. Sayers

Whose Body?

Sir William Magnay
The Hunt Ball Mystery

Mabel and Paul Thorne
The Sheridan Road Mystery

Louis Tracy
The Strange Case of Mortimer Fenley
The Albert Gate Mystery
The Bartlett Mystery
The Postmaster's Daughter
The House of Peril
The Sandling Case: What Would You Have Done?

Charles Edmonds Walk
The Paternoster Ruby

John R. Watson
The Mystery of the Downs
The Hampstead Mystery

Edgar Wallace
The Daffodil Mystery
The Crimson Circle

Carolyn Wells
Vicky Van
The Man Who Fell Through the Earth
In the Onyx Lobby
Raspberry Jam
The Clue
The Room with the Tassels
The Vanishing of Betty Varian
The Mystery Girl
The White Alley
The Curved Blades

Anybody but Anne
The Bride of a Moment
Faulkner's Folly
The Diamond Pin
The Gold Bag
The Mystery of the Sycamore
The Come Back

Raoul Whitfield
Death in a Bowl

And much more!
Visit ResurrectedPress.com
for our complete catalogue

LIKE us on Facebook for upcoming release
announcements!

Facebook.com/ResurrectedPress

FOREWORD

Cortland Fitzsimmons was best known for a series of mystery novels involving sports and other forms of popular culture. It was his novel *70,000 Witnesses: a Football Mystery,* that brought his talents to the attention of Hollywood when the novel was made into a film. This was followed several years later by *Death on the Diamond: A Baseball Mystery* which was also made into a movie. Other mysteries involved professional ice hockey, a dance band, and a stage magician. These mysteries were well written, fast paced, and entertaining, and one suspects, at least after the success of *70,000 Witnesses,* were written with the potential for adapting them to film in mind.

As successful and popular as these mysteries were, Fitzsimmons' best work as a mystery writer may be the several mysteries involving Ethel Thomas. It's hard to imagine a more unlikely detective. A seventy-five year old spinster at the time of the first mystery in which she figures, *The Whispering Window,* Thomas is a wealthy, unconventional member of New York's social elite. With the exception that she seems to know everything about everyone that matters, she bears almost no resemblance to that other famous female sleuth, Agatha Christie's Jane Marple. Whereas the latter confined most of her activities to a small English village, Thomas occupies a much larger village, the island of Manhattan. And rather than being prim and fussy, Thomas is not adverse to the occasional cocktail or whiskey and soda and fully enjoys an active social life with her many friends of a much younger age.

Considering that she was born about the time of the

Civil War, Ethel Thomas has adapted remarkably well to the twentieth century. Telephones and radios no longer amaze her, she takes automobiles and airplanes in stride, and she has reveled in the changing fashions. A woman who was at her prime during the "Gay Nineties," she has made herself at home amidst the jazz and cocktail parties of the "Roaring Twenties" and the "Thirties." Shrewdness as a businesswoman has allowed her to weather the Depression with only minor concessions. And through it all she has kept her sense of humor and proclivity for making wry observations about the world around her.

This then, is the woman that Terry Lassimon, one of the younger men with which she seems to surround herself, comes to when he comes into possession of a set of diaries that contain potentially embarrassing and possibly incriminating details of secrets affecting some of New York's social elite. The fact that he is nearly murdered on her doorstep only arouses her interest, and the two involve themselves in a tangle of blackmail, intrigue and murder as they try to determine which of the people mentioned in the diaries is responsible for the mayhem that ensues. Despite the light tone, there is a seriousness that is missing from Fitzsimmons' other works.

During the dozen or so years that mark his career, Cortland Fitzsimmons was both a successful author and screenwriter with over a dozen novels and as many movie scripts to his credit, including at least four film adaptations of his own novels. Yet today, he is relatively unknown It is therefore with great pleasure that Resurrected Press offers this new edition of *The Moving Finger*.

About the Cover
The cover of this edition incorporates re-worked elements of the original dust jacket used on the first edition of this book, published in 1937.

The cover of this book contains a re-worked portion of the original dust jacket for the first edition of the book, published in 1934.

About the Author

Cortland Fitzsimmons was born in Brooklyn, New York (possibly Queens) on June 19, 1893 and died July 25, 1949 in Los Angeles, California. After attending New York University and The City College of New York, he worked for some time as a salesman for several book distributors and publishers before turning to writing full time in 1934. Most of his works as a writer were mysteries, a number of which were based on sports themes such as *70,000 Witnesses: A Football Mystery*, *Crimson Ice: A Hockey Mystery*, and *Death on a Diamond: A Baseball Mystery*. A number of his novels were made into films and he moved to Los Angeles to work as a screenwriter. His last book was a cookbook that he co-wrote with his wife Muriel Simpson *You Can Cook If You Can Read*.

Greg Fowlkes
Editor-In-Chief
Resurrected Press
www.ResurrectedPress.com
Facebook.com/ResurrectedPress

The moving finger writes: and, having writ,
Moves on: nor all thy piety nor wit
Shall lure it back to cancel half a line
Nor all thy tears wash out a word of it

CHAPTER ONE

It is difficult to say just when a particular adventure begins but my activities started the moment I received Beth Doane's cable asking me to sponsor Althea Madison when she arrived in America. Knowing something of her story I was interested in her long-delayed arrival in the United States. I expected my contact with her to be mildly amusing, but contrary to preconceived ideas I found myself involved in a series of baffling murders with this unknown girl.

It was early July and unbearably hot. I was in no mood for a party, but having a sense of obligation to Beth and feeling sorry for this girl who was returning to her native land a stranger, I did the best I could with the material at hand. Immediately, I began calling the few people who either by accident or choice happened to be in New York. Had it been in the season, I'd have planned a reception for her instead of a cocktail party. As it was, I didn't want the poor child roaming about New York alone, depending on an old woman for her sole entertainment.

I reckoned without the girl however because I've never known any one more capable of taking care of herself. I went down to meet her when she docked. She looked and acted like a lady, but that didn't surprise me, because she came of good stock and if family and breeding mean anything the girl had had a good start. She had poise and dignity that was neither cold nor repelling. She was cordially grateful for my attentiveness and said so, but she refused to make my house her headquarters, preferring to go to the Macon-Astoria.

She was a dark and lovely child. I couldn't restrain the impulse to kiss her as we parted. If she was surprised, she didn't show it. As a matter of fact, I think she clung hungrily to my hand for a moment but that may have been pure imagination.

I'm so old myself that I think all people under fifty mere children. Althea was twenty-seven or eight. I'm not quite sure because she was born abroad. She had had a very unusual life. Her father and mother were married in Paris after Herbert Madison had followed Elsie Stewart halfway round the globe. They stayed on in Europe after the wedding until Althea was born.

When business finally brought them home, they came without the baby. If I thought about it at all, I suppose I thought of Elsie as the first of the modern mothers. The child was never brought to America. Elsie Madison made repeated trips to see her baby but there was always some reason, so she said, why it did not seem wise to bring her home.

Althea was in a French convent when the War broke out. I can remember Elsie Madison's tearful frenzy at the time. Somehow she managed to have Althea moved to England (Herbert had very powerful connections) where the child would be comparatively safe.

After the Germans began raiding England from the air, Elsie insisted that Althea be brought home. As soon as it could be arranged Herbert and Elsie set sail for England. They were lost on the ill-fated Lusitania when it went down. Neither Herbert nor Elsie had any family; they were both the last of their lines. Consequently Althea became the charge of the trustees of the estate. They seemed to think it expedient to leave her in England. Later when she was old enough to have ideas and opinions of her own, she elected to stay abroad.

As I busied myself and my household with preparations for the party during the next few days, I had no idea that I was to see the beginning of a stormy romance and would become entangled in a series of weird and horrible murders.

Althea had come to America to take over her fortune, which was a large one in spite of the inroads made on the original holdings by the depression. She was busy with trustees, lawyers and banks immediately. I called her each morning just to have a chat because I didn't want her to feel too alone. I sensed a change in her soon after her arrival. She showed none of the eager interest and excitement I had expected. Instead she was seriously preoccupied and coolly aloof. I tried to be casual in the face of her coolness and suggested dinners and luncheons which she declined politely, giving the heat as an excuse. I had no intention of forcing myself on her and decided that after the party I would let her go her own way.

The evening before the party, everything was ready. My mind should have been at ease, but it wasn't. As I think back on it now I was filled with the expectancy of things to come. That may seem sheer nonsense but I believe coming events do cast their shadows before them. At any rate, with all the preparations for the party completed, I was at a loose end. I had nothing on my mind and the unrelenting heat made me very uncomfortable. I listened to the radio, played solitaire, wrote a few notes, and finally, sometime after midnight, being weary, restless and bored with myself, I went to bed. I couldn't sleep.

Sometime after one I was propped up in bed reading a mystery story and in the midst of the most thrilling, gruesome episode, with little pin-prickles of chills and delightful shivers of terror playing havoc with my spine, the sudden settling creak of an old beam put my nerves completely on edge. Terrified for the moment, I paused in my reading to listen, but the echo of the creak had gone. The house was as silent as a tomb. Beyond the comforting familiarity of my room the deep, almost noiseless rumbling roar of the city accentuated the complete quiet of my house. From far off on one of the rivers, the deep throaty whistle of a tugboat sounded like the mournful croaking of a giant frog.

I turned back to my story. The heroine was in dreadful jeopardy. A great, horrible thing, as slimy as an octopus was creeping toward her. She was cornered. Her lover, who had been beaten over the head a few pages back, couldn't possibly hear her hysterical, agonized screams. I lived and suffered with that poor girl. My heart raced and pounded as I read each word. Would she, could she escape? I didn't know the answer to that question for days, because suddenly the telephone bell pealed, shattering the silence, to say nothing of what it did to my tensed nerves. The book flew out of my hands as my body chilled, even in that terrific heat.

When the first shock of fear was over I reached for the receiver to still that clarion call. I often make up my mind to ignore the telephone if it rings, but after several seconds of that constant jangling I lift the receiver off the hook to know the worst.

I'm still conscious of the feeling of misgiving which I had as I took the instrument in my hand. I've outlived the terror of telegrams and have grown to consider the telephone as something of a necessary nuisance (advertising to the contrary) as well as a ruthless invader of my privacy. I'm not belittling the telephone, don't think that. In this day and age, we couldn't get along without it but it does put us at the mercy of our friends and enemies if we happen to have either.

Filled with apprehension and a premonition of impending danger, I glanced at the clock. It was exactly five minutes of two. I shivered. A woman will understand the feeling I had, for, common as the telephone is today, one doesn't receive many calls at two o'clock in the morning unless something startling has happened.

It was Terry Lassimon. I recognized his voice immediately and was inclined to be annoyed. Neither of us knew then that his call was a prelude to adventure. For a moment, as I listened, I accused him of being in his cups and feeling larkish. There was something about his voice, however, which held back my first impulsive desire to resent verbally his startling call. I curbed the impulse to snap at him and listened attentively until he made his unusual request, unusual even for Terry who is well known for his pranks and escapades and absolute lack of regard for the limitations of convention. He was so earnest as he begged, I fancied I could see his fine, dark eyes.

"At this hour?" I asked with another glance at my clock. Before I agreed I warned him, "You'll be sorry, young man, if you're pulling my leg." His reply made me laugh. I won't include it here lest some of you who do not know either of us might think it slightly ribald.

He seemed relieved when I told him to come right over.

I rang for my maid, Agnes, who did a rather bad job of concealing her sleepy surprise when I told her I would be expecting a caller within fifteen minutes. I sometimes wish I could live in a nice little cottage, do my own work and have an individual and private life instead of leading a routine existence governed by my servants. That may sound ungrateful because all of them seem to adore me and I try to repay them by making them comfortable and happy in return. They are a responsibility, however, and they keep me up to their standards most of the time.

Actually Agnes has been with me too long to be startled by anything I do. She was just a little grumpy because I had probably wakened her from a fitful sleep. She moved about the room giving an excellent imitation of slow motion, an old dressing-gown of mine draped about her. She put my cream negligee over the foot of the bed and brought out my transformation, without which I'm never seen because what little hair I have left is far too scraggly for public view and I'm still vain about and proud of my appearance. I don't dress as old ladies did a few years ago. I hate poke bonnets and mousy clothes, but then I was never cut out to be a sweet old lady. I'd rather be interesting—if not to others, at least to myself.

Agnes was so slow that I became nervous. "Never mind my things," I said. "Get something on yourself and be downstairs to let him in. Have the door open," I warned. "I don't want the whole house roused. You won't have to wait up to let him out. He knows the way. Just leave the hall lights burning when you go back to bed."

I was consumed with curiosity as I adjusted the transformation—it's a blonde one. What on earth did he have to tell me at this hour of the night that couldn't wait until morning? Why was he so worried and upset?

I'd better tell you something about myself and Terry Lassimon, so you'll be able to understand the things which follow. I'm an old woman. I won't say lady because the word has been so grossly abused. I'm seventy-five, proud of my age and why shouldn't I be? I've never been ill in my life. I've lived fully and well and, like the soldier in Kipling's poem, I've taken my fun where I found it, so to speak.

My name is Ethel Thomas. Just plain Ethel Thomas, old maid. Yes, I'm one of the New York Thomases. You may have heard of me or you may have read a book which I had published last year under the title of, "The Whispering Window."

I was born to wealth and a position in society. My original fortune was large enough for any one, but it has grown to rather overwhelming proportions because I've outlived all of my family and they, poor dears, died with the quaint old-fashioned notion that money, like scandal, should be kept in the family. Where it will all go, the money I mean, when I finally make my exit I haven't definitely decided except for the legacies left to fifteen or twenty babies born during the depression and hopefully, I believe, named Ethel in my honor and in anticipation of any bequest I might make.

Most of my life has been spent right in New York City. I've known New Yorkers good, bad and indifferent for sixty years. If I hadn't, I'd have missed a thrilling adventure which came to me through Terry.

We understand each other, Terry and I. We've been friends for a great many years ... all of his life, as a matter of fact. He has always been one of my pets. His mother was the daughter of one of my childhood friends. Yes, I'm old enough to be his grandmother.

I first saw Terry about an hour after he was born. Up to that time young babies, like Chinese and Indians, all looked alike to me, but Terry, fresh from the stork, so to speak, was different. He was not a red or jaundiced little ape when he greeted the world. He was a miniature man full of his, perhaps I shouldn't mention it, sex, even then and not just a wrinkled, crinkled ball. He was unmistakably a man child as straight as a reed with a sturdy pair of shapely legs, a fine body and a lusty pair of lungs.

I'm not a fatalist and I've never worried much about predestination. In fact I've been rather inclined to let such things slide, taking my cue, I think, from an old Irish cook we once had whose entire philosophy, outside of her religion, was completely contained in one single sentence: "What is to be will be, even if it never happens."

Willy-nilly, for the past two years I've been involved in one murder after another and if that is my destiny I know of no more diverting way of spending one's time. Of course, I feel sorry for the victims and their families; but a murder, to me, is like a good fire—if they must happen I want to be where I can see them and be a part of the activity. Can you-imagine the thrill of seeing Rome burn or the excitement you would feel if it were possible for you to solve the murder of Elwell?

My thought's were broken by the hall clock which chimed the quarter-hour.

I hurried with my dressing, such as it was, because Terry is one of those people who tap on your door and then barge in with the restrained delicacy of a battering-ram. I drew the cover up over the bed and puttered about for a minute or two—you know how many little things there are for a woman to do when a visitor is about to invade the privacy of her boudoir. I fluffed up the pillows on the chaise-longue and then looked out of the window. I saw Terry swing round the corner from Lexington Avenue and stride across the street. I returned to my dressing-table to add a last dab of powder.

I live in the Thirties between Fourth and Lexington in my old house which has been a haven for the past forty years, and I believe, if I live long enough, fashion-able society will move back to me again. I'm not a person who enjoys moving. I like the stability of a home and a fixed place for my things. I've known women who not only have their houses redecorated each time the wind changes but who are constantly moving furniture all over the house. I couldn't live that way. Good heavens! One might just as well be in a series of hotel rooms. There's something about an old house and its time-worn, well-loved furniture that is warm and friendly, exuding as it does a quality that most of the modern decorators in striving for effects seem to miss. For myself I'd just as soon live in one of Sloane's Fifth Avenue windows. My house is old and the neighborhood has run down but I like it and in the forty years I have been there I've seen me fashionable populace shift from Fifth Avenue to the Drive, to Sutton Place and to Park Avenue. Why any one who can afford to live anywhere else prefers that street with the ever-constant rumbling of the railroad underneath sounding like minor earthquakes night and day, I can't imagine.

That quick glimpse of Terry pleased me. He had evidently dismissed his cab at the corner. That was thoughtful of him. Not that I care how many men drive up to my door at any hour of the night or day but it was nice of him to think of that—or did he? Was it a habit he had acquired because of his shady experiences? Well, it didn't matter. I turned away from the window and found myself wondering how he had managed to escape matrimony as long as he had. Whenever I hear a bachelor bragging about his freedom and all that sort of thing, I know perfectly well why he's never married. No woman wants him; but that wasn't true in Terry's case. Even now in his financial difficulties he was considered a good catch and I knew several women who wanted him.

I was expecting him to bounce into the room at any moment. I paused to listen, but there was no sound from the floor below. He seemed to be an unduly long time. I went to the window again. He was just stepping onto the curb and advancing toward the front door. The street was deserted. I was turning back into the room when I was startled by a slight, puffing flash which I must have seen a split second before I heard the report of the gun. My heart seemed to stop dead for an instant, a lump filled my throat as I realized that some one from the shadows had tried to kill Terry. Before I had time to think or even cry out there was a sharp sudden thud against the front door and then an hysterical ear-splitting scream from that ninny, Agnes.

I rushed to the door expecting the very worst as Agnes' cry echoed and reechoed through the house. Even in that tragic moment I found myself thinking about the neighbors and their curiosity. That cry of hers was enough to wake the dead. I switched off the lights both in my room and the hall. I didn't know what had happened but I didn't intend to invite investigation if it were not necessary. It was an instinctive automatic gesture done without actual thought. I suppose my subconscious mind must have suggested darkness as a protection from the unseen and unknown assailant who had deliberately fired the shot at Terry.

I hurried into the hall and started fearfully down the stairs. Agnes' scream had died away like the echo of a bad dream. The whole episode seemed unreal. As I turned the curve in the stairs, I could see Terry's body sprawled on the floor, prone and inert, in the checkered light that filtered in from the street through the transom and side panels of the door.

My breath seemed to stop for a moment. Tears burned at my eyeballs demanding release, but I couldn't cry. I was too frightened. I clutched at the railing to steady myself and gazed down. He looked so horribly flattened out. Was he dead? I've met death face to face, I've seen a man murdered before my eyes, yet I've never been so genuinely moved as I was at that moment when I thought Terry dead.

The next instant gladness surged through me. My eyes dimmed with tears of joy because Terry moved, lifted himself to his hands and knees and then stood upright. As he brushed the legs of his trousers, I found my relief almost as great a shock as my fear had been the moment before.

Agnes, mouth open, eyes agape, was staring at him as if he were a creature from another world. In the semi-gloom, I saw her make the sign of the cross and knew that her lips were moving in a silent prayer. It touched me, such things always do. My eyes were rimmed with unshed tears anyhow and at that simple expression of faith and thankfulness on the part of Agnes, they welled up and blinded me for a moment. A good cry would have been a relief but I was suddenly angered at Terry. Don't ask me why. I don't know why any more than the frantic mother who, believing her child lost or killed, is frenzied with worry and grief until she finds her cherub safe and innocently happy, and then gives her emotions release by spanking her bewildered offspring. I was bent on giving Terry a mental spanking.

As I reached the landing and turned for the last few treads to the main floor, I became very dramatic and said, "What does . . ."

I intended saying more than that, much more, because I was so wrought up and relieved at the same time. I wanted to scold him to release my pent-up emotions, but my speech was cut in mid-air because my mule caught in the hem of my dressing-gown and I pitched forward, head first, in an adagio dive but with none of the grace of a dancer.

Terry was as quick as a flash. If he hadn't been, my career as a detective would have ended right then and there. At my age bones are brittle and break easily. From the first blank moment of falling to the security of Terry's outstretched clasping arms seemed an eternity in which I envisioned broken hips, a fractured pelvis, and a concussion or two. The moment I realized I was safe, I began to laugh. I've been accused of having a low sense of humor because I laugh at any one who falls, even myself. I can't help it. I was probably a bit hysterical at that moment too.

"Easy does it!" Terry said soothingly as he up-ended me and I felt the floor firmly under foot.

"I fell," I said simply and then broke into renewed laughter.

"Think nothing of it," he said smugly. "Women are always falling for me." He actually poked me in the ribs, then grinned impishly.

That stopped me. To look at him standing there, you'd never have believed that just a moment before his life had hung in the balance.

He was being too jaunty. "Is that why men take potshots at you in the middle of the night?" I snapped at him. A man has no right to be as debonair as he was just a moment after escaping death.

"Oh, that," he replied, "is something else. Did you see him?"

"No. I'm not an owl! I saw the flash of the gun from the shadows."

"Whoever it was is badly in need of practice, don't you think?" he asked.

Agnes tittered nervously. She's crazy about good-looking men and adores Terry. Her eyes were admiring him at that very moment. I gave her a reprimanding look which brought her back to her senses.

"Shall I call the police?" she asked.

"I'd rather have some brandy, if you don't mind," Terry suggested.

I nodded the order to Agnes and could hear her chuckling as she left us.

CHAPTER TWO

Back in my room, I drew the blinds, turned on a lamp and settled down on the chaise-longue. Terry watched me. He seemed as cool as the proverbial cucumber.

"How do you do it?" he asked.

"Do what?"

"Manage to look so charming at this hour of the night or, rather, morning?"

I was secretly pleased. I'm not too old to enjoy a bit of blarney. That's one of the reasons I've always liked Southern men. They lie so gallantly that you're half inclined to believe them. Terry was not a Southerner but he knew all the tricks that please women—a branch of the modern man's education which seems to have been sadly neglected.

"Never mind the compliments," I said, because it's never wise to let a man know you believe his fine speeches. "You'd better begin at the beginning," I suggested tersely. "I'm eaten alive with curiosity."

"After the brandy," he replied cautiously.

His ears were sharper than mine, for the next moment Agnes appeared at the door with decanter and glasses.

She placed the tray on a stool in front of Terry and said, "Beg pardon, Miss. There's a cop and some people on the street outside."

"Pay no attention to them," Terry instructed.

"But suppose they should ring the bell?" she asked hopefully.

"Take a long time to answer, if they do, act sleepy and then tell them nothing," I advised. Disappointed, she started away, when I stopped hen "Prepare the guest-room for Mr. Lassimon."

"But . . ." he began a protest.

"You're staying here. Do you think I want my house to get a bad name? It's compromising enough to have men shot at coming in without having them murdered on the doorstep going out at the crack of dawn. That'll be all, Agnes." I dismissed her. She likes to hear all that is going on and uses every pretext she knows to linger in a room. I'm quite sure she relates everything that happens to the rest of the servants and by so doing feels she is a bit more important than they.

"Yes, ma'am." She fiddled with some cushions on the easy-chair and took one long regretful look at the closely shaded window as she moved toward the door. She loves a good gossip and I know she'd have liked nothing better than to go down into the street to talk things over with the policeman.

"And don't say anything to the other servants," I cautioned; "and close the door as you leave."

"Yes, ma'am," she answered—ruefully.

"You know where the pajamas are," I called after her.

"Don't bother about them, I sleep raw," Terry cut in quite unnecessarily, I thought, although Agnes seemed to enjoy the remark, for she stifled a giggle as she closed the door. Terry, in the meantime, had been busy with the brandy and soda and handed me one as I heard the latch click.

"I believe your hand is shaking," he remarked solicitously as the glass rattled against my teeth.

"And why wouldn't it? Roused out of a sound sleep in the middle of the night by an irresponsible young scamp who is nearly killed on my doorstep is enough to make anybody shake," I retorted.

"You weren't asleep, because I can see your book where you dropped it, and what is more, your pillows are squashed by the impress of your back rather than dented by the imprint of your fair head."

"Never mind your clever deductions," I snapped and then had to smile because his observations had been so exactly right. I went on, "What have you been doing? Where have you been—on a bender? You look like the devil and your eyes are barely more than tired pinpoints. Who fired that shot?"

"If you don't mind, I'll answer your questions one at a time. I've been at the office going over accounts. I'm in a bad way, very bad, as a matter of fact. I've made some bad guesses on the market, my publishing business is losing money rapidly and unless I do something and do it quickly, I'm quite apt to find myself a ruined man."

"If you're working up to a loan, I won't listen to a word until you tell me who fired that shot," I cautioned him.

He shrugged and said, "You're supposed to be a detective, tell me."

"Now don't act that way," I complained. "I'm not clairvoyant and besides detectives have to ask questions to get at pertinent information. Was it some one's husband?"

"I'm quite sure it wasn't," he replied promptly.

"Well, men don't run about in the middle of the night taking pot-shots at other men without a very good reason. What have you been doing?"

"Not a thing, Ethel, really! I can't understand it! I haven't been in a scrape for a long time, you know that. It's been pretty hot, you know," he ended with a broad grin.

"If you don't want to tell me, it's perfectly all right," I assured him because I didn't believe him at the moment. I felt it was probably something so flagrant that he didn't want to let me know about it.

"Honestly, Ethel," he insisted. "I can't imagine why any one should be gunning for me."

"Well, they weren't shooting at me," I said, "and there was no one else on the street. I looked out of the window just as you stepped up on the curb. There wasn't a soul in sight but you."

"Did you see the person who fired the shot?" he asked quickly.

"No. I saw the flash and heard the report almost simultaneously. I didn't look. My one thought was for you. I was afraid you had been killed."

"I was probably mistaken for some one else," he said with a sly twinkle in his eyes.

"Men don't call on me in the middle of the night, young man," I reminded him, "unless it's some scatterbrain like you. The shot was meant for you and we might just as well face it and get down to cases here and now. You've been doing something or have done something in the past which has caught up with you. Think hard."

"I wonder if this can have anything to do with the letter or the telephone calls?" he asked thoughtfully.

"What letter? What phone calls?" I literally pounced on him.

"Oh, you know the sort of crank letters you receive," he replied.

"Be explicit," I snapped.

"Well, the letter and the phone calls were probably from the same person. They all warned me to watch my step, that's all."

"That evidently was enough to give you a more tangible warning in the shape of a bullet," I stormed.

"You've been doing something. What is it?"

"But I haven't."

"Well, then, some one thinks you've been up to mischief or will be. Whoever it is, is serious."

"But, Ethel, how would any one know I was coming here at two o'clock in the morning?"

"You were probably followed," I replied.

"But that would mean that I had been watched all night," he objected.

"Why not?" I demanded.

"But I've been at the office trying to catch up with my work. It would have been so much simpler and easier for any one who wanted to kill me to have done it at the office. A smart killer wouldn't have trailed me to the door of the famous Ethel Thomas who has proven her ability to track down murderers."

There was considerable logic in what he said. I don't mean about my doorstep either. If the person who had shot at him had wanted to kill him it would have been easy to have crept into his office and have done it. That opened a new avenue of thought for me.

"Who knew you were working late?" I asked.

"The people at the office: the girl who does the billing, the bookkeeper, the stock boy, all the last ones to leave. And, oh, yes, one other! Your friend, Miss Madison."

"Althea?" I gasped. "Has she written a book or something?"

"She didn't say."

"Why did she call on you?"

"She didn't say."

"Are you trying to be funny?" I asked crossly.

"No. Just trying to answer your questions. The girl was after information; she told me nothing really. She seems to be a master at that." He leaned forward. "Say, she knew I needed money. Did you tell her that?"

"Certainly not. Why should I?"

"She said she understood my publishing business was for sale and she admitted she might be interested, but I didn't believe her. She was stalling. What do you suppose she wanted?"

"If she were a poor girl I'd say she was setting her cap for you."

"She's not that kind of girl. She wasn't interested in me. She wanted something, I'd like to know just what," he said speculatively.

"Ask her when you see her at the party," I suggested.

"I'd rather find out in my own way." His eyes danced as he said it.

"It can have nothing to do with this," I stated positively. I wanted to get back to our mystery. "Are things all right at the office?"

"Fine. We can leave the office out of it," he assured me, "I'm their bread-and-butter while I last. They nearly lost me tonight, though. That was a close shave, wasn't it? I thought I had been hit as I sprawled forward."

"What made you fall?" I asked.

"The door was open. When I heard that bullet zing past my head, I did the natural thing. I tried to get out of the way of any little brother bullets that might be following the first one. I pushed against the door and since I pushed so hard it flew away from me and I sprawled on my face. I was a bit dazed for a moment. It was a beautiful fall. You'd have loved to have seen it." He knew about my weakness for falling people. "By the way," he looked about the room, "what happened, to my briefcase?"

"What briefcase?" I asked. "I haven't seen one."

"Good Lord!" he exclaimed, "don't tell me I've lost it. I'd better take a look downstairs."

He dashed out of the room and in a moment was back, a briefcase hanging from his hand. "This," he said, patting it on the side, "is one of my reasons for coming to see you so late tonight."

"And what is the other one?" I demanded. I couldn't imagine anything he happened to have in the briefcase being interesting.

"In a way, they are linked together. I need money, Ethel, badly."

"How much?"

"A couple of hundred thousand."

I gasped, provoked by his casualness. I've a lot of respect for money. It certainly has been kind to me and made it possible for me to do, know and see the things which have made my life interesting. I didn't want him to come groveling to me begging for a loan, don't think that, but for a man to say two hundred thousand as if it were so much chicken-feed, is a bit startling.

"And what do you want to do with two hundred thousand?" I demanded.

"It'll tide me over this bad spot," he answered simply.

"And what about security?" I asked.

"Anything you want. How would an interest in the publishing business suit you? Then you could publish your own books no matter how bad they were?" He said it seriously but there was a twinkle in his eyes.

"We won't go into the quality of my books," I said icily. "I'm not interested in your publishing business. You've just told me that it's been losing money—besides, you have a partner."

"Oh, Sidney wouldn't mind having you in the firm," he answered quickly. "He'd like it. He thinks you're great."

"That's nice of him and I appreciate it, but at the moment we're talking about security for a loan that I might make you."

"I'll give you the Long Island house," he suggested.

"I've got a house," I retorted.

"You're being a bit difficult to your favorite young man," he chaffed.

"One of the reasons I have money is that I've been a careful investor," I reminded him. "Evidently, you've made a mess of your affairs. If you want a yacht, a big country house for your orgies, and other luxuries, you should be more careful of your investments. As much as I like you, I won't consider such a loan unless you can prove to me definitely that I won't lose my money." Even as I talked, I knew perfectly well that if it came to a final showdown I wouldn't see him smashed. He knew it too, knew also that I was determined to force him to pull himself out of the hole he had dug.

"All right, Madame Shylock," he said with a laugh, "I'll give you plenty of security. I just wanted to see how hard your heart was, that's all. I'm going to make a lot of money, enough to put the publishing business on its feet.

I've got a book that will do it, but I want your advice." He began fiddling with the straps that held the briefcase together.

"Don't tell me you've found another 'Gone With the Wind,'" I scoffed.

He looked across the briefcase and said, "You must have been very beautiful when you were younger."

"Don't bother about the blarney; tell me what you want. It's getting late."

"It's not blarney. I mean it. I was thinking about John Edwards," he said. "Why aren't you Mrs. John Edwards?"

"What?" I gasped, and nearly spilled my drink. I hadn't thought of John Edwards for years. "How did you know about him?"

"I was watching your face just now," he replied. "I saw you grow young again before my eyes. You must have loved him very much."

"I did," I admitted.

"He was a fool not to have married you," Terry said resentfully.

"But a grand fool, Terry, the kind a woman loves dearly. But you haven't answered my question. How did you know?"

He pulled several books from the briefcase. "It's in here. It's the book I told you about."

"What on earth?" I asked.

"Mortimer Van Wyck's diaries," he replied, holding them out to me. "He has known everything and everybody in New York for the past sixty years. Don't you think they'll sell? Of course," he added quickly, "they'll need to be carefully edited and deleted."

Mortimer Van Wyck's diaries! I was astounded. Why under the sun had Terry allowed himself to become involved with a person like Mortimer?

I remembered the day years ago when Mortimer approached me about his diaries. He threatened to expose me unless I paid him hush money. The old anger surged over me again.

Of all the parasites who prey upon society the blackmailer is the very lowest, in my estimation. Most of us have done something in our past that we want to stay buried with the past, but unfortunately we are apt to be putty in the hands of the social leach who, knowing of our indiscretion, threatens us with exposure. We become panicked with fear and instead of telling the blackmailer to go to hell and publish his facts, we pay him money to keep him quiet and live in fear and dread for the rest of our lives. I have very definite ideas about that sort of thing and believe all blackmail cases should be turned over to the police because the blackmailer's chief weapon is his victim's fear.

"You don't seem very interested," Terry challenged.

"How on earth did you become involved with a person like Mortimer?" I asked. "I'd rather lend you a million than have you mixed up in a thing like this." I made a contemptuous gesture toward the books which still lay in his lap.

"You're responsible," he said.

"Me?"

"Yes. Remember about a month ago I told you that the publishing business wasn't making money?"

I nodded.

"You weren't very patient with me or the business at the time. In fact, you were rather cruel that night the way you talked about the phenomenal sale of 'Gone With the Wind.' You seemed to think that books like that grow on bushes. You advised me to go out and find another one like it. That, I knew, was impossible, but I did some serious thinking." He lit a cigarette and took several slow puffs before he went on.

"After that talk with you I took a good look at myself, and the business. You were absolutely right about both of us, you know." He smiled for a moment. "While I was still racking my brains for an inspiration, I met Mortimer in the cocktail bar at Forty-seven. The idea came after two or three of Louis's specials. Well, I asked Mortimer if he had ever kept a diary.

"He was pretty cagey about answering my questions until he had drawn me out. When I explained to him that I thought an intimate personal panorama of New York and its society would make interesting reading, he unbent a little. He finally asked me how many copies I thought the book would sell. That, I explained, would depend upon its contents and general interest. Before he left me that afternoon, he was more enthusiastic than I was over the idea. He was very anxious, even insistent, that I read his diaries."

"I can imagine that," I said bitterly.

"They've been kicking around the office for a week or two waiting for me to look them over, but I didn't get at them until this evening."

"You weren't that careless," I protested.

"No. Wrapped, sealed and stowed in the safe, they have been innocently waiting for my attention."

"Then you've read them?"

"No. Mortimer called me late this afternoon. He seemed rather impatient. He said I'd have to make up my mind or return the books to him at once. He even suggested that I run an announcement in the papers telling of the intended publication of the diaries. He thought it would arouse interest. I told him I'd let him know in a couple of days. I thought that you—if you'd read them for me—you'd know if they were authentic or not."

"I'll read them," I answered quietly. "Tell me, is Mortimer in need of money?"

"I don't know. We didn't mention finances. Why do you ask?"

"Because I don't trust him."

"But it was my suggestion, not his. About publication, I mean. I was the one who made the overtures."

"And I still don't trust him. Mortimer has thought of most everything in the course of his life. Don't you believe for a moment that your suggestion was the first time publication of the diaries occurred to him."

"But I don't see why you're going on like this!" Terry interrupted.

"Because I have known Mortimer for sixty years or more. That's why. He's an old fox and always has been. He's using you, Terry."

"Using me?" he repeated incredulously.

"Yes. Tell me exactly what he said to you about the diaries."

"Well, he said they'd cause something of a sensation. He rather boasted about being the Pepys of New York society."

"Peeps is right," I replied unable to resist the chance to pun, but Terry ignored it. "A prying, peeping, gossip-monger."

"He warned me that they were dynamite. He made me promise not to let them leave my hands until they were read and returned to him. When I told him I wouldn't be able to get to them for several days, he insisted on my wrapping, sealing and stowing them in the office safe. I even marked them personal so there would be no chance of their being opened by mistake."

"Have you read them at all?"

"No. Not really. I sort of ran through one volume picking out a line here and there until I chanced upon your name. I read about you and Edwards. That's all. Say, do you think . . ."

"I'm not thinking," I interrupted him with a yawn. "It's getting very late. I think I'll be able to sleep. I'll see you at breakfast."

He gathered the books together before he stood up.

"Leave them here," I suggested. "I'll look them over."

He was weary as he stood before me; his eyes looked like slits. "I am tired," he admitted. He kissed me on the forehead and went on to his room.

When I was sure that he would not return, I picked up the first of the diaries feeling positive that in them I would find the answer to the mysterious telephone calls he had mentioned, the anonymous letter, and the bullet that was still lodged in my front door.

CHAPTER THREE

I didn't read the books that night. They lay unopened in my lap for a long time after he left me. I was weary and thoughtful. I reached for a cigarette and heard the clop, clop, clop, of the milkman's lonesome horse moving and resting through the quiet street. I fell asleep.

Later I was startled by a tap, tap, tap on my door. For a moment I thought it was the milkman's horse in the street below, but it was Agnes, amazed at finding me sitting up, the lights still burning. I had dozed in my chair through the remainder of the night.

"You hadn't ought to sit up all night reading," she scolded as she switched off the lights and lifted the blinds, "especially when you're giving a party this afternoon."

"Fix my bath," I answered wearily, "then call Mr. Lassimon and tell him we'll have breakfast here in my room in a half-hour."

"It's cooler downstairs," she suggested.

"Serve it here, nevertheless, and hurry." I gave a sharp command because I knew she was on the verge of asking questions which I didn't want to answer. And, furthermore, I didn't want any one to overhear the things Terry and I would find it necessary to talk about over our morning coffee.

"You look rested," I said twenty minutes later when he came in, rather disheveled in yesterday's clothes, wilted collar and all.

"I am. All ready for the fray and hungry, too." He lifted one of the silver bells and sniffed appreciatively at the bacon.

I watched him eat. It's a grand thing to be young and healthy, eager and alive. As he was sitting there, busy with his food, I didn't envy him his youth, I just appreciated it. I've heard people say, "If I had my life to live over again," their voices filled with longing and regret. How foolish! Even if I could come into the world with the knowledge and experience I now have, I don't believe I'd want to live over again. My life has been eventful and I've enjoyed all of it. I've lived through a great era in world history. I've lived through change and at this moment I'm living through great economic change, but like all the rest of you I'm too close to it to see it properly, or to fully understand the things taking place about me. In fifty or a hundred years, this time of ours will be as clear-cut to historians as the Fall of Rome, the Renaissance, or the Dark Ages.

I don't want to be young again, my heartaches and sufferings are mellowed memories.

"What's our first move?" he asked as he toyed with his .second cup of coffee.

"I'd like you to take these diaries back to your office, wrap them up, seal them and turn them over to Mortimer at the first opportunity," I suggested.

"But I thought you were going to read them!" he protested.

"I intended doing so," I replied, "but as I thought about it I decided it was too dangerous."

"Why?"

"Didn't some one try to murder you last night in an effort to shield himself? We don't know who the person was but I think you'll be safer if that person is assured that you have no knowledge of the contents of the books. Whoever it is must be desperate. There are probably a number of people mentioned in the diaries who have some horrible secrets in their pasts. Mortimer has held the key to those secrets but neither you nor I want to know what they are."

"You're dead right, of course, as usual," he grinned at me, "only "

"Only what?" I demanded.

"Well, if Mortimer has put me on the spot, I've got to do something about these people." He indicated the books where they lay on the chaise-longue.

"You can do that without reading them. You'd never be comfortable if you read and knew the secrets those books contain; neither would I. There's a better way."

"What?"

"Establish your good faith with the people mentioned in the diaries," I suggested.

"But we don't know who they are," he objected.

"But they do, and if you put an ad in tonight's paper and one in the morning papers for a week, they'll understand what you mean when you state that you have no intention of publishing any private diaries."

"They'll never believe me."

"Why not?"

"Because they don't know me. They know a Terry Lassimon who has been wild, who has been talked about, who has had a shady reputation in the past and who has at the moment a rather uncertain future."

"We'll take care of the future," I promised.

"Why don't I destroy the darned things right now," he pointed toward the fireplace, "and then advertise that the diaries I had planned to publish had been destroyed."

"You can't do that, Terry."

"Why not?"

"Because Mortimer would sue you for every cent you own and you wouldn't be able to justify yourself unless you gave good reasons for their destruction. If you were compelled to defend yourself in court, you would be forced to expose the very people you are now trying to defend."

"Not if I didn't know who they were."

"Then you would have no suit to protect yourself," I reminded him.

"I don't know why I continue to like you," he said with a smile; "you're always right."

"Then do as I say. I thought of destroying them myself last night. If ever they are destroyed, and I think they should be, it must be done in the presence of all concerned."

"That," he said quickly, "is an idea. I've got to do something, you know."

"I don't believe any further attempts will be made on your life," I said with more assurance than I felt.

"It isn't that," he said; "as you say, it's the principle of the thing. You and I hold the lives and happiness of God knows how many people in the palms of our hands. We've got to protect them, Ethel. Poor devils! They probably need it, whoever they are."

I was seeing a new Terry, one that, in a way amazed me. I'd never seen him in any but a gay irresponsible mood before. I knew he had other qualities but he had hidden them behind a debonair exterior. Isn't it strange that you can know people, live with them for years, and not know them at all because they have little secret hiding-places of their own which are never opened for public view? We do rather live on the surface, according to people's opinions of us, don't we?

"We may be wasting sympathy, Terry," I said, "but there is no other road open for you. Run along now!" I dismissed him.

He was very thoughtful as he stuffed the diaries back into the briefcase. He stopped once and looked at me and said, "What a woman you are, Ethel! Edwards was a fool not to have married you. Did it hurt?"

"At the time, yes," I admitted.

"If you were younger, or I were older, I'd marry you in a minute if you'd have me. Why don't they make women like you any more?"

Sweet child! How that speech warmed my heart. It was nice of him to say it, but Terry, like all men, is thoughtless. One of the things he likes and admires in me is my knowledge, tact and understanding of human nature. He thinks this mellowed tolerance of mine is something I've always had. It doesn't occur to him that in the process of living and growing old, life has given things to me which a young girl couldn't possibly have and would be unattractive if she did.

"They do," I assured him. "The trouble with you is you haven't been looking in the right places, but you'll find her, that is, if you want to."

"Would you think I'd gone out of my mind if I told you I'd like to be married?" he asked.

"I'd say you were growing up or settling down, one or the other."

As he snapped the catch shut and pulled the straps through the buckles he said, "Can you keep a secret? Of course you can. I've seen the girl and as soon as this mess is cleared up . . ." He paused and the queerest look flashed over his face. "What do you know about Althea Madison," he demanded suddenly.

"Althea Madison, why?"

"She's mixed up in these," he patted the briefcase. "That's why she came to see me."

"But she's lived abroad all her life," I remonstrated. "Don't be ridiculous!"

"Why should she want to buy my business? Tell me that. She knows about these and in her own way she was trying to get them."

"But, Terry! What interest could she have ..." I stopped because my memory went back to an old, old story.

"Perhaps it's a family secret that she doesn't want uncovered," he said and then asked, "Why did you stop just now?"

"Because I was remembering something."

"About her family?"

"Yes, her father. There was talk about a scandal in Washington, war contracts or something. That was before he went down on the *Lusitania*. Nothing ever came of it, so it probably wasn't true. Did she mention the diaries?" I asked.

"No, but she must have wanted them," he said thoughtfully. "There could be no other reason for her eagerness to buy the business." He looked at the briefcase for a moment. "Was it much of a scandal about her father?"

"Just one of those things you hear about, nothing important. It must be something deeper than that, more significant. The child has something on her mind. She is worried, not herself, at least not the person who came down the gangplank the morning I met her. I thought she was being aloof. Do you suppose . . ."

He anticipated my question. "It must be something to do with her inheritance. That girl is fighting to save her fortune. There must be something in these books which would make a pauper of her instead of a millionaire. I'm going to find out." He started to take the books out of the bag.

"I wouldn't do that if I were you," I cautioned. "If your guess is right, and I'm inclined to think it is, she wouldn't want you to know her secret."

"But she must know that I know," he insisted.

"Do you mean that you admitted having the diaries?"

"I told her that I was going to publish a rather startling book that would put the business on its feet."

"And gave her a fine opinion of yourself, I'm afraid," I sneered.

"But I didn't know," he protested. "Say, you don't think she tried to shoot me, do you?"

"If her fortune is at stake—" I spoke slowly because I was thinking. .

"No," he interrupted before I could finish. "She wouldn't do a thing like that."

"I think myself, she'd be a bit more subtle. Why not try to square yourself with her," I suggested, "at the party this afternoon?"

"You bet I will."

"I take it you were impressed by the girl," I said bluntly. .

"Bowled over," he admitted at once. "She's the loveliest thing I've ever seen, and smart too," he added.

"You noticed that?" I asked.

"I noticed everything about her including her rather thinly concealed contempt for me," he admitted frankly. .

"She strikes me as being a fairly direct person," I answered with a smile.

"Don't rub it in. Why couldn't I have met her under decent circumstances? The things she's going to hear about me won't add to the opinion she's evidently formed," he said with genuine regret. After a pause he went on brightly, "But I'll fix everything. I'll make her understand."

"Aren't you afraid of being misunderstood?" I asked casually.

"No. Why?"

"Since she's going to take over an estate valued at something over thirty million dollars and you're on the verge of bankruptcy . . ."

"No, Mrs. Grundy!" Laughing, he came round and put a hand over my mouth. "Just remember this. Little Terry has been in tight spots before and has come out on top. Don't you worry about me, and what do I care about the gossips?" With a jaunty toss of his hand which blew me a kiss, he started for the door.

"Don't forget about the ads," I called after him.

"I won't," he assured me, then added, "If you have the opportunity will you get down to cases with her? Find out, if you can, why she wants the diaries. If I'm going to marry her I'd just as soon she have the thirty million although I would take her without a cent."

CHAPTER FOUR

Poor Terry! Long after he left I was thinking about his problem. He had sobered considerably during the night. I rather hoped that the diary business would clear itself up. I didn't believe it was at all serious and yet how else explain the shot of the night before? I tried to dismiss the whole thing from my mind but it wouldn't be put aside. Why should Althea Madison be interested in those diaries unless her inheritance was involved? How was her fortune threatened?

I had my own problems to consider during the day. The servants were grumpy about the party and I didn't blame them, because the heat went on relentlessly.

Sometime after three o'clock Agnes brought me an afternoon paper. She actually yawned as she told me she was very tired. The impudence of the baggage! I told her to go take a nap and to let me hear no more such talk.

I hunted through the paper looking for Terry's ad and, finding it, read with interest. It certainly should have convinced any worried person of its sincerity. I was startled by the sirens of a fire truck dashing along Fourth Avenue. I rushed to the window but missed them. They go so fast you have to be right at a window nowadays to even catch a fleeting glimpse of them. Watching a fire engine has always been a passion of mine, a hangover from the old days when they really were romantic. I regret the passing of the old type engine with smoke belching from its stack and sparks scattering in the wind, as bells clanging and horses straining they raced madly through the streets.

Disgusted at having been too late, I started to draw the blinds, for the air from the street was like the hot blast of a furnace. I stopped with one blind halfway down.

Althea Madison was coming down the street. She was very early for her party. It wasn't quite four.

When she was announced I asked her up to my room. She said she came early so that we could have a little chat before the others arrived. She was perfectly turned out and looked cool and undisturbed by the heat. I envy women who can look their best no matter how hot it happens to be.

I saw her glance quickly at the folded newspaper and then turn her head away. It was done quickly, almost casually. You've seen a person look at something they wanted to see and then pretend a complete lack of interest. She may have been telling the truth when she said she came for a little chat, but I doubted her. She wanted to talk about herself but she wanted me to make the overtures. I decided I'd do nothing of the sort. I was in one of my contrary moods. Furthermore, I was afraid of a direct attack. I didn't want to spoil a chance to learn something about her plans.

We talked about this and that, France, England, and her reactions to the American scene, but it was all surface chatter. As I talked to her and had a chance to study her, I liked the girl more and more and could understand why she had captured Terry's fancy. Talking to her even about superficial things was like exploring new fields. You know how some people reveal themselves so completely in ten minutes that they can never be interesting to you again. Well, Althea was not like that. Each moment as it passed was rather breathless because you knew the next word would give you a new idea of or a new fact to her personality that would keep you absorbed. She was a deep well full of hidden springs that would never be exhausted.

Of course Terry's description of her and her conversation with him had rather prepared me for our little bout of words. Between us there was an undercurrent of expectancy as each measured the other. Just why had she come so early and what did she want to know? I'm an old hand and have considered myself rather skilful at beating about the bush to get at the thing I want, but this girl made me feel like the veriest tyro. Finally, I gave her leads which she ignored as she turned the trend of our talk back to me, society and the people I knew and the things I knew about them. Our mental fencing was delightful because you seldom meet a worthy opponent any more. The conversation we find, if any, is usually so dull or culled from the *New Yorker* and the *Reader's Digest*, that I don't wonder we play bridge and other games to fill our time.

I was determined to make her mention Terry if she wanted to talk about him. I was fully confident that I would be able to force her to do it, but she was a much better general than I believed her to be. How she knew my weak spot, unless all of us who write have the same Achilles heel, I do not know. Anyhow, whether I underestimated the girl's cleverness or was too confident of my own ability, I don't know, because she caught me off guard with an innocent statement.

"I liked your book so much," she said sincerely.

Whenever I find any one who has read the darned thing and has a good word to say about it, I open up as wide as a drawbridge. I know I beamed as I said, "I enjoyed doing it."

"It must have been fun, but wasn't the adventure itself rather horrible?" she asked, leading me on.

"Yes, but you don't think about that once you become involved. Somehow you become detached and are excited rather than horrified. It's like a bad dream —an unreality that you experience," I explained.

"Did you have any trouble getting the book published?" she asked innocently.

I jumped into the opening with both feet, knowing I was wrong as I ran on telling her that the first publisher who saw it took it at once and then went on to say, like the gabby old woman I am, rather drunk with self-interest, "Of course, Terry Lassimon has always been annoyed with me for not giving it to him."

I saw her eyes flicker for a moment as I knew she tasted success.

"But doesn't he go in for rather arty things?" she asked.

"That's why I never even considered him as a possible publisher of my book," I explained. Now that we were on the subject of Terry, I was interested to get on with it and see what she would have to say.

"Did you see his ad in the paper? I thought it rather curious, didn't you?" she asked.

"You wouldn't if you knew the reason ... or perhaps you do?" I made a direct thrust.

"It suggested fear to me," she countered.

"Of what?" I demanded.

"I don't know, do you?" she asked bluntly.

"Yes," I replied and turned the conversation back to her. She wanted to talk about Terry and I was just mean enough to make her do it because she had made me mention him first. There we were, two women dying to take our hair down, so to speak, and have a good talk and yet we sat fencing with words.

"You know him very well, don't you?" she asked.

"As well as one person can know another," I replied.

"And you know why he's afraid?" she insisted.

"Fear is hardly the word to use. Terry wouldn't be afraid of a den of wildcats," I defended. "He has been put into a rather false position and although people should know very well that he's dependable and can be relied upon to do the right thing yet he is apt to be victimized by the fear of fear."

"I don't understand."

"Oh, yes you do," I insisted. "Let's stop hedging. I know about those diaries."

"You do?" She seemed really surprised.

"And I recommend leaving the matter entirely in Terry's hands. He'll do the right thing," I said with assurance.

"You've more confidence in him than I have," she said coolly.

"That's because you don't know him. He's interested in getting rid of the diaries once and for all time."

"Then why doesn't he destroy them?" she asked impatiently.

"If, and when, they are destroyed all the people concerned should know about it," I reminded her. "Then there won't be any further attempts on his life."

"His life?" she asked.

"Yes. Some one tried to kill him last night—some one who is interested in those diaries," I ended pointedly.

She laughed. "Do you think I shot at him?"

"How did you know it was a shot?" I demanded quickly.

"There's a bullet-hole in your front door. Didn't you know it?" she asked innocently. "I noticed it while I waited to be admitted."

The girl used her eyes as well as her head. She'd be a grand person to have at your side in a moment of difficulty. There was no point to further fencing. I explained the situation to her; as much as I knew, at any rate.

She seemed relieved when I had finished.

"Why are you so interested in the diaries?" I asked.

"I believe in letting the dead past stay dead," she replied. As she went on talking, she took a small beautifully chased silver compact from her bag and dabbed at her nose and cheeks. "Those diaries," she paused for a moment and looked at me, "should be destroyed and Mortimer Van Wyck along with them." She snapped the compact shut, giving emphasis to her statement.

"If you tied them around his neck and threw him into the river you might accomplish both deeds at once," I suggested.

"That's an idea," she said.

"You didn't tell me why you were interested in the diaries," I reminded her.

"You didn't expect me to, did you?"

"Yes and no," I replied.

"If Mr. Lassimon didn't tell you, it is safer for you not to know, since the knowledge seems dangerous." She made me feel several years younger than herself. I didn't mind, however, because she fascinated me. She was in trouble and she was worried. She didn't want any help from me or she would have asked for it. I knew that when I gave up all idea of fencing with her and threw away the gauntlet.

"My dear," I said, "he hasn't read them."

Her eyes told me she doubted my word. I explained to her why I knew about the diaries and once more emphasized Terry's ignorance of their contents except for Mortimer's account of my indiscretion. "You see," I ended, "we have something in common, you and I, for I, too, am in the diaries."

"Then you must know how I feel," she said quickly.

"You don't want them published, do you?"

"No," I replied promptly, "but I'm not afraid of them."

"You're an old woman, you've lived, had your life and everything you've ever wanted," she said not without justice. "Why should you be afraid?"

"Age has nothing to do with it. Nothing is worth the price you seem determined to pay to prevent their publication. What you do is no concern of mine, of course, but please be careful. Don't do something which you may regret for the rest of your life."

"I'll regret it all my life unless I do do something," she answered, completely twisting the meaning of my words.

"Will you answer a question or two?" I asked.

"If possible."

"How did you know that Terry Lassimon had the diaries?" I asked.

"Mortimer Van Wyck sent for me immediately upon my arrival. He told me."

"And he threatened you?"

"Yes."

"Isn't it something you can fight openly?" I asked.

"No."

"You must be convinced that it is the truth."

"I don't know. I'll never know and I don't care one way or the other, but this I do know: I'll not permit that slimy old man to print those diaries if I have to kill him to prevent it."

I was thoroughly convinced that she meant exactly what she said.

"I don't believe he wants to publish them," I suggested as a consolation.

"He gave me an alternative, blackmail," she said contemptuously.

"And what did you tell him?"

"I refused to pay, naturally. I won't pay blackmail, because you pay and pay all your life. There's never an end of such things. I offered to buy the diaries and he said they were out of his hands. He meant Terry Lassimon. What manner of man is Lassimon?" she demanded.

"He grows on acquaintance," I assured her. "He doesn't intend to publish the diaries and won't."

"Then why doesn't he turn them over to me?" she demanded.

"He could hardly do that," I replied, amazed at the singleness of purpose that her question displayed.

"But how can a man who is a man be part of anything so filthy?" she demanded.

"He knows nothing about them, you must believe me. If we knew why you were afraid we could help you."

"It is a fight I must wage alone," she answered, shutting me out.

"Is your fortune threatened?" I asked bluntly.

She considered a moment and then replied frankly, "Yes, it is. I may lose it all unless I can do something to save it."

"And that something is to secure and destroy the diaries?" I asked.

She nodded an answer.

"Be careful, my dear," I cautioned.

"Care will get me nowhere. I must strike first. If your friend Terry were not such a fool I could best Van Wyck right now."

"Terry's on your side. I'd trust him if I were you," I suggested.

"I wouldn't trust any one who was playing with dynamite," she replied. "He doesn't realize his danger."

Those words were to bother and worry me later.

CHAPTER FIVE

Knowing the mood Althea was in, I was rather concerned about my party, but I worried unnecessarily. When we went downstairs to greet the first of the guests, she became an entirely different person. She played the part of a socially-minded woman with grace and skill which was a bit of relief to me. I've seen women do it before and shouldn't have been surprised by her seeming complete absorption in my guests. Women must of necessity be good actresses. How else could so many of them go on living, year after year, with the same man?

When Terry Lassimon arrived, the party was in full swing. He gave my hand an extra squeeze and said, "It's too hot to kiss you, darling."

"Then it's not the heat," I retorted, "but because I don't happen to have anything you want at the moment."

"But you have," he answered glibly, "about two hundred thousand dollars if you're in a lending mood."

"Well, I'm not. It's too hot to talk about money," I snapped back at him.

Those near us laughed and unless I'm greatly mistaken there were one or two arched eyebrows and some understanding nodding of heads. Terry was being bold and I suppose it was a wise policy under the circumstances because talk does get around. On the other hand, I don't want every Tom, Dick and Harry to get the idea that I dole out money just for the fun of it.

Terry went on with his banter. "Don't get yourself overheated," he cautioned. "Perhaps when you cool off a bit we can talk business. I'll give you adequate security."

"What?" I demanded feeling that I must go on with the game. "I understand you are down to your last yacht."

"You win! People have been talking." He took hold of my arm and eased me away from the group where we had been standing.

"Any news?" I asked in an undertone.

"All quiet." He glanced over the room which I had tried to keep as cool as possible by using all the electric fans in the house. Over the hum of conversation the whirring of the fans was barely noticeable. "Where is she?" he asked.

Althea was penned into a corner surrounded by half a dozen infatuated young men.

"She must definitely have something," Terry murmured as we approached the group, "or my partner, Sidney Kenfield wouldn't be so engrossed."

Terry was right. I had never seen Kenfield so interested in any girl before. He was doing his utmost to be charming and agreeable. I fancied I saw some of Terry's technique in Kenfield's mannerisms. I've always had an idea that Kenfield more or less patterned himself after Terry. It's just the sort of thing a younger man, anxious to get on in the world, might do.

We sailed up to the little gathering. I pried my way through the attentive young men and sent them off to pay some attention to the other women. I didn't want Althea to get off to a bad start. You know and I know that women resent a woman who can either consciously or unconsciously attract all the men in a room to her and keep them buzzing like flies over a honey-pot. If Althea was going to be a social success, she would need the help and friendship of women. The men weren't moving away very fast.

"Make way," Terry said briskly, "and give the lady some air." He grinned as he said it.

"And would you get me a drink?" Althea asked, looking up.

"I brought it with me," he answered, proffering her his glass which he had just taken from a passing tray. She laughed up at him.

She was dark and lovely and possessed of a gracious dignity and poise which was a comfort to see. I suppose her Continental education had something to do with that. "Do you always know what a woman wants?" she asked pointedly.

Terry was stumped for a moment. I felt his fingers twitch nervously on my arm as Althea went on, "You see, I've heard about you, Mr. Lassimon."

That remark may have had overtones. I don't know. At any rate, Terry took it as a challenge.

"Then for the first time in my life, I regret my past," he said.

"Has it been that bad?" she laughed. "And what of your future?"

His hand dropped from my arm.

"That will depend on a number of things. No, one . . ." he answered pointedly with a direct glance at her eyes and a flash of his habitual assurance.

"If you're going to talk about Terry's past, or his future either, for that matter," I said, "you'll be busy for some time." With a comprehensive glance at both of them, I moved away.

I knew I had seen a man falling in love. You'd have to know Terry better to understand why I felt as I did. Nothing happened. He met a girl for the second time in his life. Obviously he was not himself, was at a loss for things to say. Like males of all species he was trying to preen and in his effort he was making a rather poor showing.

A man has no license to be as handsome as he is, tall, beautifully proportioned, with a finely shaped head, perfect features, and his eyes . . . Well, I don't wonder that he has been in one scrape after another. His eyes do it. They have a melting quality when he turns them on you suggesting romance, moonlight and honeysuckle. His charms, however, seemed to fail him, at least they were having no visible effect on Althea. She didn't help him even a little bit. He floundered for words and self-control.

The girl was an enigma to me. She seemed to be giving him her undivided attention but I knew her mind was far off. Poor Terry! She would use him to gain her own ends, of that I was certain.

Well, it was time he fell decently in love and in all probability the girl was too good for him. Time would tell. Some women are born matchmakers at heart. You know the type I mean, always busy and occupied interfering in other people's lives, introducing bachelors to young girls and vice versa. I've never been interested in doing that sort of thing. The role of an aged cupid wouldn't exactly suit me. I believe that love, like nature, should run its own course.

As I moved about among my guests, I kept watching him. He was not being himself. I know of no man who can be as charming when he wants to and yet he was what I'd call a self-conscious swain, rather clumsy and awkward as he tried to hold Althea's attention on himself rather than Sidney Kenfield. Sidney's years of aping Terry were bearing fruit. He was more like Terry at the moment than Terry was himself. It was as if the two personalities had been suddenly reversed. I knew perfectly well that Sidney Kenfield would eventually run out of material, people who are not original always do. I felt confident that Terry would bounce back to be his old gay self. It was as much a part of him as his black hair and gorgeous eyes.

Althea was no novice. She played one against the other with real skill. She reminded me of a sleek cat playing with a mouse. And that, believe it or not, is a compliment because I've seen Terry when he was a handful to manage. She was taking a keen delight in making him uncomfortable. I wondered how long he would stand for her barbed coldness, but the way of a man with a maid is more than I can fathom.

I could understand why men found her so attractive. She was different. She sat erect, drank very little, smoked less and listened with a nice semblance of interest to the conversation flowing about her like a torrent of lukewarm

slush. She had a native, ready wit which was lost in the
banalities of the current wisecracks culled from popular
periodicals. I liked her in spite of the things she was
doing to Terry. Perhaps, I thought, it's time some one
took the young man down a peg or two. I had never met a
woman who could do it so well.

In my living-room now, full of gin-laden, overrouged
(that goes for nails, fingers and toes) modern American
women, she stood out like a beacon on a hilltop. Don't
think I'm opposed to American women. I like them and
think they're smart and fine under the surface. It is the
superficial pose they affect which annoys me. I'll never be
able to understand why, in the length and breadth of the
land, they dress and act like tarts of the Nineties.
Perhaps it's just a phase through which they are passing.
You know and I know that they still have the sterling
qualities dormant in them that helped to make this
country what it is today. Where would the pioneers have
been if it had not been for the women who fought with
them shoulder to shoulder?

The party was being something of a success in spite of
the heat. Conversation had become more or less general
and things were going nicely. I decided to give Terry a
chance and walked up to the group and took Sidney
Kenfield by the arm. As I led him away, I heard Terry
say, "I really have a fine collection. I'd like to show them
to you."

Althea's answer was a laugh followed by, "Is this
invitation instead of the etching one? When may I come?"

"Now, tonight, anytime," Terry answered all too
eagerly.

"Charming woman," Kenfield said as we moved out of
earshot.

We neared the hall door when Agnes came to my side
and whispered, "There's a person outside who says he
must see Mr. Lassimon."

I went to the door and peered into the hall. The man, obviously the servant type, was nervously twirling his hat in his hand. He seemed vaguely familiar.

"Perhaps I can take care of him," Kenfield suggested and went into the hall.

After a few brief sentences, Kenfield came back and said, "He wants to see Terry about some books. He'd better talk to him. I couldn't make head or tail of it. Said it was something Terry was supposed to publish. There are more things going on," he complained as I went in to summon Terry. Kenfield remained at the door, no doubt expecting some explanation from Terry.

While Terry talked to the man, Althea said, "I hope you'll forgive me. I forgot to mention it to you before. I invited a young man to your party."

"Did I miss one?" I asked with a laugh.

"He came into town unexpectedly. You probably know him, Dick Bolertho."

Before I could answer, Sidney, who had left his post at the door, said, "Everybody knows about Dick Bolertho."

"I'm glad you asked him," I told Althea. "I'd have invited him myself had I known he was in town."

"What about Mr. Bolertho?" I heard Althea ask Kenfield as I went to the hall where Terry stood beckoning me with his eyes.

He led me out into the hall. "That," he said, in little more than a whisper, "was Mortimer's man. He wanted the diaries, insisted upon having them. Mortimer has seen my ad in the evening papers."

"And what message did you send?"

"I told him to tell Mortimer I'd either return them or agree to publish them as soon as I had finished reading them."

At that moment Althea went past the living-room door. She moved slowly and I had a distinct feeling that she had been listening. My mind didn't dwell on it at the moment because Jason went to the door and admitted Philip Lassimon, of all people. I was surprised.

He barely acknowledged my greeting as he spied Terry.

"I've been trying to get in touch with you all afternoon." He said it accusingly as if Terry had been remiss about something.

"Well, now that you've tracked me down, what do you want?" Terry was definitely lacking in cordiality.

"I must speak to you privately," Philip insisted.

I nodded toward my sitting-room and Terry led the man away.

I have never liked Philip Lassimon, Terry's cousin. In this long life of mine I have found that my first judgments and opinions of people are usually the right ones. Once or twice I have allowed myself to be convinced that I had made a mistake, but nine times out of ten I have found that I was right the first time. To me, Philip was a sanctimonious hypocrite who covered himself with a mantle of righteousness which annoyed me excessively.

Philip is the run of the mill Lassimon. They have all been alike as long as I can remember, except Terry. They have always been a stodgy, uninspired, dull lot devoting their time and attention to the acquisition of money and alleged culture. A night in a Lassimon living-room is about as dull and cheerless as a seaside resort on a cold, wet winter day.

Philip followed in his father's footsteps and after college went into the Lassimon Chemical Works to be ready to take care of the business if and when old Philip should be called to his makers. As far as I know, Philip has been a good business man. Lassimon products are nationally advertised, they sponsor an air program filled with sweetness and light—Philip's idea, which is quite in keeping with the family traditions and the position of Sunday School Superintendent which he holds in one of our more prominent houses of worship.

He is married—all Lassimons, the real ones, marry young—and bring a raft of thin, puny little Lassimons into the world to make sensible people wonder if there isn't something to eugenics, after all.

Terry and Philip were barely out of sight going up the stairs when the bell rang again. It was Dick Bolertho still looking as tragically handsome as he did the day his wife, Jessica, died.

I was glad to see him and told him so. Althea must have been watchfully waiting for him because she came to the door barely a moment after he entered. Dick was really a sweet boy. He chatted with me dutifully for several moments until I gave him a slight shove toward the living-room and told him a charming girl was waiting for him.

"And I'm talking to a most charming woman," he said boyishly, but with a sly wink he left me.

You remember Dick Bolertho, surely you must? The papers were full of his story just a few years ago. I don't believe he's a day over thirty now. He was a customer's man in the brokerage office of Dunn, Dunn and Dunn. That was probably a horrible name to many investors in the late fall of Nineteen-twenty-nine.

Jessica Dunn, the daughter of one of the partners, met the boy at the office and fell madly in love with him. Theirs was one of those sudden romances which flamed and captured the attention of the world. Newspapers, of course, had a great deal to do with it. They say all the world loves a lover and I agree with the saying if the boy and girl are both handsome and look romantic. Dick Bolertho was as near to the popular idea of a Greek god as any man can reasonably be. And he was neither dumb nor vain, as good-looking men so often are. As a matter of fact, right after the tragedy he was offered a contract in Hollywood which he flatly refused. Had he gone out there, I'm sure he'd have given the Gables and Taylors a run for their money.

Of course the Dunn family (they were new-rich Irish, Jessica was only two generations removed from shanty-town on Coogan's Bluff) objected to the match, but that didn't stop Jessica. She was worth three million in her own right which old Biddy Dunn had left her probably for just such an emergency. Biddy was a grand old girl, an adorable woman whose head was never turned by the fabulous fortune she and her husband had made. Of course Biddy never got into the Social Register, but that didn't worry her. She knew her grandchildren would make the grade and they did. Jessica had some of the old lady in her, I guess, because she turned over half of her fortune to Dick Bolertho before they were married just so he wouldn't feel like a poor man.

Dick took the money without making any fuss and I thought he acted very sensibly. He must have been a rather serious-minded chap even then because the papers were full of the wills he insisted on being drawn up and witnessed right after the ceremony. They were the kind of wills that husbands and wives should make if they believe and trust in one another. Each left their entire fortune to the other. I'm sure it was a nice motive which prompted him to do that. He evidently wanted to be sure that the Dunn money would return to the Dunn family.

Three days later the world was shocked by the news that Jessica had died. She fell from her horse and broke her neck while they were riding. It was a sad and horrible tragedy. The boy was beside himself with grief. He never married again and as far as I know took no interest in women. He has lived decently and respectably and has done, I've been told, a tremendous amount of good with his money.

One or two household matters demanded my attention just then. My guests were ravenously hungry, it seemed, because the hors d'oeuvres vanished almost as soon as they were taken into the room. It was getting late and cook wanted to know if she should make more. The ice too was running low and they wanted my advice about that. Much to my surprise, I was enjoying the party and hoped they'd stay as long as they liked. I'd just finished detailed instructions to Agnes when Terry and Philip came downstairs looking as solemn as two boiled owls.

"Come in, Philip, and have a drink," I invited.

I know he was about to say "I don't drink," as I hurried on, "You look like a man who needs a stiff one."

"I believe I do," he agreed. I took him inside, fixed the drink for him myself, introduced him to one or two people he didn't know and then returned to Terry, who had remained in the hall.

"Things are beginning to pop," Terry said quietly. "Philip is in the diaries."

I gasped. I couldn't believe my ears, yet I know you can't always trust the quiet God-fearing type of man.

"Been weeping on my shoulders about the family name and all that sort of bunk. Demanded that I destroy the books at once."

"What on earth has he done?" I asked.

"He didn't say, but it must be pretty bad. He's scared to death. He even threatened me."

"He did?"

"Yes. He said I wouldn't live long enough to regret my stubbornness unless I destroyed the books."

"I'd like to know where Philip was last night when that shot was fired at you."

"Probably safe in his bed."

"What could Philip have done bad enough to make him threaten you?" I speculated.

"Search me. Maybe we should read them, after all," he suggested.

"Where ignorance is bliss ..." I started to quote but was stopped by the departure of a guest.

Ten or fifteen minutes later the party began to break up. Looking for all the world like a disappointed faun, Sidney Kenfield came away from the group and joined me at the door.

"Leaving so soon, Sidney?" I asked.

"Might as well. There's a conspiracy going on over there in the corner." With a jerk of his head he indicated the group clustered about Althea and Terry.

"Conspiracy?" I asked.

"Yes. Say, do you know anything about the ad Terry ran in this evening's paper? Several people have asked me and I know nothing about it. I've asked Terry, but he told me to wait. Am I his partner or his office boy?" he complained.

I felt sorry for Sidney. "It's probably something quite private and personal," I suggested. "Terry usually knows what he's doing."

"He doesn't have to be secretive about it," Sidney objected.

We chatted for a few minutes. Just as he turned from me, Terry came hurrying up, calling him.

"Say, old man," he used his best wheedling tone, "if any one asks you about diaries tell them you know nothing about them, will you?"

"I don't, do I?" Sidney asked with a growl.

"No and just stick to that story, will you? If you are forced to say anything, just say they aren't in the office."

"Okay," Sidney agreed grudgingly.

"I'll tell you all about it tomorrow."

"Why not tonight? How about dinner?" Sidney insisted.

"Tomorrow," Terry promised. "I'm dining with Ethel tonight. She's going to lend us some money."

That made Sidney beam as he departed.

Philip Lassimon, Dick Bolertho and Althea left together. They were the last to go. Relieved, I sank down into a chair. Terry stood near the door watching the group outside the house. He said with a sigh, "They look like a band of conspirators. I don't like the company she keeps."

"Meaning which man?" I asked unable to resist the chance to tease him.

"Looks like Bolertho's after another fortune," he said bitterly.

"You were fairly attentive yourself," I reminded him, "and any young man who's so badly off that he needs a loan of two hundred thousand is apt to get himself talked about if he is overly attentive to an attractive young woman who is about to take over a fortune which is in the millions."

"Right," he said tersely. "It was a rotten thing for me to say about Dick. I'm sorry. I don't know what's the matter with me. I'm worried, I guess."

One of the things I've always liked about Terry has been his willingness to admit himself in the wrong. I've never known him to shirk it, either.

"Forget it," I suggested.

"I will, but do you know I've a sneaking suspicion she arranged it all," he said regretfully.

"Arranged what?"

"Those people, your uninvited guests, Philip, Bolertho."

CHAPTER SIX

Our dinner together was not a success. I wasn't hungry and Terry picked at his food, eating only a little of the chicken mousse of which he is supposed to be inordinately fond. Conversation was as slim as our appetites. I was tired, and his mind was miles away from my dinner table.

Over our brandy, I suggested, "You'd better take Sidney into your confidence, partially at least; he is feeling slighted and abused."

"He'll be all right," Terry assured me. "There's no point in having him mixed up in the mess, too."

"But he is your partner and is entitled to some explanation. The young man is annoyed."

"He's often like that. Imagines he's being slighted when no slight has been intended." He sighed, which made me wonder if Sidney was something of a problem, but I said nothing.

Terry helped himself to another brandy, lit a cigarette, toyed with it for a moment and then snuffed it out. "I say," he finally managed to get it out, "do you mind if I run along? I'm no good to you or myself. I think I'll go up to the apartment and try to get some sleep."

"Is it cool up there?" I asked.

"Er—oh, yes, cool enough, I guess. I hadn't noticed." He came round the table to plant a rather dutiful kiss on my brow.

"Run along," I said. "I'll sit here, have a cigarette and finish my brandy."

"I say, I'm sorry. I thought you had finished. Forgive me, please."

"Run along." I patted his back. "Call me if you have any news. You should be in the clear by tomorrow. Don't forget," I called after him as he went into the hall.

I inhaled my brandy and smoked for at least a half-hour after he left. Agnes hovered about making pretenses of helping the waitress clear the table. "It was a nice party for such a hot day," she qualified.

I agreed.

"Do nice people go to parties uninvited?" she asked.

"Sometimes, even the nice ones do it."

Agnes laughed. "You don't think Mr. Philip Lassimon is nice, do you?" she went on, getting bolder.

"That's enough, Agnes."

"Yes, ma'am." She held my chair as I left the table.

"What are you angling for?" I asked.

She laughed self-consciously as she always did when I outguessed her. "Cook and I would like to see Robert Taylor tonight. It'll be cool there, too, if you don't mind."

"Go, by all means. You both deserve a treat," I agreed. She beamed, waiting for my next move which had been the same for years. I opened my purse and looked for two one-dollar bills. I was out of change. I handed her a five. "Three dollars change, remember," I cautioned.

"Yes, ma'am."

I was about halfway up the stairs when the telephone rang. I waited undecided whether to take the call in my room or at the hall switch. Agnes looked up at me and said, "It's Mr. Terry. He said to hurry."

I went back to the hall and lifting the receiver said, "Yes, Terry."

"Ethel, something terrible has happened at my apartment! I don't know what to do." His voice was barely above a whisper.

"What is it?" I demanded. "Talk louder."

"I'm afraid. I don't want any one to hear. I should call the police but thought I'd wait until I talked to you. Will you come up?"

I assured him I would. Police! Will a bull charge a red flag? Did he think wild horses could keep me away? I turned to Agnes as I rang off and said, "Tell Malcolm to have the car at the front door in ten minutes." I scurried up the stairs. "You and cook may ride up town with me if you're ready," I called back to her.

In ten minutes they were in the hall waiting for me. Malcolm was at the curb, the car door open. My car is an old Lincoln limousine. I've had it ten years and have become quite attached to it and although it is something of an antique as cars go, I like sitting up high and seeing things. I never thought I'd live to see the day when I would rather have one of those low slinky models but then one never knows what will happen.

When Malcolm saw cook and Agnes, I saw his nose tilt upward at least a quarter-inch. He is an excellent chauffeur but a terrible snob. He doesn't approve of my occasional habit of giving some of the servants a lift if we happen to be going in the same direction. His nose has an habitual tilt due to long years of sniffing disdainfully at what he considers my plebeian laxness. He takes awfully good care of me but I'm quite sure he thinks I'm not quite right in the head and need looking after. He's very conventionally-minded, having been in service on the other side for Lady Some-thing-or-other who was, I'm sure from all he says, a perfect lady and probably as dull as dishwater.

"Where are you going?" I asked the girls.

"The Strand," Agnes replied.

"Cook, you ride with Malcolm," I suggested.

"They can both ride with me," Malcolm offered.

"It's too hot. Stop at Forty-seventh and Broadway and then take me to Mr. Lassimon's apartment. You know where it is."

On that ride uptown through the early evening traffic, I tortured myself with questions that I couldn't possibly answer. What on earth had happened at Terry's apartment?

In just about a half-hour after he telephoned me, I left the automatic lift on the sixth floor of the old apartment building on Central Park West which the Lassimon family has owned for years. I rang the bell of Terry's apartment. There was a considerable wait which worried me. I was on the verge of pounding on the door, the bell seeming to have been without effect, when I heard Terry's hushed voice asking, "Who's there?"

At the sound of my voice, he opened the door narrowly and closed it quickly after me.

"Why the caution and secrecy?" I demanded. "What on earth has happened?"

He led me across the small foyer to the door of the living-room. He didn't have to say a word. The place was topsy-turvy. Every possible hiding-place for anything as large as a pin had been investigated. His desk was littered with papers and books, drawers yawning open had been rifled, cabinets, their doors swinging wide, attested the thoroughness of the search which had been made.

"What has been taken?" I asked.

"Nothing," he replied. "What they wanted wasn't here."

"Why should they search this place for the diaries?" I demanded.

"Because I gave Mortimer's man the impression that I was reading them here."

"Then you think this was Mortimer's work?" I asked.

"I don't know. It hardly seems possible that Mortimer would have done this if his man were searching for the diaries." He led me further into the room and stopped a few feet from a large divan. "What do you make of this?" he asked, pointing down to the floor in front of the couch.

On the floor about a foot in front of us on a small white rug lay a revolver, its nozzle jutting into what was evidently a splotch of blood. I moved closer and gasped. Under the edge of the divan there was a man's felt hat, but that was not the thing which made me cry out. Just beyond the edge of the divan on the floor lay Althea's silver compact. There could be no mistaking that compact. It was silver, chased and flat. I know perfectly well that there are hundreds of compacts all made alike, but this was not one of the common type. It had been made by a silversmith and was probably the only one of its kind in existence.

"Pretty tough, isn't it?" he asked, not understanding my reason for gasping the way I did. I wanted to get hold of the compact without his seeing it. Since he fancied himself in love with the girl there was no reason for letting him know about that compact until we had all our cards ready to put on the table. I was wondering if she had been in the apartment and asked, "Has any one been here?"

"Obviously," he replied, which annoyed me, but I knew I had to be patient because he couldn't possibly understand what I meant.

"You haven't called the police?"

"No, and I don't want them," he replied vehemently.

"Why not?" I asked. "Your apartment has been robbed, there has been a tussle of some sort here, murder for all we know."

"It couldn't have been murder," he denied.

"Why not?" I demanded.

"Because there's no body. I'm surprised at you, Ethel."

"You're right about the body," I agreed. "Now tell me who the two people were who were here?" I felt certain that I knew the identity of one of them. Had Althea been wounded? Or was she the person who had fired the shot?

"I suppose there must have been two people," he said.

"Unless the person who was making the search shot ..." I very nearly said herself but caught the word before it was uttered and ended, "himself."

I knew there had been two people in that room. Althea wouldn't wear the hat we had found.

"What do you think we should do about this?" he asked.

"We'd better call my friend, Detective Peter Conklin," I suggested. "He'll help us."

"No, thanks," he said decisively.

"But, Terry," I remonstrated, "I'm a firm believer in conforming to the rules of law and order." I meant it then as I said it, with no idea in my mind how far afield from law, order, and normality I would go before the night was actually over.

"We're a little outside law and order at the moment," he reminded me. "We're toying with dynamite. What could I tell the police?" he asked with absolute reason.

"Have you looked through the apartment?" I asked as I moved closer to the end of the divan and the compact. I don't see how he missed seeing it himself.

He glared at me. "Looked! I've searched every closet and corner of the apartment, even looking on the shelves, and found nothing. Do you think this is just a plant to frighten me?" he ended.

"I hope so," I answered and bent down and pulled the hat from under the edge of the divan. Then I sat on the edge of the couch to conceal the compact from him. I examined the hat. It was just an ordinary gray felt with an initial J pasted on the sweat-band. I tossed the hat toward him. While he examined it, I reached down for the compact and dropped it into the pocket of my skirt. I wear rather full flounced skirts and; always have a pocket made along one of the seams. Such a pocket is convenient and a much better place for your handkerchief than down your neck, up your sleeve, or constantly picking it up from the floor.

He twirled the hat in his hand thoughtfully after he looked at that enigmatic letter. "J what? Is it a first name or a last name?" he asked.

"Let me see it again," I asked getting up.

I took the hat to a lamp, pulled out the sweat-band and studied it carefully. "It's a first name," I announced. "See where a second letter has been pasted and rubbed loose? It was one of the following, B-D- E-F-H-I-K-L-M-N-P-R." I rattled the list off quickly.

"My, you do know your alphabet, don't you?" he grinned, becoming more normal.

"I was taught that way when I went to school." I retorted. "I've no patience with people who make such a fuss about not knowing the alphabet."

"What a memory!" he teased. "But tell me, why one of those letters?"

"Because the leather hasn't been discolored in one place indicating clearly that the second letter pasted in here had a vertical line at its beginning."

"Excellent reasoning, my dear Watson, excellent. Just rest while I go through the alphabet, with your help. J. B.," he muttered and paused, "J. D " He went through the list carefully and thoughtfully until I was a bit bored by it and him. Finally he looked at me and said, "I don't know any J anything that will fit the hat, do you?"

I didn't. And furthermore, I couldn't make rhyme nor reason out of the problem which confronted us. I knew that some one searching for the diaries had turned his apartment inside out. I knew that Althea had been there. Was she the person who had made such a thorough search? I rather doubted that because I didn't believe a fastidious woman (and she was one) would have made such a mess of things. If she hadn't made the search, was she the person who had shot the searcher?

"Where are the diaries?" I asked.

"Just where you told me to put them, in the office safe, wrapped, sealed and marked personal," he replied.

"How many people believed they might be there?" I asked.

"Mortimer, his man and . . . That's all."

But was it? I remembered that moment in the afternoon when Althea crossed the living-room door. Had she been listening to us? If she had stood there in the door she could have heard Terry's report to me. Had Althea arrived at the apartment to find Mortimer searching the place for his diaries? Had she in a moment of rage shot at him feeling that with him out of the way she would have a clear field to get the diaries and destroy them? I recalled her rather cold-blooded remark of the afternoon when she said throwing Mortimer overboard would be a good idea. But the hat, and that initial J? Mortimer wouldn't be wearing another man's hat.

"Why not let me in on your thoughts?" Terry suggested. "I'm as bewildered as you are."

"I'm just trying to make sense out of a situation which in unexplainable," I replied. "Two people were here. One of them was wounded. There's something unreasonable about that. The two people who were here in search of the diaries had something in common. There is no sign of a struggle. Why the shot?"

"Nothing in common if one of them was Mortimer," he reminded me.

"That's true, but at the moment a dead Mortimer would mean additional danger for you as the sole holder of the secrets."

"Why a dead Mortimer? I don't follow you."

"I'm fishing for something. I feel certain the meeting here was not premeditated. It must have had a surprise element to it."

"Are you trying to say that if some one was killed here I'd have a difficult time explaining the evidence without a body?"

"Something like that. It seems a ridiculous thing for a murderer to do but it would put you in a most embarrassing position, wouldn't it?" I asked.

"Embarrassing!" he repeated. "You understate. What are you driving at, anyhow?" he asked irritably.

"Suppose a person wanted you out of the way for some very good reason which we don't understand at the moment," I asked.

"Well?"

"One attempt which failed has been made on your life. That failure makes it dangerous for the person to carry on any further direct attempts but he still wants you out of the way."

"I don't follow your reasoning," he interrupted.

"Your enemy knows I'm in your confidence. Don't you see if you were killed, I'd be able to give the police a clue which might eventually lead them to the criminal? Your enemy is smart, Terry. He has thought of things from every angle. I'm assuming at the moment that a man was killed here. You'd have less difficulty explaining these bits of evidence with a body to corroborate your story than you have at this moment."

"He wants me out of the way, in jail, waiting a conviction for a crime which I didn't commit. Is that what you mean?"

"Something like that," I agreed.

"But what good would that do him?"

"He could get at the diaries without you in his way."

"But why get me out of the way?"

"I wish I knew," I answered, completely baffled. The next moment I had a sudden inspiration. "Terry," I cried, "we must do something and do it quickly! The police are apt to be here any moment and we sit wasting precious moments talking. If our reasoning, any of it, has been right your enemy will send the police here under some pretext or other. Get me a small hand-bag, quickly, one about the size of a dressing-case," I ordered.

He hesitated a second. "Hurry," I cried, excited, "they may be here any moment! I'll take care of the evidence." I bent down and started to fold the rug.

"But I can't let you do that!" he protested.

"You can't do anything else. Will you hurry? I'll take the stuff home with me, drop it in the river, burn it, or do something. Don't you worry about me," I called after him.

He was back in a jiffy with a medium-sized black pin-seal suitcase.

We worked quickly. Fortunately, the rug was on a thin rubber pad so we didn't have to worry about any stain on the floor itself. The rubber mat and the rug had absorbed all the blood. I folded the rug and the mat into a flat bundle and squeezed them both into the bag, then put the hat and revolver on top of them and snapped the lid shut. Then we placed another small rug in front of the divan so that the floor wouldn't seem so bare. That done, we were considerably relieved.

We then began putting the room in order. "That gun," I asked, "ever see it before?"

"It's mine. It's been in the top drawer of the desk for years."

"Was it fired?"

He shrugged.

I opened the bag, took out the gun and fiddled with it. I've heard of breaking a gun and all that sort of thing, but it wouldn't break. I should have known better than fool with the darned thing, for the first thing I knew it went off with a terrific-bang. Terry jumped forward and took it from me. It had been fired once before. While Terry put the gun with the other things, I went back to the divan and tried to discover angles from which the gun had been fired. I found the telltale mark. There was a hole in the divan near the top. I pointed to the hole. We were about to move the divan when the doorbell rang.

Automatically our eyes went toward the small handbag.

"Put it in the hall near the door," I whispered. I took a chiffon scarf from my shoulders and dropped it over the hole on the back of the couch.

"It's too dangerous," he whispered, hesitating, the bag in his hand.

"Do as you're told. I'll pretend I'm ready to leave. I'll go out and take the bag with me. Get along now and open the door." I moved behind him, all ready to make my exit speech in case it was the police.

Reluctantly he opened the door and there, smiling on the threshold, stood Althea.

CHAPTER SEVEN

"Are your etchings at home?" she asked facetiously in greeting. Then spying me, said, "How nice so see you so soon again! You two are quite inseparable, aren't you?"

That girl had the self-possession of the devil. She had missed her compact and had returned to get it. Well, I'd fool her this time. I'd let her look. She followed Terry into the room. He began to apologize for the appearance of the room.

"Have you lost something?" she asked looking about very carefully but pretending to be innocent enough.

"No, have you?" I demanded.

"How could I?" She tried to worm out of an answer by laughing.

"Don't hedge. What are you doing in a man's apartment at this hour of the night?"

"I might ask you the same question, but I won't," she retorted.

"Because you know the answer," I replied. "What do you want?"

"Ethel, please," Terry begged, not understanding.

I was annoyed with myself. I intended to let her show her own hand instead. I began forcing the issue at once.

"We've been a little upset," Terry started to explain.

"Save your breath," I cut in. "She knows all about it. She's seen all this and a lot more." I was definitely opposed to the girl at the moment. If it were to be a choice between Terry and Althea, I was more than willing to throw her to the dogs.

Her best defense was to say nothing and she knew it. She did a very good job of being amazed and puzzled by my speech. Terry was dumfounded. He looked at me as if I had suddenly gone mad. I reached into my pocket, drew out the compact and handed it to her, saying, "Here it is, the thing you returned to get. It was on the floor at the end of the couch. I didn't want him to know about it at first, but I've changed my mind."

"Thank you so much," she said as she took it from my hand. "That was careless of me."

I would have enjoyed slapping her; her poise annoyed me and yet I admired her for it.

"But I don't understand," Terry said, eying us both. "Would you mind letting me in on this?"

"Sit down," I suggested to Althea. I selected a straight-backed chair for myself. I always feel at a disadvantage both mentally and physically when I'm slumped down in a soft squashy overstuffed chair.

"I prefer to stand," she replied and stood facing me.

"Have it your own way." I looked at her sharply. "Now, young lady, perhaps you'll tell us what you were doing here earlier this evening."

Terry moved between us and spoke to her. "You don't have to answer questions. You needn't tell us why you were here, if you were, what you did, or anything about it. I don't want to know. We know you've been worried and upset. We don't know why and we don't want to learn your secret. I'm sure that whatever you may have done was done for a legitimate reason. It's all right, really it is."

I snorted but he paid no attention to me. What a fool a man can be when he's in love!

"Pay no attention to her. I don't care what you've done in the past or what you may do in the future. If you'd only trust me, I'd be able to take care of and protect you. I want to do it. Won't you believe me?"

Her reply was just about as warm as a breeze from a glacier. I felt sorry for Terry. His little speech had been a declaration of love which she ignored completely as she said, "That's very nice of you, but I believe in taking care of myself. I don't approve of your tactics. When there's danger which threatens I believe in removing it if possible. I did come here hoping to find the diaries. I heard you tell that man this afternoon that you were reading them."

"That was Mortimer Van Wyck's man. I did that to stall Mortimer. I have no intention of reading them, honestly."

"I couldn't know that. I came here hoping to find the diaries. I'd have destroyed them, too, but I came too late," she ended, sweeping the room with her hand.

Terry sighed with relief. He was being a bit heroic and I think he meant what he said, but you know, and I know, that we don't want to think a person we love is guilty of murder. The girl had information which we might find useful. I changed my tactics. She wasn't exactly on our side and she'd make a better friend than enemy. I had to protect Terry if he wasn't interested in protecting himself.

"Perhaps you could help us understand a few things," I said with a complete change of tone. "I'd like to ask you a few questions."

"Certainly."

"What time did you arrive here?"

"About eight."

"Had you ever seen the man before?" I asked, hoping to catch her in a trap.

"I didn't see his face," she answered.

I was dumfounded by her answer.

"Whose face?" Terry shouted.

"The man's." She looked toward the couch and shuddered slightly. "He was there on the floor face down, a revolver beside him, his hat half off his head. I see you have removed the evidence," she ended accusingly.

"What did you think?" I asked.

"Since he seemed to be quite dead I supposed there had been a murder," she replied. "I see you have covered the bullet-hole with your scarf."

My, but she was a sharp one! "And yet," I said, "realizing that there had been a murder, you did nothing about it?"

"Why should I? I could have no interest in the murdered person when I realized it was not Mr. Lassimon."

"You thought it was me?" Terry asked.

"Only for a moment. When I moved forward and looked more closely I realized it was not you."

"Why didn't you do something about it?" I insisted.

"Why should I call the police and expose some secret of Mr. Lassimon's? I'm not interested in the secrets of others."

"Neither are we," I replied. The implication was too pointed to let it pass without notice.

"You have such an odd way of proving it," she retorted.

"Did you see any one in the halls or the elevator as you came up?" Terry asked.

"No one."

"How did you get in here?" I demanded.

"First, I rang the bell and waited for a long time, then I rang again. There was no answer. I thought I heard a movement inside, so I rang the third time. After a long interval, I turned away. My elbow grazed against the door and it opened just a little. I pushed the door open further and called but no one replied. Then I came in here. I was amazed at what I saw. I knew I was too late. I left at once because I didn't want to be connected in any way with what, on the surface, seemed to be a murder."

"You didn't leave until you came all the way into the room. Your compact was under the far end of the couch. Why did you bend down?"

"To see if the man was Mr. Lassimon. It was then that I noticed the bullet-hole in the couch."

"You're very observant," I admitted grudgingly, "but tell me, if you didn't want to be connected with this murder, why did you come back this time?"

"Blackmail," she replied shamefacedly.

We both gasped.

"You see," she explained, "I thought that Mr. Lassimon had killed some one."

"You don't believe that?" Terry cried.

"Why not? You both think I did it!"

"But we don't! We know you had nothing to do with it, don't we, Ethel?" he pleaded.

I nodded in agreement. "Go on about the blackmail," I urged.

"Perhaps it's in the air," she said wearily. "Anyhow, as I thought it over, I knew that Mr. Lassimon would be in a difficult position. I called your house and learned that he had left. I came here to demand the diaries for my silence," she stated boldly.

"But I have nothing to hide!" Terry cried.

"Then where is the body, the rug, the gun, and the hat?" she demanded. "Why haven't you called the police?"

I countered with a question, "Are you quite sure that you didn't come back here for your compact?"

"Naturally, I wanted to get that too. I knew I could find it while I was putting my proposition to Mr. Lassimon."

"But unfortunately for you I found the compact, so your little scheme has fallen through."

"Not exactly. You've given me the compact. You can't prove now that it or I was ever here before."

"And since you don't know where the body, the rug, the gun or the hat are, you have no story either," I reminded her. "We've sort of squared accounts, haven't we?"

"You don't believe me, do you, Miss Thomas?" she asked point-blank.

"Not completely." I was just as direct. "If you only came in for a moment, how on earth did you lose the compact?"

"I suppose it fell out of my bag when I tucked it under my arm. The end is quite open. See, it's a silly bag, really." She held it up to give me a demonstration which made her answer reasonable enough. The end was quite open. She was either as deep as darkness or naively innocent. I didn't know which, but I knew she was no fool.

"I'm glad you came back," Terry said honestly. "It's cleared up a number of things for all of us."

"I didn't search your apartment and I didn't kill any one," she said bluntly. "I came back because I wanted to get the diaries or to know exactly what has happened to them. Were they stolen?"

"No. I still have them," he replied.

"Then give them to me," she demanded, "or I'll tell the police what I know about this apartment."

"You wouldn't," he said, trying to make himself believe his own words.

"Wouldn't I? Aren't you afraid?"

"Very much," he admitted, "of a number of things. ..."

He didn't finish because the bell rang and was immediately followed by a peremptory rapping on the hall door which cut him short.

"That," I suggested, "is probably the police."

"Police?" she asked unbelievingly.

The rapping grew more insistent. Terry moved toward the door.

"Yes," I explained quickly. "We think the murderer is trying to put Terry on the spot. Now's your chance. Tell them your little story. The rug, gun, and hat are in the black bag there in the hall. We know nothing about the body. He may as well hang for a sheep as a lamb. Go ahead." I turned away from her and stood near the desk as the clattering at the door died away.

Two policemen marched into the room like Tweedle-dum and Tweedle-dee and in chorus asked about the robbery.

Our guess had been right. Terry's enemy had sent them. But why had he waited so long? Had he been busy with the body?

One of them, the shorter of the two, was very businesslike as he took out a little book and began asking questions. The other moved about the room investigating.

When Terry admitted that nothing had been stolen they lost interest at once and seemed rather disgusted.

"I guess you came in and scared them off," the little one suggested. "Is there a back way out of here?" he asked.

"Yes, a service stair and elevator," Terry replied. "Would you like to see it?"

The man nodded and off they went. The other man continued to move about the room. He looked over at me and said, "They sure made a mess of things. Didn't they take nothin'?"

"Mr. Lassimon says not," I answered with a look at Althea, who seemed fascinated by the policeman.

"Well, I'll see if they've found anything out back," he said and wandered off.

"Why didn't you tell them?" I asked bitterly.

I believe her eyes were rimmed with tears as she said, "You know I wouldn't do a thing like that. I don't want to get any one into trouble. It's too horrible."

Terry and the officers came back. "Sorry to have troubled you, boys," Terry was beaming, "but I always think it's best to call the police in a case of this kind."

"Right you are, sir. Glad they didn't get anything."

"How about a drink?" Terry suggested with a wink. "It'll cool you off."

"Or make us hotter," the little one replied, "but hot or cold, what's the difference, as my wife always says."

They rattled around in the pantry for a few minutes and then with a cheery goodnight left.

We all sighed with relief when the door closed behind them.

"Would you like a drink?" Terry asked.

"I don't want anything but the destruction of those diaries," Althea answered. "Will you do it?"

"Not until all the people vitally concerned meet in one place with Mortimer and see them destroyed," he answered firmly.

"Mortimer won't consider their destruction. I've offered to buy them," she cried in desperation.

"If all concerned make their offer large enough, I'll see that they are destroyed," he promised.

"And in the meantime, you jeopardize my future and risk your own life for people who don't care whether you live or die," she said scornfully.

"I do care, and I've very good reasons for knowing that some one member of those interested cannot be trusted with any secret. While the books are in my possession, you are all safe from Mortimer and the unknown."

"How can you be so contrary? You'd put an end to it all if you'd destroy them," she cried in exasperation.

"I'm sorry, but it will have to be done my way now. As soon as you or Mortimer or any other person concerned can contact all the others and bring them together in one place, I'll produce the diaries. You'll come, of course."

"If it isn't too late," she replied, thoroughly beaten for the moment. "Goodnight, Miss Thomas." She turned, marched to the door and left, making no effort to conceal her contempt for Terry.

I had a drink with him. We both needed one and together we mulled over the situation which confronted us. Our hands were tied. There was nothing we could do about the affair without incriminating ourselves. Any question, action or movement on our part would be equivalent to an admission of guilt. Painful as it would be, we had to sit and wait for the next move from the man who seemed more determined than ever to remove Terry from his path. Why? Terry didn't know and neither did I. He would have to muddle along torn by fear and worry wondering who the victim was, where his body had been taken and how we would be connected with his death.

I felt certain that Terry had suspicions of one sort or another and I tried to draw him out, but he was as silent as a desert sunset. I had nothing upon which I could work. I had seen only a vague shadow from across the street the night of the shot. I found myself wishing I had read the diaries. At least then we would have had something to go on. All we knew at the moment for certain was that Philip Lassimon was interested in the diaries along with Althea.

Of course we should have called the police right at the start but we didn't and our muddling along alone made no difference anyhow. The crimes would have been committed in just the way they were because the murderer was overconfident of his ability to fool us all and he had very good reason for his assumption. I still get angry when I think of our blindness as we groped our way through the fog of the following events.

After a fruitless talk during which Terry' refused to return to my house to stay until the whole thing had blown over, I started home alone. He wanted to go down to the street with me, but knowing that Malcolm would be there, I refused. Things would have been different if he had insisted, but he didn't. I'm not blaming him because I'm very definite about things like that and hate people to make issues of them. With the little bag clutched tightly in my hand, I started down in the automatic lift.

When I reached the ground floor, I had some difficulty operating the inner and outer door with one hand, but I was determined to keep hold of that black bag.

The air was breathlessly hot as I reached the door. I could see my old Lincoln pulled up against the curb a few feet down the street. I rather expected Malcolm to come running forward, but I reached the car without a sign of him. I then realized that he was slumped down under the wheel asleep.

It isn't often that I can catch him napping. I decided to give him a shock. I opened the rear door quietly, put the bag on the floor and started to climb over it. I must have been a queer sight from the rear for I know one of my legs hung in midair for a minute or more. I couldn't move in or out, neither could I believe my eyes, for the body of a dead man was slumped across the rear seat.

CHAPTER EIGHT

When I finally managed to get back on to the curb and had slammed the car door shut to keep prying eyes from that inert body, I hurried round to the front of the car expecting I knew not what. Poor Malcolm, would I find him as still and dead as that thing on the back seat? Now, don't say, "Why didn't the old fool call an officer?" I thought of that but I couldn't call the police without a long explanation which would involve Terry. I needed no chart to tell me that the man on the back seat of my car was the man who had been murdered in Terry's apartment. I didn't stop to look at the body to identify it. I was too taken-back by the unexpectedness of it. Where had the murderer been with the body from the time he left the apartment until my car arrived? The whole thing was fantastic and why in heaven's name pick on me? Of course I knew even as I walked to his side that if Malcolm were dead I'd have to do something and do it quickly. If I had been less conscious of all the things which had happened I probably would have called the police right then and there although if I had known the identity of the man nothing in the world would have prompted me even to consider such a step.

Fearfully, I felt for Malcolm's heart, he was breathing heavily. What a relief! I suppose he was really snoring. I gave a great sigh. Poor soul! My eyes filled with tears. We're very fond of each other, Malcolm and I. He's been with me for so many years. I opened his shirt collar and loosened his tie. He'd have been scandalized if he had been conscious. I shook him and called into his ear. He just went on snoring heavily, paying no attention to me. Have you ever tried to do anything with a man who is unconscious, slumped under the steering-wheel of a car? I tried to slap his chest but without much success. It was then that I noticed the piece of wadding. It had fallen to the seat between his sprawled legs. From the position they were in, I imagine he must have struggled for a moment.

I lifted the wadding and sniffed. Chloroform!

There were people passing up and down the street and I was afraid I'd attract attention. You know what people are in New York. An Indian could walk down Broadway in full war-paint and no one would pay any attention to him, but let a woman or a man, normally dressed, do anything even slightly out of the ordinary and a crowd gathers. I had to have help, so I went back to the apartment for Terry.

For a moment, after I gasped out my story, he acted as if he thought I had lost my senses or had had a touch of heat.

"How do you revive a man who has been chloroformed?" I cried. "Do you know? If you do, come along."

He went to the kitchen and came back with a bottle of ammonia and some ice cubes wrapped in a napkin. He slipped into his coat and together we went back to the car. I held the ice and bottle while Terry managed to slide Malcolm out from under the wheel. As I crawled into the car to hold him upright, I took one hurried glance at the thing in the back but couldn't recognize the man. Terry went round to the other side and climbed in under the wheel and held the bottle to Malcolm's nose. In the meantime, I rubbed his wrists with ice cubes which felt like pieces of glass in the heat.

After a few minutes, Malcolm began to stir. I sighed with relief as his eyes flickered open.

"We'd better ride about a bit, to give him plenty of air," Terry suggested.

We drove round and round the park with the front windshield partially open until Malcolm regained consciousness. When he opened his eyes and realized I was holding him in my arms he blinked in amazement and went off again. The next time he came out of it, he slithered himself a bit and I let him sit alone, steadying him with one hand on his arm. He was upset when he realized that his shirt was open and his tie undone.

"Take it easy, man," Terry advised. "You've had a rough time."

We kept circling the park until I felt the place was a huge merry-go-round. After an hour or more Malcolm said, "I think I could drive, now, sir."

"What's the matter," Terry chided, "don't you like my driving?"

"It's all right, sir, but you're a bit rough on the curves for Miss Ethel. She's fussy about her curves, sir."

Terry let go with a guffaw that very nearly ran us into a tree.

"Never mind about the curves and, Terry, take it slower," I ordered. "Now, Malcolm, tell me what happened."

"I don't know, Miss. I was sitting there and all of a sudden somebody plumped something over my nose and there I was. I struggled for a bit but it didn't do me any good. What did happen?"

"You were chloroformed, Malcolm," Terry explained.

"But why?" he asked naturally enough.

"Can you keep a secret?" Terry asked.

"I think so, sir."

"We have a dead man in the back of the car," Terry said quietly.

"A what, sir?"

"A corpse."

"Good heavens! Miss Ethel!" he exclaimed turning to me. "You've haven't gone and killed some one, have you? What are we going to do with it?"

Bless his old heart! He thought me mad enough to commit murder but he was ready and willing to help me in spite of his fears.

"It's not my corpse," I started to explain.

"That's good," he sighed with relief.

"You were chloroformed so that the body could be placed there. We've got to get rid of it somehow," Terry explained.

"Could we give it to the police or take it to the morgue?" he asked innocently.

"Neither of those things. You know what the police are. We can't answer questions. They're too involving," Terry explained. "I'm in a bit of a jam, Malcolm. Miss Ethel is helping me. I didn't kill the man but he is my responsibility. We've got to get rid of it."

"Yes, sir."

"Any suggestions?" Terry went on.

Malcolm was immediately helpful. "There's the river, sir," he said, "or a bench here in the park. There are dark alleys and vacant lots and just the other day I read in a book where they took the body and left it in an empty store. We might put him in an empty cab, sir, if we can find one which the driver has left while he's having a bite to eat." He went on, "I read in another book where the body was put in a police car in front of the police station. That would be a good trick, don't you think?" he ended hopefully.

"What do you say?" Terry grinned across Malcolm to me.

"I couldn't dump him into the river, Terry."

"No, ma'am, I suppose not." It was Malcolm who agreed with me.

We were probably making our tenth round of the park when a siren sounded behind us and a motorcycle policeman pulled alongside. I must admit that my heart jumped into my mouth. I felt Malcolm shiver. Terry pulled over to one side. The officer rested his foot on our running-board and suggested, "Why don't you take a trip up Pelham Parkway or over the new bridge to Long Island. It ought to be cooler than the park."

"That's an idea," Terry grinned. "I never thought of it."

"The truth of it is," the cop smiled, "I'm sick of seeing this old bus running around. Aren't many of them left."

I leaned over and looked at the officer. His voice sounded familiar. Sure enough, he was the man detailed to give me escort to Harlem when I was on the Doane case. "You should know this car," I chirped. "You led it all the way to Harlem a little over a year ago."

"Miss Thomas, ma'am!" he grinned. "How are you? Working on another case? Who was killed this time?"

I felt Malcolm squirm. I know I gulped before I replied, "No case. Just trying to keep cool. Too bad you can't come with us."

"Well, to tell you the truth, for two cents I'd like to put my bike on the back there and go along with you, only I have to watch the park. We're busy tonight with the heat and all. Well, so long." With a roar he sped away. The three of us sighed with relief and Terry headed out of the park at 110 th Street.

"You're not really going to the new bridge, are you?" I asked.

"No, but he may change his mind and want to go for that ride."

"That gave me a bad turn," Malcolm breathed. "I thought he had us sure."

I liked the way Malcolm included himself in the conspiracy. Terry turned onto Fifth Avenue. We headed downtown. "There may be an empty bench somewhere near the Museum," he suggested.

Malcolm and I peered at the benches which seemed so well shaded by the trees. There was only one vacant and that was in a pool of light from a street lamp.

"What do you think?" Terry asked as we slowed down for the bench.

"No, Terry," I cried. "We can't risk it. Some one would be sure to notice this car and remember it. No matter where we leave the body, if we are seen at all, this car will give us away. You might just as well put the Eiffel Tower on Times Square and expect it to go unnoticed."

Just then some people sauntered out from the shade and moved toward the bench.

"Standing room only," Terry muttered. "I never saw so many people at this hour of the night."

"It beats all, doesn't it?" Malcolm said. "Wouldn't you think some of these people would go home?"

Terry chuckled and we went grimly on.

"Couldn't we leave him at your office, sir?" Malcolm suggested.

"No. That wouldn't do. You see, in a way he's my corpse."

"A bit of a nuisance, sir, and that's a fact. Now let me see . . ." Malcolm was trying to be helpful. After a moment, he said, "How about Battery Park?"

Down we went through dark canyon-like streets, past sleeping buildings, but each time we thought we had found a likely spot, a policeman or a stroller spoiled our plan. Battery Park itself looked like a Sunday School picnic-ground. Every New Yorker seemed to be looking for a cool spot.

"I've an idea," Terry said hopefully. "I've a key to Gramercy Park. Surely in that staid neighborhood we'll find some peace and quiet."

We were wrong again. The park was full of people trying to find relief from the heat.

"You wouldn't mind leaving him on a pier, would you?" Terry asked quite as if that were the last straw. I didn't blame him a bit. You've no idea what a difficult job it is to dispose of a body during a hot summer night in New York.

We went over to the East River to a pier somewhere in the twenties right near Bellevue Hospital but the place was jammed with people and a policeman on guard wouldn't permit us to drive the car onto the pier anyhow.

"I've an idea, sir. Let's take him over to the Pennsylvania Station. We could go in from the Eighth Avenue Subway entrance. It's quite deserted there at this time of night between trains. There are a number of telephone booths along the passage. We could put him in one of them and leave him there." Malcolm was just full of ideas.

"You've got something, Malcolm," Terry replied. "The trouble with us is we've been afraid. We must be bold. We'll drive to Thirty-third Street right beside Gimbel's and you on one side and I on the other, will trundle him down the steps and into that long alley. There won't be many people there. We'll deposit him in a phone booth."

"It's risky, Terry," I objected.

"But we can't drive about all night," he retorted. "Before you know it, it'll be daylight and then what will we do?"

"On to Gimbel's," I cried with more bravado than I felt.

We pulled up alongside the curb on Thirty-third Street and Terry slid out from under the wheel. Malcolm adjusted his coat and stepped to the curb. I held the fort. I heard Terry open the rear door and grunt once. Then I heard a low whistle.

In a moment Terry was at my side. "Jumping catfish, Ethel," he whispered. "Do you know who we've been trundling around the town? Mortimer's man, Fergus! The one who called on me this afternoon at your house!"

"No!" I exclaimed.

"Yes."

"Wait, Terry, let me think." I heard Malcolm close the rear door. I knew he would be standing at attention. I wondered if people who passed were looking at us and my old towering car.

"We can't stand here very long," Terry reminded me.

"And we can't put Mortimer's man in a phone booth. It might come right back to us too quickly. After all, he's Mortimer's problem, isn't he?" I asked pointedly.

"You mean take him back to Mortimer?" he asked.

I hadn't meant anything of the sort, but I knew at once that it was an excellent idea. "Why not?" I challenged.

"Do you think of the right things!" Terry beamed. "Get in, Malcolm. As usual Miss Thomas has solved our problem."

Mortimer lives in an old brownstone house in the West Eighties, between Amsterdam and Columbus Avenues. Fortunately, the street seemed deserted. I suppose one of the reasons was due to the fact that the people who live in that section can afford to go away for the summer if they want to do so.

We stopped in front of Mortimer's. I looked back fearfully. A car turned in from Columbus Avenue. We waited. It was only a cab. A man popped out, paid his fare and ran up some steps into the shadow of a vestibule. The cab sputtered away, the street was clear. Terry and Malcolm got busy at once. They lifted the man, Fergus, out and between them they carried him to the basement door and left him on the step. They were back in a minute. Malcolm went round and slid under the wheel.

"We'll drop Mr. Lassimon off at his apartment," I said.

"Yes, ma'am." Under normal conditions he would have been shocked to have me sitting on the front seat with him. As a matter of fact, I rather expected him to suggest that Terry and I get into the tonneau, as long as the body was gone, but he didn't.

We turned into Central Park West when I happened to think of the bag. "You didn't lose the suitcase, did you?" I asked.

"I didn't even notice it," Terry grunted.

We rode on in silence, each busy with our thoughts, Malcolm watching the traffic. As we rolled up to his apartment and Terry prepared to leave he said, "You're

a brick, Ethel." Then he turned to Malcolm, "If Miss Ethel ever fires you, you know where there's a job waiting for you."

"Yes, sir. Thank you, sir," Malcolm replied.

"Just check on that bag, Terry," I suggested. "It's been on my mind ever since we left Mortimer's."

He opened the door and said, "There's no bag here."

I was aghast and cried, "There must be." I bounded out of the car and looked myself. I even foolishly moved the robe which is on the rail winter or summer. Terry was right, the bag was gone.

We looked at each other blankly for a moment, then Terry laughed. "We're damned if we do and damned if we don't, aren't we?"

"But I put the bag in there. I did it myself. I thought Malcolm was asleep and I was going to surprise him," I explained. "You didn't take it out to get at the body, did you?" I asked anxiously.

"No."

"Are you sure?"

"Positive."

"Then it was taken while I ran back for you to help me with Malcolm."

"But why?" He laughed.

"It's no laughing matter, young man," I reminded him. "That bag belongs to you and that gun and hat are full of our fingerprints. Once the body is found and that bag turns up our goose is cooked for sure. No one will believe us now."

"I wonder," Terry said, "if we haven't added ourselves to Mortimer's list of victims tonight."

"I'm afraid so," I agreed, then added, "I need a drink."

"Come up. I couldn't sleep anyhow. Come along, Malcolm," he invited.

"I'll stay here, sir, and get the air," Malcolm replied.

"Come along, Malcolm," I ordered. "We don't want anything to happen to you again, and for pity's sake lock the car," I warned.

In the apartment Malcolm became the perfect servant once more. When he realized that Terry was without a houseman he offered to serve the drinks.

"Miss Thomas will have brandy and soda, sir," he said. "What would you like?"

"The same," Terry replied, "and have one yourself."

"Not while I'm driving, thank you, sir."

It was not until the drink began to have some effect that we spoke at all. We had been through so much. I know my mind teemed with ideas and possibilities but I had nothing definite to say.

"What's the next move?" he asked finally.

"I'd say watchful waiting," I answered. "There's very little we can do at the moment. We certainly can't ever admit knowing anything about Fergus, can we?"

"No, that's true," he admitted. "But I'll go crazy waiting. I can imagine now how a condemned man feels waiting for his death sentence."

"Don't be morbid," I scoffed.

I was thinking, however, about what he had said when the telephone bell jangled sharply. I jumped and spilled some of my brandy down the front of my gown. I was suddenly cold. I laughed hysterically.

"Quiet!" Terry barked as he lifted the receiver.

"Lassimon speaking," he said and then listened attentively for a moment. He put his hand over the mouthpiece and whispered. "It's our friend. He says unless I give him the diaries he'll turn the bag and evidence over to the police."

I shook my head. Terry nodded approvingly, then said with force and emphasis, "I'll see you in hell first!" and slammed down the receiver.

"The time has come ..." I started to quote.

"For another drink," Terry finished.

CHAPTER NINE

I puzzled over our problem all the way home and long after that. We were certainly hung on the horns of a dilemma.

Once when I was undressing, I was tempted to telephone Terry and suggest that we call up the police and take our chances once and for all on the right side of the fence, but the next moment I realized how silly that would be. We made our initial mistake at the moment some one shot at Terry and we did nothing about it. We had nothing to conceal then, but since we had involved ourselves in a story far too fantastic for ordinary belief.

Terry had been drawn into the situation because he had those diaries in his possession and now heaven and earth wouldn't move him from his plan, which was to protect Althea's secret.

I felt helpless. I regretted over and over again that I had not read the accursed things when I had them in the house. I was sure that in the diaries we would somehow find the answer to our problem. As it was, we had two suspects—Althea and Philip Lassimon and possibly Dick Bolertho. I'd have read the books then and there had they been in my possession. We had no definite clues whatever and couldn't possibly be in a more ticklish spot.

The person who had shot at Terry, searched the apartment and killed Fergus was much smarter than we were at the moment and knew much more than we did. And furthermore, he was a determined individual who wanted Terry out of the way. But why Terry? I couldn't rationalize that act in the light of what had happened. Why was Terry in danger and why was Mortimer apparently safe? Why should Mortimer be safe when for years he had had the information which had just come into Terry's hands? It didn't make sense at all. And why kill Fergus?

The murderer had displayed fiendish subtlety in promoting fear. One of the Borgia women couldn't have done better. With the death of Fergus, the murderer had fashioned a powerful weapon with which he hoped to control Terry's future actions. What would his next step be now that Terry had defied him? I was sure it would be clever and unexpected, but what? Why put the body in my car? Also, since it was there and I would be faced with the problem of getting rid of it, or calling the police, why take the bag? How did the murderer know that he would need the bag? How did he know what was in that bag?

He had probably been watching Terry's apartment from the time he had left it with the body. He had chloroformed Malcolm, put the body in my car, and then gone back to watch and listen. The service entrance! That was it. He had probably heard everything we said. Even if he hadn't heard us talking and planning, when he saw the police arrive and leave so matter of factly a few minutes later, he must have realized that we had outsmarted him for the moment. A man less clever than this person had proved himself to be would have no difficulty in guessing where we had hidden the evidence. When he saw me leave with the bag, he knew the things were in it.

I knew there would be a tremendous stir once the body was found. Would our enemy then send the bag to the police or would he wait hoping that Terry, driven to desperation, would give up the books? Why did he want them? Was it self-protection, or was it for purposes of blackmail? The question staggered me.

Could one person have done all those things alone and unaided? Althea, was she in cahoots with Philip Lassimon or Dick Bolertho?

I just went round and round in circles trying to find answers to the questions until I finally fell asleep plagued by dreams of horror.

In the morning, the first thing I did was to scan the papers quickly looking for news about the murdered man, Fergus. There wasn't a line. The body should have been discovered in time to make the late morning papers. The milkman, at least, should have found him squatting there at the basement entrance. The very lack of news filled me with misgivings.

Terry rang up before I had my coffee. He, too, was puzzled by the lack of news.

"I'm going to see Mortimer right away, bright and early," he said.

"I don't believe I'd do that," I warned.

"I might as well," was his reply. "We should know all the things that are going on. I want to get what information I can while I can."

"What do you mean?" I asked quickly.

"If I go to jail, I'll be rather limited in the things I can do. I'm going to get my work in first. Do you want to do me a favor?"

"If I can. What?"

"I'd feel safer if those diaries were out of the office. Would you mind getting them and depositing them in your own safe-deposit box until further notice from me?"

"Why do you want me to do that?" I demanded.

"I think it will be safer in case I am arrested. . . ."

"Althea's secret, whatever it is, won't be exposed," I finished for him.

"Bright girl," he chuckled over the wire.

"I hope she's worth it."

"Go early, will you, Ethel? There'll be some one there at nine. The quicker the better. You can't miss the parcel. It's done up in brown paper and has red sealing-wax all over it. You'll recognize it at once. I'll call you as soon as I've had my talk with Mortimer. And, Ethel, don't say anything to Sidney if you see him. I don't want him mixed up in this. It's our show."

After he rang off, I called Agnes and told her I was going out.

"In this heat?" she objected.

"Hush up! Fix my things and stop mumbling under your breath."

"Do you want the car?" she asked.

"No. I'll take a cab. Have one here at eight-thirty."

My bath finished, I began to hurry. Agnes hovering about me suggested that I leave off the transformation. She'll never suggest that again. Why, I'd as soon go in the street in my chemise! I wanted to be at Terry's office before nine or the very minute it opened. I don't know why I was suddenly seized with the urge for haste. All I knew was that haste was imperative.

There's nothing more distressing than dressing in a hurry, particularly when it's hot and you're hotter. I did the best I could with the tiny rivulets that streamed down my body. Agnes kept annoying me by insisting that I have some breakfast. She knows that, nine mornings out of ten, I'm bad-tempered until after my coffee. Impatiently, I took a cup and sipped a little just to please her because she was standing over me in much the same manner that mothers assume when they try to make their children eat spinach. It seemed hotter than usual and scalded my lips. I put it aside and descended to the hall to find Malcolm waiting for me.

"I have the car ready," he said.

"I intended taking a cab, didn't Agnes tell you?"

"Yes, ma'am, but . . ."

"All right, come along." Together we stepped into an inferno called a street.

We drove up Lexington to Forty-ninth Street and then west to the building which Terry had converted into an office for his publishing business. It was about ten minutes of nine when we arrived. Listless men and women were dragging themselves along the street. Poor souls! They should have had a holiday. Near Radio City some women were walking their panting dogs. It was going to be another unbearable day. As I stepped from the car, a figure down the street arrested my attention. It was a woman who was walking briskly. I felt quite certain it was Althea. Was I too late? Telling Malcolm to wait, I ran up the steps to the front door.

Terry's office building is an old converted residence. The main offices are on what had once been the parlor floor, but then I don't need to tell you about such buildings, you probably have been in dozens of them during prohibition times.

The entrance doors, the type which open in the center, yielded to my hand. I went in. The building was strangely quiet. I looked into the empty reception-room first, then went on down the hall hoping to find some one in the back office. The room was as empty as a tomb. I called once, but there was no answer. There was nothing to do but wait, for I knew I couldn't get into the safe alone, safe-cracking being an accomplishment I neglected to learn in my youth.

It was fairly cool in the dark hall. I sat on the bottom step of the stairs facing the front door. It was a long twenty minutes sitting there waiting in the gloom. I had reached the point where inactivity was beginning to bore me. I lit a cigarette and toyed with the dead match.

I've never learned to throw matches or cigarette butts down in public places as so many people do. It makes me wince when I see supposedly nice people drop burning cigarettes on the carpets of theater lobbies and hotel corridors. Most of them do stop to press the cigarette with the toe of their shoe, I'll give them credit for that much care, but it's something I can't do. I often wonder if those people are as careless in their own homes.

A sudden noise in the basement startled me. I walked back to the stairs and called down. In a moment, a freckled-faced, engaging youngster of about seventeen poked his head round the partition and grinned up at me, saying,

"We ain't open yet, lady. Did you want a book?"

I felt like telling him I had a book, but didn't because he may not have heard the one about the chorus girl.

Instead I said, "I've just had a message from Mr. Lassimon. I'm a friend of his. He wants me to get something from his safe."

The boy came up the steps then, giving me a rather thorough and inclusive eye-raking as he advanced. When he reached the top he was seized by a thought. "Say, how did you get in?" he asked.

"Through the door, of course. Do I look like a ghost?"

"I dunno," he replied not too flatteringly after a speculative glance. "Anyhow, it's funny." He swung past me without another word and went to the front doors. He stopped to inspect the lock. After a moment he whistled and said, "Holy gee!"

I moved forward. He was bent down rubbing his finger over the wood. "What are you doing?" I asked.

"Nothin'. This door's been jimmied. No wonder you got in." He looked at me again and then as if satisfied that I had no jimmy concealed about my person said, "I'd better call the cops."

"You'd better not," I said quickly, "not until you're sure you're right."

"I'm right, all right, look!" He pointed at the lock dramatically. "See the marks."

He was right. There were marks there, plenty of them, showing how the lock had been forced open. My heart pounded with excitement and annoyance. I was evidently too late. Had Althea Madison taken the diaries? I was certain she had been in the office before me.

"I'll call the cops," he said eagerly.

The police were the last people I wanted to see at the moment, because I couldn't offer an explanation. "You'll do nothing of the sort," I snapped with a last look at the jimmied lock. My lack of experience with burglaries made me miss an important point right then and there.

"But . . ." the boy began a protest.

"Let's look around a bit first," I suggested. "You don't want the police unless something has been stolen. Where's the safe?" I asked.

He hesitated a moment before he decided to bow to my assumed authority. With a come-on, semi-friendly nod he moved down the hall and opened the door to what, in the old days, was called the middle room of the parlor-floor suite. It was a dark room sandwiched in, as it was, between the two parlors. He turned on the light. The walls were lined with filing cabinets topped by shelves holding supplies. In one corner behind the door, there was a small commercial safe. From its size I judged that publishers either didn't make or had no necessity for keeping large sums of cash on hand. The safe was closed.

Another shrill whistle turned my attention to the opposite wall, where a large, tall, steel safe stood with its double doors gaping wide open. The boy ran to my side and inspected the smaller safe.

"They didn't get in this," he said gleefully. "This is where they keep the money. Must have been scared off," he mused.

I wasn't interested in the little safe. I knew what the robber had wanted. I crossed to the large safe, wading through manuscripts scattered over the floor. I poked about them with the toe of my boot hoping to find one wrapped sealed package, but I knew before I looked that it wouldn't be there. I made a diligent search, however, inspecting everything.

We were still rummaging fruitlessly when Sidney Kenfield came in. He was amazed at what he saw. "Looking for something?" he asked facetiously.

I explained my errand quickly without telling him anything about the package itself.

"What was in it?" he asked.

I lied convincingly. "I've no idea. He just asked me to get it for him. It isn't here, we've searched everywhere."

"Has it anything to do with the mystery?" he asked.

"What mystery?" I demanded innocently.

"Whatever it is that's going on. The thing Terry's being so secretive about."

"I don't know any more about it than you do," I evaded. "I've been looking for the package he wanted, that's all."

He glanced at the helter-skelter disorderly pile of papers and manuscripts littered about the floor and said with a wry smile, "When you look, you do a good job of it, don't you?"

"Don't be an ass!" I snapped. "This safe has been ransacked by an expert."

He must have thought I was trying to be funny because he replied, "I can see that."

"Heaven above, man!" I cried in exasperation. "This office has been robbed!"

"Robbed?" His echo annoyed me and yet it is something we all do. Why do we get annoyed at others for faults so common to ourselves?

"The front door's been jimmied, Mr. Kenfield," the freckled-faced boy interrupted. "It's robbers, but they didn't take any money because the cash safe ain't been opened."

"Your package may have been put in there," Kenfield suggested and crossed to the small safe. He bent down and began twirling the dials.

I waited anxiously while he fiddled with the combination. He had always been exceptionally agreeable to me, a little too friendly I felt, sort of suggesting a camaraderie similar to Terry's and one I was not willing to give him. He was feeling hurt by Terry's secrecy and I felt rather sorry for him, knowing just exactly how he would feel. He was very thorough as he hastily sorted the contents of the small safe.

He stood up, showing no sign of stiffness from having been bent over and said, "No package here. What was in it?" He repeated the question as if he hoped to trap me.

"I don't know," I lied glibly for the second time.

"What happened to Terry?" was his next question.

"He didn't say."

"I haven't seen much of Terry for the past week. Is anything wrong, Miss Thomas?" he asked anxiously.

"I rather imagine he's in one of his usual jams."

I'd forgotten all about the boy who stood there taking it all in. When I turned and glanced at him, he colored a bit and said, "Should I call the cops, Mr. Kenfield?"

"I wouldn't if I were you," I said to Kenfield.

"Run along to your work, Jack," Kenfield ordered. "I'll attend to this."

With the boy out of the way, he asked, "Is it serious trouble?"

"I don't know." His endless questions exasperated me.

"What's on his mind, anyhow?" he continued. "He wouldn't even explain those ads he ran in the paper. He's made me feel rather useless."

"Don't worry about that. He'll probably tell you all about it when the right time comes. You know him well enough to know that he wouldn't think of involving you in anything that might be at all serious."

"He's not in danger, is he?" He was genuinely troubled.

"I don't believe so."

"It isn't anything shady, is it?"

"Haven't I told you I don't know?" I barked, making no effort to conceal my annoyance.

"You know more than you're telling me. I respect you for being loyal to him. I wish he were as loyal to me. If anything crooked is, or has been, going on, I ought to know about it."

"Don't be childish."

"But you didn't want me to call the police. After all, this place has been burglarized," he protested.

To avoid further conversation, I went back to the manuscript safe and stood in front of it, puzzled by something, I didn't quite know what. I was looking for clues and didn't find any. During my experience in the Doane store when those awful murders were taking place right under my very eyes, my wits were sharpened and my eyes trained to look for the little tell-tale bits of evidence which can be seen everywhere after a crime if you know where and how to look.

As it was, I was thinking about Terry and wondering how I could help him. He was in danger. We had to get those diaries back in our possession. I suppose I was thinking about Mortimer, too, and the man Fergus.

"Is there anything at all I can do?" Kenfield asked.

"Yes. Stop asking me questions. This is Terry's affair. He asked me to do him a favor. I have failed. When he wants either of us to know what it's all about, he'll tell us."

"Very well," he said and turned away.

I was sorry for my snappishness. I caught hold of his arm. "Forgive me, Kenfield, for being so rude. I didn't sleep well, it's this heat. My nerves are on edge. You know Terry as well as I do, perhaps better. I know you want to help him as much as I do. If he hasn't told you about this latest escapade of his, he must have a good reason. In fact, I know he doesn't want you involved. He told me so himself."

"Let's forget it," he suggested. "I suppose I did seem to be prying into things that didn't concern me. But I've been puzzled by his actions—those ads and the mysterious way he has been acting."

I felt relieved that he showed no resentment toward me. I had been testily impatient with him. From his smile I think he realized that I had been under considerable stress. I have been a firm believer in the old saying, "It's better to have a friend than an enemy."

As my hand fell away from his arm, I automatically brushed some dust from his sleeve. I gave it several light pats with my hand. "You need a housekeeper here," I sniffed disdainfully. "Dust over everything!"

"I'll take a brush to it," he suggested as I tried vainly to remove the discoloration.

A girl came to the door. "Is this Miss Thomas?" she asked. "Mr. Lassimon wants to talk to you."

I took the call at the switchboard. He said, "I've only a minute. Something unexpected has developed here at Mortimer's. The police are holding me. You'd better go home and wait." He rang off.

Go home! Indeed!

CHAPTER TEN

Terry's news came as a terrific shock. Why was he being held by the police? It didn't make rhyme nor reason in the light of the things that had happened.

Kenfield stood at my side. I didn't want him to see my face at the moment. I did my best to seem casual. I leaned over the switchboard and asked the girl to call the Macon-Astoria.

When the hotel operator answered, I asked for Althea. I waited several minutes before I was told Miss Madison did not answer. Althea was out. That fact convinced me that she was the person I had seen going down the street as I arrived at the office a short time before. Had she taken the diaries?

As I turned from the switchboard, Kenfield said, "You didn't tell him about the theft."

"I forgot," I replied.

"Where is he?" he asked.

"At Mortimer Van Wyck's," I answered absently and moved toward the front door.

Malcolm was surprised when I told him to drive to Mortimer's, but he said nothing like the good servant he is.

People who have sense enough to mind their own business never get involved in other people's troubles. I'm quite sure Terry didn't want me at Mortimer's, but I had no intention of letting him fight the thing out alone. What had happened? What of Fergus' body? I was dying to know. Why had there been no notice of his death in the morning papers? Had his body been discovered? And what of that bag of evidence? Had that been unearthed to confound us?

We had turned into Mortimer's street when Malcolm interrupted my thoughts.

"I can't get in front of the house, Miss. There seems to be trouble of some sort. I'm afraid," he said with a tremor that caught in his throat, "it's the police. It is! They are keeping people back."

I didn't answer for a moment.

"Shall I drive on?" he asked rather hopefully.

"Certainly not! Stop here!" I commanded.

From the back seat of that old Lincoln, I had the equivalent of a grandstand seat. Ahead of us, I could see a curious crowd clustered near the front of Mortimer's house. They were standing wide-eyed, their weary New York faces slightly upturned, their mouths open, gazing blankly at the front of the house.

What were they doing to Terry? I had to get into that house, but how to do it? I decided on boldness first and if that failed, I'd think of something else, but get in I would.

'

"Now, Miss Ethel," Malcolm begged as he recognized the glint of determination in my eye.

"Be still! Wait for me! I'm going in there."

He slammed the door behind me. I went briskly down the pavement knowing that if I stopped or seemed undecided my chances were nil. I elbowed my way through the damp, sticky people, sailed up to and swept past the policeman on guard, before he realized I was there. My foot was on the bottom step leading up to the front door when his hand reached out and caught my arm rather roughly.

"Not so fast! Where do you think you're going?" he demanded gruffly.

I had a plan. If I asked to go in, I would be refused.

"Take your hands off me!" I flared indignantly and gave that man a look that ran hot and cold, if you know what I mean.

"You can't go in there," he said a trifle less sure of himself.

"Well, I've been doing it off and on for fifty years and I'd like to see you stop me," I flung at him and took a second step upward.

"Oh, you have, have you?" His eyes lit up as he gave birth to an idea. I kept my own smile of gratification hidden. My plan was working.

"I certainly have," I replied. "Mortimer Van Wyck is one of my oldest friends," I lied glibly.

"Was, you mean," he said.

"Is," I insisted.

"Do you know anything, lady?" he asked.

"That depends," I answered.

"About the murder, I mean," he said.

"Murder? What murder?" I repeated with a gasp of surprise.

"Van Wyck. He was murdered this morning."

I hadn't counted on that but I took immediate advantage of it. "Murdered! Not Mortimer! ..." I cried. I tried to make it sound as startled and shocked as possible. Then I tottered forward.

"Here, here!" he cried. "None of that!"

In spite of his warning, to all intents and purposes I fainted. At least, he thought I did. He caught me as I sagged toward him and called to the other officer: "This old bird has fainted. I'll take her into the house, the Doc's in there."

My eyes were closed but I could hear the crowd surge forward. I smiled inwardly. I was going to get inside and that accomplished I would have to depend on my wits to keep me there. I felt no resentment toward the man for having called me an old bird. I hate to think of what he would have called me if he had known of my deception. Bless his heart! He helped me get inside. Normally, I have little patience with women who use fainting spells (vapors they were called when I was a girl) or tears, to have their way with men, but I guess I've been wrong. I suppose the end always justifies the means.

Schultz, the policeman, gave me a bad bump as we went through the door and I very nearly said, "Ouch," but caught myself just in time. He dumped me rather unceremoniously on a sofa in the front parlor, and muttered, "Fainted," to some other person in the room and left, calling for Doctor Burton. I opened my eyes rather cautiously to see the other occupant of the room. It was Althea who was crossing toward me! The room was in semi-darkness. She didn't recognize me until she was at the couch side.

"Miss Thomas!" she exclaimed with genuine surprise.

"Shh ..." I cautioned.

"Van Wyck has been murdered," she whispered.

"I know," I whispered back. "Where's Terry?"

"With the police."

"What are they doing?" I started to get up.

"Easy," she warned. "I'm glad you came. Take this, will you, and hide it? They may search me."

She slipped me a crumpled wad of onion-skin paper which I stuffed down the neck of my dress.

"Will it be safe?" she asked anxiously.

"Safe as the Bank of England," I replied. "Remember I'm an old-fashioned girl who still wears the unmentionables that went out of existence with the World War. I have a waist-line too and nothing has ever gotten past it yet. Don't worry! It'll be safe until I reach for it or undress. What is it?"

"I don't know. Terry gave it to me before the police arrived. He said they might search him." She explained as much as she knew.

"Have they been asking you questions?" I asked.

"The detective just came a few minutes ago."

"Where's Terry?"

"The policeman who came first is holding him incommunicado in a room at the back."

"What are they doing now?"

"I don't know. An army of men came with the detective. They went upstairs where he . . ."

I heard the heavy tread of men's feet on the stairs. "Sh ..." I warned. I lay back on the sofa, closed my eyes and whispered, "When they come in, say I'm reviving."

The footsteps grew louder, a voice asked, "Where is she?" Althea replied, "She's coming to." She was holding my wrist and pressed it reassuringly.

I began to do my little act. I was tempted to say, "Where am I?" but thought that would have been a little too thick. I sighed and moved my free hand when I heard a familiar voice say, "Well, I'll be damned! How did she get here?"

I opened my eyes and sure enough it was Detective Peter Conklin, my friend and team-mate of the Doane Store Affair. "Peter Conklin!" I cried happily, my voice ringing.

The doctor started to bend over me, but Peter stopped him saying, "She'll be all right, Doc. She's got the constitution of a horse, the nerve of the devil and will outlive all of us. As a matter of fact, I don't believe she fainted." He placed himself squarely in front of me and demanded severely. "Just how do you fit into this picture?"

"You know how interested I am in murders," I answered, sitting up. "I came to call on Mortimer and the man on guard wouldn't let me in. He said there had been a murder. That made me curious. If I had known that you were on the case, I wouldn't have had to resort to trickery to get in here." I slid off the sofa and gave my dress an adjusting twitch, smoothing the skirt over my hips, what's left of them. As my arm moved, I heard the slight crinkle of the wad of paper.

Schultz, the policeman who carried me in, gasped in amazement. His consternation was so ludicrous that even Peter chuckled and said, "She put one over on you, Schultz, but that's all right. She's done it to me too."

"But when I said the guy had been murdered, she did a flop," Schultz tried to explain in an attempt to justify himself.

"It's all right. Get outside and forget it," Peter said kindly. As Schultz left with an uncomprehending glance back over his shoulder, Peter, the kindness gone from his voice, said, "So you're the one Lassimon called. Had I been here, you're the last person I'd have permitted him to call."

"Now, Peter! You know that isn't true. Why say such things? Aren't we friends? Didn't we work well together once before? If you've a riddle on your hands, you're going to need some help. I won't get in your way."

"What do you know about this?" he demanded.

"Nothing yet, but between us, we will," I suggested brightly.

"Is Lassimon another of your pet young men?" he asked.

Peter knew of my liking for and interest in young men. I nodded in reply before I asked, "Is it a good murder, Peter?"

"With you mixed up in it, it should be a honey," he replied. "Come on, what do you know or out you go!"

"Nothing," I answered innocently.

"Why did Lassimon call you?" he insisted.

"Perhaps he has more faith in my abilities as a detective than you have," I evaded.

"Don't try to fool me. You didn't just happen to come here."

"Certainly not. Terry Lassimon told me he was being held by the police. I needed no further invitation."

"No, I suppose not. Did Lassimon ask you to come?"

"Oh, no! He simply said he was being detained. I could tell from the sound of his voice that he was in trouble," I explained.

"I'll say he is, and you won't be able to protect him either."

"He doesn't need protection," I retorted.

"That's what you think. It's not going to be so easy for this guy to get out of the scrape he's in. We've got him cold. He hasn't a Chinaman's chance. If I could discover

what it was he came back for, I'd have the case cinched."
Peter was very sure of himself and was spiking my guns
in advance.

"Came back?" I asked. "What are you talking about?"

"That's my secret. I've work to do." He turned away.

"Let me work with you?" I begged. "I haven't had any
excitement for ever so long and beside, Terry Lassimon is
a very good friend of mine. Please, Peter," I cried.

"No." Peter's denial sounded absolutely final.

"Very well. Come along, Althea." I started to follow
Peter's retreating back.

"Not so fast. She stays here and I think I'll keep you
for a little while. I don't exactly believe you." There was
an understanding smile lurking at the corners of his
mouth.

"You sound a bit uncertain. What's the trouble, Peter?
A bad puzzle?"

"Not so bad. I have the murderer."

"A cut and dried case, eh?" I asked innocently.

"Perfect."

"Motive and everything?" I asked.

"I'll get that," he answered cockily.

"I wonder," I put a great deal of doubt into my voice.

"I suppose you know all about it?" he flashed.

"I might have an idea," I said. "Let me stay. I won't
interfere with your work. If you'll do that, I'll tell you
something you really want to know."

I saw fear creep into Althea's eyes. I flashed her a
reassuring smile. "Is it a bargain?" I asked.

"I suppose so," Peter agreed reluctantly.

CHAPTER ELEVEN

Peter led the way to the back parlor where Terry was confined under the watchful eyes of a policeman. Terry was standing in the bow window gazing thoughtfully down into the yard. His face was drawn and haggard. Poor lad, he showed he had had very little sleep. No wonder, with the things he had on his mind.

"Hello, Ethel!" he cried, genuinely surprised to see me. "How did you get in?"

He made me think of some splendid wild animal that had been captured and caged. I wanted to let him know about the diaries and did a little explaining by double-talk. "If you don't get what you go after, you go after it."

Terry didn't blink an eye and my remark evidently went over Peter's head because he said to Terry, "She doesn't have to be brought. She has a nose for murder." Then to all of us, "Sit down."

Althea and I took chairs. Terry stood near Althea in a protecting pose. I've seen Terry in and out of affairs but never before had I seen the look which now glowed in his eyes as he gazed down at that lovely girl. I know nothing about so-called love at first sight. I can understand spontaneous passion which at best is little more than a flash in the pan or the sudden union of chemical elements. Quick love has always seemed particularly uncertain to me because it fails to take into account all the little things that go toward making love durable. I've been in and out of love dozens of times hoping each episode would be the last but there was always another because I was never really properly innoculated.

When we were all settled, Peter went on, "Now, Miss Thomas, suppose you tell me what you know."

Terry scowled at me. Althea was agitated. I ignored both of them and looking at Peter said, "Who killed Mortimer Van Wyck?"

Althea, poor child, opened her bag to get a handkerchief. She was so nervous she had to be doing something with her hands. She was fumbling. Her bag slid from knees and spilled to the floor. Peter was very quick springing forward to pick it up. He beat Terry to it by a fraction of an inch. As Peter lifted the bag, a wad of fresh clean new bills slid out and fell to the floor. You know how stiff new money can be. I was fascinated as I saw that roll settle to the floor and then unfold. There was a thousand-dollar bill staring us all in the face.

Peter picked up the bills and flipped through them quickly before handing them back to Althea. "That's a lot of money," he said; "too much to be carried loose like that."

Althea took the bills and put them back in her bag. "Taxi fare," she said glibly.

Peter chuckled, then turned to me. He wanted an answer to his question. You can very often keep a dog quiet by giving him a bone instead of the whole roast. I decided to feel my way carefully.

"Now," I suggested, "why not get on with the investigation? I have nothing to tell you."

Peter had Delia, Mortimer's maid, brought in. She was an Irish girl who faced Peter boldly.

"I want you to tell me exactly all the things that happened here this morning," Peter advised her.

"Mr. Lassimon phoned about seven," she began at once. "When I took Mr. Van Wyck his coffee soon after, he told me to send Mr. Lassimon up the moment he called."

"Did Van Wyck seem worried?" Peter asked.

"No, sir. As a matter of fact, he was quite cheerful, rather elated, I should say. He was like that when things were going well. He told me he expected several visitors within the next few days."

"Did he give you any names?"

"No, sir, but I rather imagined they were the people he had written to."

"What people?"

"I don't know, sir. He mailed the letters himself. There were carbons on his desk this morning, I think, sir."

"Are you sure?" Peter asked eagerly.

"I couldn't say positively, sir, but there was something under the paper-weight. I never touched his desk. He was very secretive about his things. Fergus attended to all that."

"Who is Fergus?" Peter asked quickly.

"Mr. Mortimer's man, sir," she replied.

"Where is he?"

"I don't know, sir. He went out yesterday and didn't come back. Mr. Mortimer was worried last night."

I didn't dare look at either Terry or Althea.

"Why?"

"I don't know. He kept ringing for Fergus every few minutes and each time I told him Fergus had not returned, he became more impatient than ever."

"And yet you say Van Wyck was in a good humor this morning?" It was a good point Peter made.

"He seemed very pleased, yes, sir."

"Did he mention Fergus?"

"No, sir."

"Have you heard from Fergus?"

"No, sir."

"Did Mr. Van Wyck hear from him?"

"I don't know. The telephone switch is turned off downstairs in the evening. We never hear it ring after dinner-time."

"Do you know where Fergus went yesterday afternoon?"

"No, sir. Fergus was very secretive. Never talked. He was proud of his confidential position with the master and treated the rest of us very proud-like."

"Umm . . ." Peter considered a moment before he asked his next question. "How was Fergus yesterday before he went out?"

"Testier than usual," she answered promptly.

"We'll forget about Fergus for the moment." Peter paused. "This morning when Mr. Lassimon arrived, did you show him upstairs?"

"No, sir. I sent him up alone. Mr. Van Wyck was expecting him. I rang the bell to warn him that some one was on the way up."

"I see," Peter said. I'm glad he did for I was completely in the dark. After a moment, Peter asked, "How long did Mr. Lassimon stay?"

"I'm not sure, sir. It was several minutes."

"Did you see Mr. Lassimon leave?"

"I did and I didn't, sir."

"Explain, please."

"Well, Mr. Lassimon was coming down the stairs when I heard the whistle on the speaking-tube begin to blow. It sounded impatient-like, the way he was blowing. I hurried to the rear of the hall to answer it. I didn't want to spoil Mr. Van Wyck's good humor. I knew Mr. Lassimon could find his way out all right."

"Haven't you any idea how long Mr. Lassimon was upstairs?"

"Do you mean the first or the second time?" she asked.

"Both," Peter said.

She considered a moment. "I couldn't say, sir. You see, when I answered the speaking-tube I supposed Mr. Lassimon had gone out."

"And hadn't he?" Peter asked.

"No," she stated boldly.

"Are you sure?"

"Well, I took the message at the tube and busied myself at the back of the house for a minute or two. Some time later I returned to the front hall and was surprised to see Mr. Lassimon coming downstairs for the second time."

"Did Mr. Lassimon offer any explanation?" Peter asked.

"No, sir. I said, 'I thought you'd gone,' but he didn't answer me. He went out, banging the door."

"Go on," Peter urged.

"I had thought to go up to remove the coffee things and would have done so only Mr. Van Wyck told me he didn't want to be disturbed for a few minutes. I started for the kitchen and was halfway down the back stairs when the front doorbell rang again. When I opened the door there was Mr. Lassimon with the young lady. She came in saying she had an appointment with Mr. Van Wyck. Mr. Lassimon said, 'I've changed my mind. I'd like to speak to him again.' I told him he'd have to wait. He went into the front room and sat down. I told the young lady to go to the third floor rear. I went to the end of the hall and pressed the button to warn Mr. Van Wyck of the arrival of a guest."

"You didn't go upstairs at all?" Peter kept insisting on that point.

"No, sir."

"It's your turn now," Peter indicated Terry.

"What do you want?" Terry asked.

"From the beginning."

"I arrived some time after seven, as Delia has told you, and went directly to Van Wyck's room on the third floor. He was up and dressed, drinking coffee. We talked for ten minutes or so."

"During which time you were enraged," Peter suggested.

Terry looked from Delia to Peter and replied, "Well, I did lose my temper once, I'll admit that."

"And you threatened Van Wyck?"

"Probably," Terry admitted.

"Go on." Peter was too positively sure of his case against Terry to suit me.

"Van Wyck and I had reached an impasse. Talking or arguing could accomplish nothing. I walked out. I came down to the lower hall and then regretting my haste and temper, I decided to try again. I went back, but when I reached the third floor I heard voices in Van Wyck's room. I hesitated a moment, then turned and came back down the stairs. Delia did seem surprised when she saw me. I left immediately." Terry stopped for breath.

"Then what happened?" Peter asked.

"I paused at the top of the steps and looked hopefully for a cab but there was none in sight. I was thinking about my unsuccessful interview and had started down the street, when I realized a cab had turned in from Madison Avenue. It was coming slowly. You know how they drive when they're looking for a house number. I paused and waited. The cab stopped in front of this house and Miss Madison got out."

"You recognized her?" Peter asked.

"Yes," he answered honestly. "When I saw her ascend the front steps, I decided to come back."

"Why?"

"Because I hated to think of Miss Madison as one of Van Wyck's possible victims."

Terry had made a mistake and realized it immediately. He would have hurried on but Peter stopped him by saying, "Explain just what you mean by victims."

"Van Wyck was a blackmailer," Terry answered boldly.

"Oh, he was?"

"Yes."

"How long have you been paying him hush money?"

"I've never paid him any money."

"Was he trying to force you to pay him?" Peter insisted.

"No."

"Then why were you here?"

"I had some private matters to discuss with him."

"But he was not trying to blackmail you?"

"No."

"Then how did you know he was a blackmailer?" Peter demanded.

"Miss Thomas told me. As a matter of fact, she sent me here."

For a moment I was annoyed with him, but the next instant I knew why he did it. He was throwing the responsibility of telling what we knew to me. It was rather clever of him to get out from under that way by dropping it in my lap.

"So you were just being a Galahad, is that it?"

"That's a good way to describe it," Terry answered with a grin. Then he went on, "Delia has told you what happened when she let us in. There was nothing for me to do but wait. While Miss Madison was upstairs I sat in the parlor. Delia, I believe, was in the hall. In a short time, I heard a scream. I met Delia at the foot of the stairs. We both dashed up to meet a terrified Miss Madison on the verge of hysterics stumbling along the hall on the second floor."

"I suggested calling the police at once," Delia burst in on the recital, "but Mr. Lassimon told me to wait a moment."

"Why?" Peter asked.

"Because I had no idea what had happened. I wanted to investigate first."

Delia took up the narrative. "We put Miss Madison in the sitting-room on the second floor and went up together. Mr. Van Wyck was very dead, sir."

"Right," Terry agreed. "While Delia called the police, I went back to Miss Madison, who was feeling pretty jittery."

"They were whispering together when I returned to tell them that the police were on their way," Delia continued pointedly.

"You don't shout just after you've seen a murdered man," Terry fired contemptuously at Delia.

"He asked me to get some strong coffee for Miss Madison," Delia ignored Terry's remark and went on. "I went below. Cook had just made some. When I returned, Mr. Lassimon was coming down from the third floor."

Peter gave Terry a quizzical glance.

"That's right. I thought that I might be able to do something for Van Wyck, but as Delia has so aptly put it, he was terribly dead."

"This was your morning for philanthropical duties, I take it," Peter said sarcastically.

"Take it any way you like," Terry flung back.

"What did you do in that room after the murder?" Peter demanded.

"Nothing."

"Were you wearing your gloves when you were in there?" That sounded like a catch question to me.

"No."

"Did you touch anything?"

"Only Van Wyck. I listened for a heart beat."

"What was under the paper-weight?"

"What paper-weight?" Terry asked quickly.

"The one on his desk, the one that is full of your fingerprints."

I gasped at that. Terry had slipped up there. I was on the point of making a clean breast of the whole thing when Terry said, "I must have toyed with it while I talked to Van Wyck."

"The voice talking to Van Wyck when you went back the second time," I cut in, "was it a man's or a woman's?"

"A man's," he replied.

"There was no one in the house, sir," Delia objected quite unnecessarily I thought.

"Of course not," Peter said. "That's just a flimsy alibi you cooked up to cover yourself, isn't it?" Peter asked Terry. "Delia admitted two people to this house this morning, you and Miss Madison, no one else."

"It's the truth," Terry cried in exasperation and I believed him.

Peter's next move was a surprise to me. "Let's assume for a moment that you're telling the truth," he began innocently enough. "If you are, that gives us another angle to the case, an old one used rather successfully in murder stories and once or twice, I believe, in real life."

I didn't know what to expect but was amazed when he went on, "Miss Madison went upstairs, stabbed Van Wyck, ran out into the hall and halfway down the steps before she screamed. You say you found her on the second floor. She must have moved fast."

"No, no!" Terry cried. "She didn't do it! She didn't have time."

Althea had turned a dead white as Peter flung his rather logical accusation at her. Except for that sudden pallor, I had no means of knowing if Peter had made a direct hit. I could only remember what she had said.

"How do you know so much about the time it takes to kill a man?" Peter demanded.

"Oh, forget you're a cop for a minute and think!" Terry said scornfully.

"Just a minute!" I cried and jumped to my feet because I didn't want a fracas between them. "Were you in the room with Miss Madison when Delia brought the coffee?"

"Yes, ma'am, he was," Delia replied for him.

"Were any of you watching the hall?" was my next question.

"No," was the reply.

Peter sensed the drift of my questions and said, "Very smart, but it won't work."

"Why not?" I asked defiantly. "Was any search made of the house before the police arrived?"

"Not until after, Miss," Delia said.

"Then a person watching his chance could have left the house without being seen," I flung at Peter.

"But there was no one in the house," Delia insisted.

"That you know of," I reminded her and gave her a look that kept her quiet for a moment. I turned to Peter, "You've missed a bet, Peter. Why don't we begin at the beginning?"

"It's no use, Miss Thomas, one or the other of them killed Van Wyck. Either he did it on his second trip up there or she did it."

"Delia," I called.

"Yes, miss."

"You told us that Mr. Van Wyck gave orders he didn't want to be disturbed for a few minutes and yet you sent Miss Madison up the moment she came in. Had you forgotten your instructions?"

"No, miss, the call button rang just as Mr. Lassimon left."

"There, you see," I cried gleefully to Peter. "Dead men don't ring bells!"

"Why didn't you tell me that before?" Peter barked at Delia.

"I didn't think of it, sir, and besides, you should have known that a good servant wouldn't disobey instructions."

"Rats," Peter growled. "You've been a great help," he threw over his shoulder at me. He began to squeeze his lower lip between his thumb and his first finger—a trick he has when puzzled.

"Now," I suggested, "why don't you and I go to work since we know who didn't kill Van Wyck?"

"How long were you out of the house?" Peter asked Terry.

"Not more than two or three minutes," Terry replied.

"And how did Delia seem when she opened the door to you, Miss Madison?"

Delia leaned forward anxiously.

"I don't remember."

"Birch!" Peter raised his voice in a loud call.

The door opened and a policeman entered.

"Go to the foot of the hall stairs. Have one of the men time you. Go up to the room on the top floor, stay in it about fifteen seconds and then return to the lower hall. Let me know how long it takes. Come in when you've finished."

I didn't know which of them Peter was checking, Delia or Althea. I moved over to the bow window and looked down at the yard. I'd have to have some story for Peter, but what? I didn't want to tell him about the diaries. It didn't seem fair that all the people mentioned in them should suffer because of one man who was a murderer. I firmly believe in letting dead dogs lie. No matter what those people had done, it had been forgotten except for the diaries and a rehash would only make many innocent people suffer.

Terry came and stood beside me. "You've put Althea on the spot," he whispered. "Isn't she wonderful the way she's taking it? What are we going to do?"

I wasn't thinking about Althea. At the moment, I had diverted Peter's suspicions away from Terry, which was all I wanted to accomplish at the time.

Althea, her hands folded in her lap, waited. She seemed terribly alone. I was sorry for her. Peter's timing would probably involve either her or Delia. The idea evidently hit Terry at the same moment, for he turned.

"No whispering," Peter snapped at us.

The next instant we were in a panic. It started with an impact against the window-pane followed by a sharp zing. I don't know how else to describe it. Althea gasped. Terry gave me a sudden yank which nearly dislocated my shoulder. Delia screamed in sudden pain, and Peter barked, "Get away from that window!"

It all happened instantaneously. From the seclusion of the side wall, I could see a round hole in the glass through which the bullet had entered. Peter, from the other side of the window, was looking out at the buildings in the rear.

"That's the second one," I said to Terry without thinking.

Delia was on the floor gasping with pain and shock. Birch opened the door and started to speak.

"Never mind, get Doc Burton in here quickly," Peter ordered and crossed to Delia.

We all converged toward the poor girl still clutching her leg.

"Second what?" Peter asked me as he bent over Delia.

I ignored the question as I knelt beside him.

The girl had suffered a bad flesh wound in the calf of her leg and was terrified. Peter pulled the girl's skirt up from her knee and pressed his thumb on a vein to stop the flow of blood. The doctor came bustling in. Delia was placed on a couch and the doctor went to work.

I went to the bow window and looked up. The house next door had an addition on the back which made it extend thirty or forty feet into the yard beyond Mortimer's house line.

"You haven't answered my question," Peter reminded me as he led us back into the hall.

"I suppose I meant a second murder," I answered vaguely. "I don't remember saying anything."

"In time of stress, people give themselves away," he reminded me.

CHAPTER TWELVE

It was at least ten minutes before the excitement subsided. I should have liked a moment or two alone with Terry and Althea but Peter seemed to take particular pains to watch us every moment. Unfortunately, he gave all his orders while he was with us.

I know Peter likes and believes in me, but he doesn't quite trust me when my friends are in any way involved in a murder. He thinks my effort to clear them of the crime is an attempt to frustrate justice. I suppose it is, in one sense, but you know, and I know, that justice being blind, clutches at the first thing at hand and hangs onto it so tenaciously that often the truth is never seen.

Without meaning to, our enemy had done us a favor. That bullet, coming as it did, took Peter's attention away from Terry and Althea for a short time at least and eventually gave us a clue which ended the whole outrageous affair. In this day and age in one of the largest cities in the world we were and had been in unpredictable danger that only civilization can fashion.

Terry's escape was miracle number two. For the second time in a few days a bullet, intended for him, had barely missed its mark. While I'm not at all superstitious, I found myself wondering about the third attempt on his life. When and how would it come? Would he escape the third time?

Birch had been hovering near us anxious to make his report. His complete trip, up and back with a few seconds spent in the murder room, had taken a fraction over two minutes.

Peter considered the information thoughtfully and said, "Delia might have killed him."

"She didn't," Althea denied immediately.

"Why not?" Peter demanded, giving Althea a curious speculative look.

I rather fancied I knew what he was thinking at the moment. He suspected either Althea or Terry of having killed Mortimer and yet Althea had quickly sprung to the defense of the serving girl who had done all she could to incriminate both of them.

"He was alive as I climbed the stairs," Althea answered.

"You can't be sure of that," Peter denied.

"I heard voices," she insisted.

"You did?" Peter was aghast. "Why didn't you say so before?"

"You didn't ask me," she answered, "and I thought the information would be rather useless since you so obviously didn't want to believe Mr. Lassimon's story."

"Tell me about it now," Peter invited.

"There were two people talking. One man's voice was rather high-pitched and seemed excited. He was protesting vehemently about something."

"That was Mortimer," I said positively.

"And the other man's voice?" Peter was extraordinarily eager.

"If Mr. Lassimon had not been in the room downstairs, I'd have thought it was he speaking," she replied. Terry and I thought of the same person at the identical moment. Philip Lassimon! We exchanged a quick understanding glance which Peter intercepted. He turned toward me blazing mad.

"Are you going to tell me what you know about this case, or are you going to continue to hide things?" he demanded.

We were saved the immediate necessity of making a reply by a disturbance on the stairs. Mortimer was being carried down on a stretcher. As the grim procession went through the front door, Peter turned to me once more. "Well?" he demanded.

"We can tell you what little we know any time," I said icily. "Of course, it's none of my business, but if I were you, I'd be a little more concerned about that bullet, who fired it and where it came from."

"I'm having that checked," he growled.

"Did you send a man to the roof of the building next door?" I asked. "If you did, I didn't hear you do it."

"What has the roof of the building next door to do with it? The shot could have come from any one of a dozen rear windows on the next street," he answered.

"It could have, but did it?" I insisted. "Why not ask the doctor about the direction of the bullet? That may save you some time."

Peter knew my suggestion was a good one and followed it immediately. He went back to the room where the doctor was working over Delia. We had only a minute to ourselves, but one weighted with new anxiety.

"I'm sunk," Terry said.

"Sunk?" both Althea and I gasped.

"Yes. I rented a furnished apartment in that building this morning," Terry announced.

"Don't mention it," I cautioned. "We must have time to think. I've been too clever," I said regretfully.

"You didn't know," he whispered.

Peter came back. "The bullet came from a direct overhead angle," he announced. "Thanks for the suggestion," he flung at me and started for the stairs.

I fell in behind him and beckoned the others.

"I can't," Althea said.

"Come along, Terry," I whispered. "I may need you."

I saw him give Althea's hand a reassuring squeeze before he left her.

When we arrived at the scene of the murder, Peter asked several questions of the men who had been at work in the room.

"They heard no shot," he said when we were alone.

"That doesn't prove anything," I retorted. "You've heard of silencers, haven't you?"

"I have," he answered.

"Give me a few minutes to think, Peter?" I begged.
"But first may I ask a few questions?"

"Go ahead," he said with an amused tolerant smile.

"I'm not working against you, Peter," I said. "I want to
catch this murderer more than you do. Be patient with
me, please. I don't know who did it but I do know who
didn't."

I went on with my questions. Peter was patient.
Between them, Peter and Terry gave me all the details
concerning the position of the body when it was
discovered. Mortimer had been stabbed in the back. He
was slumped forward on the desk top when Terry dashed
into the room.

I considered all the facts for several moments.

"What do you make of it?" Peter asked a little
impatiently.

"The murdered man was behind the desk. He never
moved from that position. The quick thrust of the knife
came as a complete surprise to Mortimer. He was off
guard and had no reason to suspect the murderer."

"Very pretty, but why?" Peter demanded.

"Sit at the desk, Terry," I ordered. "You take the role
of observer," I instructed Peter. "I'm going to play the
part of the murderer for the moment."

"What am I supposed to do?" Terry asked.

"Remember this. You are Mortimer. You and I have
been having a heated argument. I want to kill you but
you don't know it. Act naturally when I come toward
you."

I took up a position in front of Terry. Then I moved
over to the end of the desk. As I did, Terry, who had been
facing me, turned sideways. I moved toward the rear of
the room. Terry swung in his chair still facing me.

"I get you," Peter said.

"Good," I said gratefully. "Turn around, Terry, and
face forward." I stood at his side. "Now, if I had been
standing here and we had had our last word, Mortimer

would have swung away from me in disgust. Then I would have had the perfect chance to stick the knife into him," I ended.

"It's reasonable," Peter admitted.

"Where's the exit to the roof?" I asked Peter.

"I don't know. Probably in the hall, they usually are," he replied.

"That won't do," I answered.

"Why not?" Peter demanded.

"Because both Althea and Terry say they heard voices in this room. Althea heard them as she came up the stairs. Mortimer was killed before Althea reached the top step. The murderer never crossed this room."

"He could have concealed himself in a closet when Miss Madison came in," Peter objected.

"I don't believe it, Peter. The murderer was gone before she entered the room." I began to search the area behind Mortimer's desk. In a dressing-room I found the very thing I was sure had to be there. Concealed in a closet was a narrow staircase which led directly to the roof.

"You're right again," Peter cried and started up the stairs.

Terry followed Peter. I waited below. I had had enough of stair climbing for one day. I could hear Peter tugging at the door and looked up the narrow passage. He was forcing it with his shoulder. The door finally flew open and for a moment there was a draft of air that came as a momentary relief from the heat which, in the excitement, I had forgotten.

As their voices faded away, I decided to go down to Althea. Terry had followed Peter. I went back into the room. My heart stood still. How on earth had I missed seeing it before? Standing innocently against the side wall, a few feet from the desk, was the suitcase I had taken from Terry's apartment. I couldn't mistake that bag. What to do with it? How to get it out of the house?

How had the police missed it thus far? Would it show in the photographs that had been taken?

I lifted the bag and left the room. I made the first landing without either trouble or qualms. As I started down the final flight of steps, I began to worry. If I could make the first-floor landing unobserved, I'd be safe. Birch came through the hall from the rear. He looked up at me and smiled faintly. I thanked fortune for my roomy voluminous skirt. By letting my hand lag backwards the bag was not seen by Birch as he went outside. With a sigh of relief, I dropped it on the floor near the old-fashioned clothes-rack and turned toward the living-room and Althea.

I had no time to spare. I heard voices and footsteps from overhead. Althea was not at all communicative. She told me flatly that I must not mention the diaries. Our discourse was interrupted by the arrival of the men.

"Why did you run away?" Peter asked as he entered the parlor.

"It was so hot up there," I answered. "Find anything?"

"Not a thing," he replied, "but we will have a look at the place next door. I think you're on the trail of something. The murderer could have come over the roof."

"Good heavens! You're a sight, both of you!" I exclaimed. I brushed Peter first and then Terry with my handkerchief. "You won't want us any more, will you, Peter?" I asked when the dusting was done.

"Why do you want to get away from me?" he demanded suspiciously.

"I don't. There's nothing we can do about the house next door. Surely you're convinced now that neither of these people had anything to do with the murder?" I suggested hopefully.

"I wouldn't say that," he answered promptly. "Let's say that my suspicions are allayed for the moment. Lassimon didn't fire that shot at himself."

"Then may we go?"

"All right, go ahead. But no funny work, understand," he cautioned as we went into the hall.

"Why not come down for cocktails this afternoon, Peter? We can talk it over dispassionately then," I suggested.

"I'll see," he half promised.

"Don't forget your bag, Terry," I warned casually as we moved toward the door.

Terry stopped, looked sideways, bent down and lifted the suitcase. "Thanks," he said; "I'd have forgotten all about it."

It was as fine a piece of acting as I ever hope to see. Terry was surprised but he didn't show how much. Neither did he register by sign or sound the startling recognition of that bag. As we started down the steps, I called back to Peter, "Come about five."

Malcolm was standing at attention when we reached the car. We settled down with a sigh of relief, that awful bag at our feet.

It was Althea who broke the silence. "If he comes at five, what are you going to tell him?"

"I don't know," I replied.

"Are you going to tell him about the diaries?" she asked.

"Do you know anything about them?" I returned pointedly.

"No," she replied hopelessly.

"You know they have been stolen?" I went on.

She nodded.

"What are you talking about?" Terry demanded.

"I went to your office this morning," Althea replied, "to steal the diaries, but some one had been there before me."

"Why don't you trust me?" he asked.

"Because there is too much at stake," she said.

"And now more than ever," I added.

Althea looked at me inquisitively.

"Let's know all the bad news," Terry suggested.

"The man who is working against you, Terry, is a fiend. He has the imagination of the devil himself. Who but a fiend would have, could have, thought of leaving that bag in Mortimer's room? Don't you see how diabolical it is? I can't understand its not having been opened unless the police were so busy with surface things, pictures, fingerprints and things like that that they passed the bag for the time being. Thank fortune, we found it."

"You found it, you mean," he said.

"Well, we have it once more and let's try to keep it as long as we can this time."

"I don't understand," Althea said.

I explained about the bag to her. "If they had opened it," I went on, "they would have soon realized that the hat belonged to Fergus. Then they would have traced the gun to Terry. From that to the finding of the body of Fergus would be but a step and then Terry would be in jail and how could he ever get out of such a fix?"

"It's quite bad enough as it is," she said.

"What about the apartment next door?" I asked Terry.

"I thought it would be a good idea to have a place handy to Mortimer so that I could keep an eye on him. I had no idea of the things that would happen. I rented one this morning when I saw the 'For Rent' sign."

"Then we'll be hearing from Peter before five o'clock," I said hopelessly.

"Perhaps not," Terry said. "I rented it in the name of Theodore Martin."

"Why?" I demanded.

"I don't know," he replied.

"But they'll describe you," I insisted. "Peter will recognize your description at once. There is a perfectly sound police case against both of you. Either one of you could have killed him."

"But . . ." Althea protested.

"Look at the thing clearly. Terry might have killed him when he went up the second time. It would have been possible. You could have killed him before you screamed and Terry ran up to you."

"But surely the detective is too intelligent to believe that?" Althea objected.

"They believe the obvious things first," I replied. "You must remember that Peter will realize that Terry is the man who rented the apartment next door."

"But Terry was with us when the shot was fired this morning!"

"That will make no difference to the police. It has nothing to do with Mortimer's death. Peter will think that Terry might have dashed into the house next door, raced up the stairs or taken a lift and succeeded in killing Mortimer before you reached the landing. Peter Conklin won't forget what you said about a voice that sounded like Terry's," I reminded her.

"I'm sorry," she said. "I didn't mean to incriminate you." She flashed a quick smile at Terry.

"Of course you didn't," he answered promptly.

"It's going to be incriminating testimony nevertheless. They will play you one against the other," I said thoughtfully as I tried to see some way out for them.

"But it's ridiculous," Althea objected. "All of it."

"Of course it is, but there are any number of things to be explained." I turned to Terry. "You were on the roof with Peter. Could a man get from the house next door easily?"

"Yes. They are level."

"But what has that to do with it?" Althea was full of objections. "Terry didn't shoot himself this morning and it is too unreasonable to suppose that he could have raced up there and killed Mortimer while I was climbing the stairs."

"I know all that," I answered patiently. "Peter Conklin is no fool. He'll know very soon, just as we know, that the person who killed Mortimer is the one who fired the shot at Terry this morning."

"Well, then," she interrupted.

"Don't forget Peter will want to know why Terry rented the apartment." She irritated me. "He still thinks that Terry was being blackmailed by Mortimer. As long as there is the slightest chance of Terry's having killed Mortimer, Peter will ask questions. He'll investigate this morning's shot later. We must decide now how much we'll tell Peter when he calls this afternoon. We can't keep quiet. You will be forced to talk, both of you. If we tell Peter about the diaries he'll want to know why you're so interested in them. You may be arrested on suspicion. Peter will do most anything to get to the bottom of this. I don't see how you can keep quiet any longer."

"There's one thing we can do," Terry said quickly. "Get married."

Althea gave him a quick, faintly amused look. His eyes twinkled as I seized upon the idea and added my arguments to his. He was right. If they were married neither one could be forced to testify against the other. "It is something you should do," I agreed.

"Are you willing to marry me?" Terry asked Althea.

She was engrossed by the sudden turn of the tide.

"It isn't the kind of a proposal I had hoped to make," he said, "but it will help both of us, me more than you. They can't force either of us to talk about the diaries if we do it."

"It will protect you from the menace of the man who holds the diaries," I added my argument to Terry's.

"It probably won't be for long," Terry went on. "This murderer is determined to get me out of the way. I'll probably be the next one on the list of his victims. For some reason, I know too much."

"He probably thinks you've read the diaries," I said, "and wants to be rid of you for that reason."

"But why should you be murdered?" Althea asked. Terry shrugged.

"He won't be," I pronounced with more conviction than I felt at the moment.

"How do we get married?" she asked.

I loved her for that simple question. I stopped the car. I have a great deal of respect for Peter Conklin. If he had connected Terry with that apartment next door he had doubtless by now sent out an alarm for my old Lincoln. We could take no chances until after they were married. I sent Malcolm home. He was displeased because he felt himself part of the conspiracy, but I explained quickly that I rather expected the car to be picked up by the police. I told him to act indignant but to say nothing if questioned. If they wanted to know where we had gone, he was to say he left us at the corner of Park Avenue near Pierre's.

With Malcolm on his way, we took a cab and started for City Hall. The ceremony took very little time. Isn't it odd that a thing as important as marriage can be accomplished so easily? I've attended all sorts of weddings from shotgun to pure romance in my day, but I'd never seen such a solemn or curious one before. They were like two people in a dream repeating the oath after the clerk in unfeeling singsong voices. The clerk tried to put a little spirit into the affair by demanding his right to kiss the bride. Althea submitted gracefully. Then he nudged Terry in the ribs with a sly poke and told him to go ahead. As Terry kissed her chastely and with reverence the clerk winked at me and said, "He'll get over it."

I was just as sober as they while Terry signaled for a cab in the hot sun on Park Row. The bag was a good prop to have had with us for the wedding, but we had to dispose of it before we returned to my house. We drove over to Pennsylvania Station, where Terry checked it in the Long Island baggage-room. Then he put the check in an envelope and sent it to me in care of my niece at her summer camp at Lake Piseco. We would be rid of the bag and the check for a week at least, which was a pleasant thought.

The bride and groom were a silent preoccupied pair. Terry became diffident and shy. Now and then, I could see his adoring eyes seek the girl hungrily but I never once saw her look in his direction.

"We better talk over plans," I suggested as we started across town in a taxi. "We may not have much time. You two must give the impression that you're in love and living together. The marriage must appear to have been consummated."

"I didn't think that would be necessary," Althea said.

"For a few days at any rate," I went on. "Would you like to live with me?"

"We'd better go out to Roslyn," Terry suggested. "The house is large and we can have all the privacy we want and at the same time give the effect of being happily married."

"A good idea," I agreed.

"Very well," Althea acceded.

Terry was thoughtful for a moment. The cab was dragging along the street behind a big truck. Without looking at Althea, he asked, "You have those papers I gave you?"

"I was afraid of being searched. I gave them to Miss Thomas," she replied.

"Good girl!" he said admiringly.

In the excitement I had forgotten all about the papers which Althea had given me. I drew them out of the front of my dress and smoothed them on my knee. Althea and Terry leaned toward me and we read together a letter which had been sent to six people. It read:

"My diaries are in the hands of Terry Lassimon, who is editing them with the intention of publication. As you know, they contain facts and information of the greatest importance to you. For a consideration I might be persuaded to stop publication. Since there are a number of people vitally concerned, I suggest that you see me personally not later than the yth of July."

The letter had been sent to the following people:

Richard Bolertho
Philip Lassimon
Archie Van Nuys
Daisy Williams
Florence Gunner
Tom Andrews

"At last," Terry said, "we have something definite to work on."

"Do you know these people?" Althea asked.

"All of them," I replied.

"What on earth could that charming Bolertho man have done?" Althea asked.

"What did you do?" Terry asked quickly, too quickly I thought, for I seemed to sense jealousy in the question.

Althea made no reply. She turned and looked out of the cab window at the stores lining the street. I looked down at the letter still spread in my lap. It was dated July first. "There has been plenty of time," I said.

"For what?" Terry asked at once.

"For any of these people to have done the things that have been done so far," I replied.

"Four men and two women on that list," Terry said thoughtfully. "I think a man has been behind all this, don't you?"

"A woman might have conceived the plan," I suggested, "for some man to execute."

"If we only knew what had happened to the diaries," Althea said wistfully. "What is the financial status of these people?"

Terry took another quick look at the list and replied, "They have plenty of money, all of them, with the possible exception of Tom Andrews, my cousin Philip and Archie Van Nuys. I'm not so sure of them."

"Then wouldn't that make him a likely suspect?" she asked.

"You mean that the diaries might still be used for blackmail?" he asked.

"Can any of us who are mentioned in them be safe until they are destroyed?" she asked. There was no accusation in the words but Terry rose to his own defense immediately.

"I couldn't destroy them, under the circumstances," he said.

I didn't want them to get into an argument. After all, it was their wedding day. "We've work to do," I said quickly.

"What now?" Terry asked.

"We must contact each of the people mentioned in that list. If I only knew what they had done," I said regretfully.

"We've made mistakes, haven't we?" Terry said.

"We must get the diaries," Althea stated positively. "We won't be safe until they are in our possession."

"How?" he asked.

"If they were taken by a person in need of money . . ." she began.

We had crossed Fourth Avenue and, clear of traffic, the taxi shot down the street. "Oh, oh," I cried and crumpled the papers into a wad and stuffed them back into the dress.

"What's the matter?" they both exclaimed.

"We have company," I said and pointed to the police car parked in front of my house. "Undoubtedly Peter has made some discoveries concerning you."

I leaned forward and instructed the driver to go on beyond my door without stopping.

"What's the idea?" Terry asked.

"Do you want to be arrested?" I asked testily. "Give me a minute to think." I signaled the driver to turn into Third Avenue and park at the first opportunity.

"You must keep out of sight for some time," I said to both of them. "I'll try to manage Peter. If I can't, I don't know what we will do."

"You mean hide like an ordinary criminal?" Terry asked.

"Yes, although you'd probably be safer in jail."

"Why?"

"Because you're still in danger. I'm going to get out here. You keep this cab. Drive round for an hour, then telephone me. I'll know by then what will be best for you to do." I slipped out of the cab and left them rather amazed at the suddenness of my decision.

CHAPTER THIRTEEN

Peter was sitting in the hall when I opened the door.

"Well, Peter," I cried, pretending surprise, "you've come early. Have you had a drink?"

"I don't want a drink. What have you done with Lassimon and that girl?" he demanded.

"They've gone up to the Macon-Astoria," I answered.

"Where's the telephone?" he asked.

"Wait a minute, Peter." I put a restraining hand on his arm and smiled up at him.

"Don't try any of your wiles on me," he growled. "You've already made a fool out of me."

"Now, Peter, don't be absurd. What on earth do you mean?"

"Why did you switch from your own car to a cab, tell me that?" he asked.

"Because I knew you'd discover that a man answering Terry's description had rented an apartment in the building next to Van Wyck's," I answered honestly.

"Why didn't you tell me that up there?" he demanded.

"Why add fuel to a fire that's blazing well enough?" I countered. "You want to believe that either Terry or Althea killed Van Wyck. I happen to know that they had nothing to do with it. You're jumping at conclusions."

"That girl said the man's voice in the room sounded like Lassimon's," he barked, "and it could have been Lassimon."

"Don't sit there, Peter Conklin, and tell me that you think he could have raced from one building to the other while she was climbing the stairs. What do you think she is, a snail?"

Peter laughed at my explosive indignation.

"Strange as it may seem," he said, "it could have been done."

"Bosh!" I cried.

He went on. "We timed it, working on the theory that Miss Madison moved slowly because of the heat. There's an elevator in the house next door and if it had been on the ground floor waiting he could have made it in time."

"You don't believe that," I scoffed. "If you do, it's because the heat has done something to your head. Suppose he had galloped up there as you suggest in a frenzy of haste. He would have made a great deal of commotion. Do you think Van Wyck would have sat quietly at his desk waiting to be stabbed in the back? You know all that is absurd. You're just trying to take the easy road, Peter, and I'm ashamed of you. I don't blame you, however, in this terrific heat. I wouldn't work at all if I were you."

"You seem to be interesting yourself a great deal and getting around quite a bit in the heat," he grumbled. "I've got to get to the bottom of this."

"Of course you must. I know Terry Lassimon didn't kill Van Wyck. And neither did Althea Madison. Let's look at this sensibly. Better have a drink and cool off. Come along in here." I rang for Agnes as we went into the living-room.

"Since you're so sure they didn't kill Van Wyck, who did?" he asked.

"That's exactly what I would like to know and hope to find out if I can be left alone," I answered.

"So you think you're smarter than the police?" he asked accusingly.

"You don't mean that, Peter."

"Well, what do you know about the case? Why was Miss Madison being blackmailed? What has Lassimon to do with it? Why did he rent that apartment next door?"

"Just a minute," I stopped him. "I've no idea why she was being blackmailed. You know as much about it as I do."

"I know nothing about it," he growled.

"Which is what I know. When she mentioned Van Wyck to me I suspected blackmail at once and warned her against him. She did tell me that Van Wyck could put obstacles in the way of her inheritance. That's all I know."

"Which is reason enough for murder. She's due to get thirty million or so," he said.

"If she contemplated murder, she wouldn't have had the money with her this morning, would she?" I insisted.

"No, I suppose not," he admitted grudgingly. "Where does Lassimon fit into the picture?"

"A blind man could see that he's in love with the girl," I answered. "Naturally he has been attempting to protect her."

"It's a good thing they're not married," he stated.

"What difference could that make?" I asked fearfully.

"It would be such a swell set-up for a double motive."

"But you couldn't make them testify against each other," I said.

"I wouldn't even try. I'd arrest them on a double charge. She provided his alibi while he killed Van Wyck."

"Ridiculous!"

"It isn't and you know it. It would be a nice tight case with thirty million involved."

"It's no case at all. It's a possible motive—nothing else," I scoffed. "Van Wyck was a cagey cuss. . . ."

"Say—" He leaned forward. "How do you know so much about Van Wyck?"

"If you promise not to use the facts against me, I'll tell you," I replied.

"Don't be silly."

"I had a motive, as far as you're concerned," I answered. "Mortimer tried to blackmail me."

"Did you pay?" he asked quickly.

"I told him I'd see him in hell first."

Peter guffawed at that, which pleased me. Up to then he had been much more difficult than I had expected. Agnes came with highballs which gave me a little extra

time to think. I was positive that we must be free of the
police or the mystery would never be solved. My problem
was to think of arguments convincing enough to make
Peter agree to give us plenty of leeway. It was to be more
difficult than I imagined.

He turned to me after the first sip of his drink and
asked, "What did you do with that suitcase?"

I reacted badly. I jumped. The question was so
unexpected. I had hoped the absence of the suitcase from
the room would go unnoticed. "I put it in a safe place.
Why? " I answered bluntly.

"Why did you take it?" he demanded.

"It belonged to Terry Lassimon," I answered.

"So, you admit that?"

"Why not?"

"I was wondering what you would say, that's all. The
initials T. L. showed up on the photograph. I was sure I
had something until I found it gone. What was it doing in
that room at the top of the house? How did it get there?
He had no bag with him when he arrived in the morning."

"The bag," I replied, "is part of the mystery."

"You carried it downstairs, didn't you?" he asked.

I nodded.

"Why?"

"I didn't want you to think that Terry . . ."

"How did you know the bag would make me think that
he . . ."

I made a snap decision right then and there. I
interrupted him because I knew that our only chance was
to tell him the truth and trust that he would be willing to
play along with us for a little while. I realized that we
couldn't fight the police force and hope to reach a solution
of the case. I told him all the things that had happened
up to that morning. The one thing I kept from him was
the identity of the people mentioned in those letters
Mortimer had written.

"And the one person who might be of assistance to us
is dead," he said when I had finished.

"Fergus, you mean?" I asked.

He nodded. "Van Wyck's cook identified a body that was picked up in the Sound this morning."

I was relieved to hear about that. Poor Fergus! How shabbily his corpse had been treated, but then, I didn't suppose he knew anything about it. "Poor devil!" I said, "he knew too much."

"If we could get our hands on those diaries," Peter said eagerly, "we'd know what to do."

"That's the one thing you must not do," I said quickly.

"How are you going to get to the bottom of this in any other way?" he asked. At the moment there seemed no ready answer to refute the logic of his question. We did need the diaries, but I knew we would never get them if the police were involved in any effort to find them.

"Will you do me a favor, Peter?" I asked.

"I don't think so," he answered warily, "but tell me what you want?"

"Please don't interfere in this case for a week or ten days. Give us a chance to work it out in our own way."

"I thought you liked the Lassimon chap? You realize he is in danger."

"I do. He won't be killed if we are let alone. I feel positive of that."

"Well, I don't," he retorted.

"Listen, Peter," I begged. "We've no idea of the secrets contained in those diaries. If we make a fuss about them, there's no telling what will happen, don't you see that? At the moment, there is probably only one person interested. If the fact of the diaries is made known, there will be any number of people who will be concerned."

"You can't trifle with criminals," he objected.

"I realize that. I have the greatest respect for the police, law and order." He grunted at the statement but I paid no attention to him. "Some things are best done without police and if it's a question of human life . . ." He wanted to interrupt me, but I hurried on. "I'm thinking of kidnaped children who have died because their captors have been so terrified by the hue and cry of police, detectives and newspaper publicity. I know the police and government men have captured most of the guilty parties, but what of the children? We're in a somewhat similar situation. I don't want kidnapers to go free—I don't want this murderer to escape. I'm arguing about method and technique. I want to give our man plenty of rope."

"What makes you so sure the murderer will expose himself?" he demanded.

"I don't know, but I feel certain that the diaries were taken for the purpose of blackmail. Why else should both Mortimer and Fergus have been killed?"

"What has it to do with Lassimon?" he asked.

"Isn't that rather obvious? One way to get the diaries was to get rid of Terry. That won't be necessary now."

"But suppose the murderer is one of the people mentioned in the diaries? Lassimon isn't safe as long as that person thinks Lassimon knows his or her secret."

"That's why I want you to give us some time. Don't you realize that the murderer will be watching us every minute? If he or she thinks we are in collusion with the police they will stop at nothing to protect themselves. You must give us a chance, Peter."

"I wish I knew what was in your mind," he said, looking at me searchingly.

"Nothing at the moment. I'm just hoping some plan will come."

"Of course I don't believe you," he replied.

"Well, I have an idea," I admitted.

"Why not tell me?" he asked eagerly.

"I can't yet because I'm not sure. If you'll promise to leave us alone, I'll call you as soon as I'm at all reasonably sure. Will you do it?"

"I don't see how I can."

"I don't see how you can refuse. You won't get anywhere if you arrest either Terry or Althea on the slim evidence you have. You'll only make things difficult for them and warn the murderer to protect himself. Just give us a week," I begged.

"I'll tell you what I'll do," he said after a moment. "I'll forget all the things you have told me about Lassimon and the diaries. We'll go along trying to unearth a clue on our own. In the meantime, you must promise to keep me posted on anything new you may learn."

I agreed to that heartily. Good old Peter! It was an unusual thing he was doing and I was grateful to him.

CHAPTER FOURTEEN

When Terry telephoned, he was greatly relieved at the good news I had to tell him. "That's fine," he said, "now we can go ahead."

"With what?" I asked.

"I'm going to do a little sleuthing on my own account," he said.

"Don't take any unnecessary risks," I cautioned.

"I won't," he promised. "I'll take Althea out to Rosyln and leave her there. In the meantime, I'll be busy."

"Doing what?" I asked.

"This time I'm working alone," he answered mysteriously.

"But how will I get in touch with you if I should need you?" I asked.

"You won't need me. I'll keep you informed if I make any progress. I wish you'd forget the whole thing and let me handle it from now on," he said.

"There's nothing I can do now," I said.

"That's fine. Take it easy. You'll hear from me. It's make or break this time. I'm risking everything on an idea." He rang off.

What on earth was he going to do? He was an impetuous lad and I was fearful of what he might bring down on his head.

It would be necessary for us to act and act quickly. Of course, I had an idea in mind all the time, but I had had no intention of telling either Peter or Terry. Peter would not have consented to my working alone, neither would Terry, for that matter. I was rather grateful to know that Terry would be out of my way for a day or so.

I admit I was worried about their marriage. If Peter chanced on the notice of their sudden wedding, he would be doubly suspicious and might spoil all my plans. I was afraid that we had outsmarted ourselves.

I tried vainly to fit the pieces of the puzzle together. Why had Mortimer been killed after the diaries had been stolen? Why had the murderer risked possible exposure by taking the second shot at Terry while we were at Mortimer's? If all the events had taken place in one day, I would have believed that the murderer didn't want Terry and Mortimer to compare notes. Why had it suddenly become necessary for the murderer to kill both Fergus and Mortimer? The answer, of course, was obvious. First Fergus and then Mortimer had the answer to the problem which was vexing us. There was so much to be done and so little time left to us! I had made a promise to Peter which must be kept, after a fashion. I was taking a woman's license there in the hope that the end would justify the means. I did fear for Terry's life. I knew we must have the diaries to protect Althea's fortune.

What I planned to do, I couldn't very well do alone. I needed help. I called Sidney Kenfield and asked him to come over at once. I told him as much as it was necessary for him to know and then announced that I was going to get the diaries back in our possession.

'Then you've an idea where they are?" he asked.

"No," I replied, "I think I know why they were taken. I'll advertise and offer a reward."

"Are they that important?"

"They're worth a lot of money to some people."

"But will the thief risk exposure now?" he asked.

"Thieves do it every day. How do you suppose stolen jewels are recovered? I'll advertise and be my own contact man."

"Be careful," he warned. "You shouldn't be doing this, it's dangerous."

"I've done dangerous things before," I replied.

"I won't permit it," he stated boldly.

"You won't what?" I tried withering him with a glance but he wouldn't wither.

"It's all connected with our publishing business, isn't it?" he demanded.

I nodded.

"Then certainly I should have something to say about it. There's no reason for you to "

"Don't be an ass," I cried. "You've no money and something must be done. I'm going to advertise in all the papers tonight and tomorrow morning. You can take care of that for me while I arrange with the bank for the cash. Will you help me?"

"All right," he agreed finally.

"You can also keep in touch with each of the papers and arrange to have the answers, if any, sent directly to me by messenger service. We'll work all night if necessary."

"Good! Now I feel I'm a part of whatever it is."

"Run this ad." I handed him a slip of paper on which I had written: "*A good price will be paid for the right diaries.*"

He smiled as he read. "Are these the same diaries mentioned in Terry's ad?" he asked.

"Yes, worse luck," I replied.

"You can depend on me," he promised.

"One other thing. Don't mention this advertising scheme of mine to Terry if you see him. He wouldn't like it, would probably fuss about danger and all that sort of thing."

"Don't you think he should know?" he asked.

"He has enough on his mind. We'll do this together, just you and I."

"Partners," he agreed. "I'll keep you posted."

At the bank I arranged to have two hundred thousand dollars in cash ready for the next day. There were to be four packages of fifty thousand dollars each. I was willing to pay it all to get those diaries and save Terry from the danger which was closing in on him. Also, and I admit it without blushing, I had two hundred thousand dollars' worth of curiosity gnawing at my vitals. Those books would never get out of my hands again before I read them.

During the balance of the day, Sidney Kenfield and I called each other every hour on the hour with the precision and regularity of trains leaving New York for Philadelphia.

At six o'clock a messenger came -with some of the first answers to the ad. None of them were right, however. At seven, another batch arrived. They also were blanks written by people who were hopeful that they had the diaries I was interested in. I rather expected some more at eight but none arrived.

Nine o'clock! At last! I had an answer. There could be no question about the authenticity of the message. The person knew what I wanted. The message was composed of words formed by letters cut from glazed paper. It read:

SUCH SECRETS COME HIGH. IF YOU HAVE $100,000.00
BE IN THE DRUGSTORE AT THE CORNER OF YOUR STREET
AND FOURTH AVENUE AT 10:30 TONIGHT. WORK ALONE
OR BEWARE.

I don't believe I was afraid of the threat but for a moment it gave me a chilly feeling. Perhaps I had been a fool to keep my plan from Terry. Well, it was too late now to bother about that. He phoned to say he was leaving town but refused to tell me where he was going. Later I talked to Althea. She, too, was worried about him and his secretiveness. I called Sidney to tell him that I had received an answer to the ad. He wanted to know all about it but I refused to give him any information, explaining to him that I had been threatened and must work alone.

I went down to the drugstore about ten fifteen and bought a few articles. I had a limeade at the soda fountain, looked over magazines and chatted with the manager about the heat.

What would happen? Would a man walk in and speak to me? Would a messenger boy come with a note? As I was asking myself those questions, one of the telephones rang in a booth. The manager answered it. "Yes, she's here," I heard him say before he beckoned to me.

So that was it. I'll admit I was nervous as I entered the booth and pulled the door shut behind me. "Ethel Thomas speaking," I announced.

"Why do you want the Van Wyck diaries?" the voice asked.

"They must be destroyed to protect innocent people," I replied.

"What people?"

"I can't say," I answered, "but those vitally concerned will know."

He considered a moment. "My price is $200,000. Will you pay it?"

"Yes," I answered. "How do you want it done?"

"Do you have the money now?"

"No. I can get it tomorrow."

"I'll give you instructions tomorrow," the voice said and the line went dead. I didn't hear him hang up. It left me with a sense of emptiness which lasted all through the night.

My own excursion the next day was to the bank for the money. Later I tried to get in touch with Terry. No one knew his whereabouts, not even Althea. Where on earth had he gone and what was he doing?

The papers were full of the double murder of Mortimer and his man, Fergus, but none of our names were connected with the crime.

I spent the rest of the day watching the telephone, wondering when it would ring. Each time the bell rang I reached for it hopefully. It was nine o'clock when my instructions arrived. A messenger brought the note. It was done in the same manner as the previous one and read:

TAKE THE FLUSHING SUBWAY FROM GRAND CENTRAL
STATION. GET OUT AT WOODSIDE. -GO TO TWENTY-ONE
FORTY-NINE KENT AVENUE. ENTER GARAGE AT END OF
DRIVEWAY. BE THERE AT TEN-THIRTY TONIGHT.

I hated the idea of the hot sticky subway but I had to obey instructions. I was generous with my time. I arrived at the Woodside station a little after ten. I made inquiries about Kent Avenue from a man in a cigar-store where I bought some cigarettes. I had twenty minutes to kill. I looked in shop windows for a little while. Bought a limeade and then started for Kent Avenue. I walked up the driveway beside an empty house at exactly twenty-nine minutes past ten. The garage was at the end of the lot. There was a car in it. Inside, it looked as black as a pit. I moved in beside the car and waited.

There was no one there. In the distance, I could hear the rattle of subway cars and the more solid rumble of the Long Island Railroad trains. There was a slight purring sound within the garage. The motor was running. It startled me. Was the man going to make off with me? Well, not without a struggle, I was determined. I heard a spring creak and turned quickly. The garage door was closing behind me. I turned, and ran back and pounded on the door with my hands.

"Quiet!" a voice commanded. Then, "You have the money?"

"Yes."

"The diaries are on the floor of the car," the voice said.

I sidled along the car, opened the door and found the package. I tore it open and felt the books. He had brought the diaries. I went back to the door.

"Here's the money," I said.

The door opened slightly at the bottom. I bent down and pushed the money through the opening. It vanished into a gloved hand.

The voice said, "I'm putting a thin piece of wood through the hasp of the lock. It will take you a minute to break it. By that time I'll be gone."

The door banged down again. I could hear something scraping at the lock, then footsteps melted into the night. I pushed at the door frantically. It wouldn't budge. I tried again. What a fool I had been! I was trapped, caught like a rat in a trap. My head began to spin. I slid along the car again and felt for the ignition key. I couldn't find it and dared not waste time hunting in a strange car for something that might not be there.

There were no windows in the garage to break. I'd heard it said that a person dies in about four minutes from carbon monoxide poisoning. How long had I been there? There was one asset I had that the murderer didn't know about. I knew how to drive a car. Malcolm and I were in the Adirondacks years ago. We were caught in the mud. He got out to look over the ground and fell and sprained his leg, which left me absolutely helpless. I made up my mind at that time to learn to drive so that I wouldn't be useless again in a case of emergency.

I suppose you are wondering how much driving I expected to do in a narrow one-car garage. I climbed into the driver's seat and turned on the headlights. There were about three feet between the rear of the car and the door of the garage. I put the car into reverse and jammed my foot on the gas pedal. I released the clutch, the car shot backwards toward that door. We hit it with a crash that must have wakened the neighborhood. I pulled forward a little and ran back again. The door was splintered at the bottom. I tugged at it with my hands. It moved upward reluctantly, creaking and groaning. It cleared the car and opened all the way. I ran back to the car, picked up the diaries, and started out of the driveway more thankful for my release than I can ever express in words.

CHAPTER FIFTEEN

It took two full days to read the diaries. I was particularly interested in the lives of the people to whom Mortimer had written. The secrets were dangerous. It's a great wonder to me that he lived as long as he did. As I read I could understand why attempts had been made on Terry's life. Any or all of the people concerned in the diaries had reason enough to commit murder to protect themselves.

Was Daisy Williams really a murderess? Mortimer stated that she had killed her husband. Did Mortimer know the truth? Whether his statement was true or not the fact remains that Daisy could have killed her husband and done it very easily. The stage was all set for her and as Mortimer pointed out her chances of being caught or even suspected were practically nil. He didn't say how he gathered his data. It would be interesting to know exactly how he arrived at his facts. If he had lived, could he have proved his statements? I'd love to tell you exactly how Daisy was supposed to have accomplished Roger's death but I don't think it a fair thing to do. Who knows when you might be tempted just as Daisy was tempted?

Innocent or guilty, Daisy couldn't afford to have the story published; but then that was true of all the cases. In each story there was enough of truth to make things extremely uncomfortable for Mortimer's victims. Daisy probably overplayed her hand at the time of her husband's death. If Roger Williams' death and burial had been normal, Daisy would have nothing to fear, but it wasn't that simple. Daisy had given poor old Roger a grand funeral. Then the body had been cremated and Daisy, sadly, in her widow's weeds, surrounded by satellites, took the ashes to Mount Beacon and scattered them to the four winds. Those funeral rites would give Daisy a bad day or two in court. It would be extremely difficult for her to explain to a jury of her peers why she ignored the Williams' tradition of the family vault in Woodlawn. If she is innocent, it is rather ironic that her chance of proving it has literally gone with the wind. If she is guilty she knows the case against her is a black one. I could readily understand her willingness to go on paying Mortimer to keep him quiet. Also I could see the worm turning. Daisy is the type who can be driven just so far before revolting.

It is quite possible that Roger Williams might have died of kidney trouble. The Williams family have been famous for years because of their weak kidneys, but poor Daisy couldn't prove that she hadn't murdered her husband in exactly the manner described by Mortimer in the diaries. Fear of exposure would drive her to any means to protect herself. That was the whip which Mortimer held over her head.

Archie Van Nuys, poor asthmatic Archie, no wonder he was afraid. About ten years ago there was talk of running him for governor. There was a great deal in the press for a short time presenting Archie as a great educator, a man who molded the lives and destinies of American youth. Just as I grew tired of that publicity, the campaign died quite suddenly. I never knew why nor did I care. I think since we are such a great nation we should be careful about the people we put into office. I prefer gentlemen to politicians at any time and I'm a little fussy about my gentlemen. I can't imagine a wheezing asthmatic public official lending grace to any occasion. If Mortimer was the man who kept Archie from, running for governor, I think the citizens of New York State owe him a vote of thanks.

Archie had a great deal to lose. He owns and runs a large well-known school for boys. If the things stated in the diaries ever became known, every boy in his school would be taken out immediately.

What a contrast Archie's implied decadence was to the accusation filed against the vitally young Dick Bolertho. I didn't want to believe Mortimer's story about Dick. In fact, I refused to believe that he deliberately frightened the horse his wife Jessica had been riding and so brought about her death. What had he to gain by such a move? Jessica had given him a million and a half just before their wedding. He had all the money he needed and he was in love with her. Mortimer's accusation didn't make sense. Jessica had been so madly in love with Dick that she'd have given him her last cent if he had wanted it. He knew that. Could it be possible there was some other reason why he wanted her out of the way?

Mortimer didn't give the reason for the crime he claimed had been committed. It couldn't have been another woman because the world would have known about it long before now. What a clever way to kill a person, though, if Mortimer were right. Jessica was an excellent horsewoman, which was one of the things that made her death so tragic. When a novice falls from a horse and is permanently injured or even killed, one is apt to have the feeling that it serves him right, but when an expert is killed it is difficult to be rational. I can see her now taking the hurdles at the horse show, riding with ease and grace as her horse soared through the air.

Innocent or guilty, Mortimer's accusation must have been an awful shock to the poor boy. Dick would have been justified in trying to keep the diaries from being published.

The Dunns, Jessica's family, in spite of their money and two generations of the Social Register, are still fighting Irish. The veneer which covers the Dunns is thin and takes but a scratch to bring out the belligerent qualities of their ancestors. The Dunns would probably have believed Mortimer's statement and the rest of the world would have followed suit. The story of Dick's and Jessica's romance would be retold, only this time Dick would be made to appear as a sinister figure seducing and

luring the girl to a horrible death. He would be taken to
court, tried and even though a jury might fail to convict
him, his entire life would be ruined.

I could conceive of Archie, under pressure of exposure,
doing most of the things which had been happening to us,
but somehow I couldn't imagine Dick Bolertho stooping so
low. I dismissed him from my mind as the murderer. Of
Daisy I couldn't be so sure. I didn't believe for a moment
she had done the things herself, but she is the sort of
cackling hen that would jump from one side of the road to
the other. It would be just like her to put herself in the
hands of some unscrupulous man who would take her last
cent away from her after she had tried to protect both her
fortune and her secret.

I was somewhat inclined to feel that way about
Althea. After all, a tremendous fortune was at stake as
well as the family reputation. Mortimer claimed quite
baldly that Althea was not a Madison. Mortimer said
Althea was actually the child of a Frenchman with whom
her mother had had an affair while she was in Paris.
According to Mortimer, the Frenchman wouldn't marry
Elsie, so in desperation she married Herbert Madison. If
Mortimer's statement were true, it would explain Althea's
unusual childhood. It would make Elsie's unmotherly
actions understandable. The world would nod its head
and say, "Of course; no wonder she never brought the
child to America."

Can't you see how, under the circumstances, every
person who thought they had even the slightest claim to
the Madison fortune would try to have Althea's
inheritance set aside? Poor child. It must have been a
terrible blow to her pride. I know if I were in her position
I would fight to the bitter end to protect not only my
mother's name but the fortune as well.

I was quite willing to believe everything Mortimer
said about Philip Lassimon, Terry's cousin. I never liked
him. He isn't my type at all.

Philip, as I've said, is a run of the mill Lassimon. They've always been dark, almost swarthy and rather dried up, full of inhibitions, we say now that we are aware of modern psychology. I like people who seem clean, fresh and bright both inside and out. Haven't you noticed that some people seem to be unhealthy and nasty just beneath the surface of their skins?

There had never been a breath of scandal connected with his name. He had a large family and if he chose to use his wife as a breeding machine and she liked it, surely it was none of my business. Philip had always been such a devoted family man that it made Mortimer's charge a little difficult to believe. But, as I say, I'm inclined to believe it because I don't like Philip in the first place and knowing old Philip for the tight keeper of the money bags that he was, I can conceive of Philip being tempted. Even before his father died, Philip seemed to have plenty of money. I had always believed that by canny and doubtless crafty investments he had been able to build up what little money he had of his own into a sizable fortune.

Mortimer insists that Philip is in the dope racket. And what is more, Mortimer speaks with the voice of authority, even giving in detail the methods used to bring cocaine and codeine back into the country. I won't tell you what the plan was because if dope runners haven't already thought of it there is no point in giving them new ideas.

I thought I hated a blackmailer about as much as I could hate any low person, but I think men who traffic in dope are at the top of my hate list. Imprisonment is too good for them. They should be hung, drawn and quartered for the things they do.

It would have been so easy for Philip to operate in the way described by Mortimer. He had every opportunity to handle the drugs through the chemical works. With his skirts clear on this end, he had devised a scheme to bring the narcotics right back into the country. It was a method that had doubtless baffled Federal Agents for a long time. Then, too, Philip would be in a position to keep posted, because Federal Agents were probably in and out of his office trying to track down the original source of supply. It was a clever if unsavory business.

How Philip would hate to be uncovered! Can't you see headlines reading something like this: "Prominent Society Man Heads Dope Ring." What a ruin it would make of his life! If Mortimer's story were true, then a little thing like a murder or two wouldn't stop Philip if he could keep his secret covered.

I think we can sometimes forgive a man for murder when we learn just what factors led to the crime, but for dope running there can be no excuse. I wanted Philip Lassimon caught and exposed for the things he had done. I wanted him behind prison bars where he would be unable to victimize poor and weak people.

Right then and there I knew that we should turn the case over to the police. It was not our problem. On the other hand, it was not our business either. Both Terry and I had been dragged into the sordid mess quite by accident. Who am I to stand in judgment on others, even Philip? The moral aspect of the thing bothered me for sometime.

I do believe in permitting the dead past to bury its dead. If the things I had learned by accident had remained undiscovered up to now, why should I want to expose them? There are hundreds of crimes and scandals that are never made public. Why should I torture myself about the ethics of this particular problem? I was determined to stop Philip's drug traffic, however, no matter what else happened. After that my chief interest was Terry's safety. Nothing else really mattered. I had pledged myself to help him and I would. I tried to console myself with the thought that murder will out.

Will it? Perhaps that was why Florence Gunner was so afraid of the diaries.

Florence was a gorgeous blonde, not the cold antiseptic type but a fully developed glowing woman. The type that turns men's heads and she has turned them by the dozens. Florence was the most-often-engaged girl I've ever known. Certainly she was the most talked about. I understand that at one time you could get bets on the street for and against the probability of her marriage. When she had exhausted the supply of eligible and gullible young men in America she went abroad and became engaged to a few counts, earls, dukes and even a prince or two. The last story I had heard about her was an account of a growing romance between her and an Englishman. Those who seem to know assured me that Florence was in love at long last and would go through with the venture. The man was reputed to be one of England's wealthiest peers. If it was a romance, the world couldn't say that it was a case of poverty-stricken nobility looking for good sound American dollars. Dollars are sound, aren't they, in spite of all the talk we've heard to the contrary about inflation?

Do you remember the Alderman Case? Of course you do. The papers all over the country were full of it at the time. Alderman was shot to death in his living-room. When the body was found, it was without wig or false teeth. It became definitely known that there was a woman in the case but her identity was never disclosed. I've heard people say that the police knew who she was but because she was rich the whole thing was hushed up. It is one of the famous unsolved murders in New York records. Yes. You've guessed it. Mortimer definitely accused Florence Gunner of being the woman in the Alderman case and seemed to be possessed of very definite information.

If she loved her Englishman, such a scandal had to be suppressed. A thing like that, if known, would most certainly squash any chance of marriage. We've just had a recent example of British squeamishness.

Almost every crime known to man was represented by the diaries. Tom Andrews' game was traffic in souls. Sounds melodramatic, doesn't it? Horribly so. I was inclined to believe the accusation. Tom was a man about town. He was a theatrical promoter. I know he did send chorus girls to South America and other places. According to Mortimer, the theatrical business was merely a cover for an extensive White Slave Traffic. A man who makes money in that way is a loathsome beast to me.

After learning all the secrets I was sorely troubled by a new problem. Why had the diaries been sold to me? I tried to rationalize that question. Had fear and greed been mixed in the motives for turning the books over to me?

When I assured that unknown voice that the diaries would be destroyed, did he really believe me? Why else give them to me? The answer was obvious as I thought about it. The man expected me to die in that garage. He had probably lurked outside waiting for those deadly fumes to make an end of me. I'm sure that he planned to creep back to the garage after my death and take the diaries. In that way he would have the money and the diaries and with me out of the way could go on with his plans.

It was a bold plan and a risky one. Why was he so sure that I was working alone? Would a man like Philip risk his secret once he had the diaries in his hands? Perhaps if he were clever enough he would do it. Possession of the diaries would carry a double murder charge in addition to the secrets contained in them. Would I, if I were Philip, Andrews, Van Nuys or Daisy, release the diaries once I had them in my possession? I could conceive of Althea, Florence Gunner or Bolertho doing such a thing, but I wasn't at all sure about any of the others.

As I thought about the problem, I regretted that I had had no means of checking each of those people on the night I had recovered the diaries. How simple it would have been to pin the crime on the one person who had no alibi for the hour or so I spent over in Long Island in that beastly garage.

I was restless. I wanted action. I tried to contact Terry but he had vanished completely. I was annoyed with him. What on earth was he doing? Where had he gone? Why didn't he let me hear from him?

CHAPTER SIXTEEN

I heard from Terry the next morning. I've had all sorts of letters in my day, but Terry's note, which catapulted me further into the adventure, was the most unusual and startling I had ever received. I didn't believe a word of it. You wouldn't have either if you were as furious with him as I was at the moment. He had been gone for days. No one knew where he was or what he was doing. He knew nothing of my adventure or the recovery of the diaries. Peter Conklin was in a peeve about him. Althea was all at sea, and goodness knows I was reaching the breaking-point.

The letter was on my breakfast tray the Thursday morning which happened to be the day the all-time heat record for New York City was broken. I'm not claiming a sense of prophecy when I say I knew record heat was coming. Dawn, after another murky night, was heavy and depressing. If you've ever spent a summer in New York you know what I mean. It was and had been hotter than Tophet with an overdose of humidity thrown in to keep a sodden humanity gasping and mopping. It had been like that for several days, baking, blistering hot under the rays of a brooding sultry sun which pierced the low-hanging blanket of haze—a combination of fog, smoke and city dust. The days of waiting anxiously to hear from Terry were bad enough, but the nights—damp, depressing, breathless black pits of torture—left me worn and frayed each morning and in no mood for flippancy of any sort and certainly not Terry's type represented by the note.

I looked at the weather forecast before sorting my mail.

Each night and morning that practical jokester, known as the weather man, had promised us relief, but the promise had not materialized. As much as I loathe thunderstorms, I fervently hoped each day we would have one because they usually clear the air and bring relief. I wonder how the meteorologists feel when the elements laugh at their predictions day after day. I suppose it's like any other riddle—if you keep guessing long enough you find the right answer.

The papers had been unusually dull for days. There had been much speculation about the deaths of Mortimer and Fergus, but nothing that I didn't already know. The rest of the news was negligible. One gets weary of headlines about heat and dust storms, burning crops and all that sort of thing. I wouldn't have been interested in a new murder that morning. No, that's not sure because I'm always very much interested in murder. What I wanted was the promise of a good rousing thunderstorm, but instead there was a headline to inform me that the Midwest heat wave was moving East.

I believed it. The idea of another ten degrees of infernal heat added to the high nineties which we had been having was just too much to bear. I tried to convince myself that there was no reason for. me to stay in New York and swelter, but steam tractors couldn't have dragged me away, though I did play with the idea of going places. For years I've belonged to that school which believes New York is as comfortable or vice versa as any other place in summer. Certainly there is much to be said for the satisfying comfort of your own good beds, personal things and the privacy which is so necessary if you're at all uncomfortable.

I knew I wouldn't be able to go anywhere and escape the heat unless I decided to rent an air-cooled theater and move into it for the balance of the summer. As I listlessly sorted my mail, my mind played with the idea of Bar Harbor or Newport. Then Terry's dashing scrawl promised me respite from the anxious boredom of the last few days.

At least it was news. Eagerly I opened the strange and challenging note which told me nothing and made me furious at the same time. No man, not even Terry, has any license to write such a note.

I was most annoyed. I knew that young man and his bag of tricks, or rather, I thought I did, but this was something quite different.

Once before I had accepted one of his intriguing invitations to a party out at his estate in Roslyn and on my arrival there found things in a frightful condition. It was just before five in the afternoon when I arrived and you've never seen such people, on the surface at any rate, as swarmed all over the place. I stood in the hall and looked at his guests with a contempt in my eyes that I made no effort to conceal.

One jovial cove, in his cups—slightly pie-eyed, I believe is the popular expression—was in a hurry to get somewhere. He barged into me on a leeward lurch. As I tottered from the impact, after all I'm rather frail, he put out a fat pudgy hand to steady me and gave me the most accusing look and said, "Grandma, I'm surprised at you! Steady, old girl!" and went on his way.

For a moment my sense of humor deserted me. I know I glared . . . something I do quite well after long years of experience. I've been wrongfully accused of many things in my life but I can take my liquor and hold it as a lady should. To be twitted of being tight at five o'clock in the afternoon when I hadn't had a drink was too much for me, and what is more I hate being called Grandma. I turned my sudden wrath on Terry and told him I was going home. He wheedled me into staying by saying, "You know, Ethel, you lend a bit of tone to this party which might otherwise be completely shoddy."

I stayed. Wouldn't you? I'd heard about wild parties, read descriptions of them in books, but I'd never been invited to one before. Shoddy the party was, in one sense, and wild in a way but not nearly as bad as I thought it was going to be (secretly I was a bit disappointed). It was never dull and always diverting because the people were what you call ordinary until you knew them. They were a revelation to me. Fundamentally, we're all alike under the skin. It is just our stage settings and degrees of social education which make us seem different.

They were Terry's idea of a diversion. He had always been anti-Social Register. His tastes had led him into the highways and also the byways of life. I didn't blame him too much, however, because so-called good society can be an awful bore without even half trying. It was one of his by parties and I must admit I had a good time. I had never known the warm, inclusive big-hearted friendliness of a burlesque queen up to that time, nor the fascinating camaraderie of a racetrack tout, to say nothing about the facts of life which I gleaned from some chorus girls over a nightcap.

This incredible note, however, was a different matter. What on earth did he mean? Why write me a note like that? I was determined to show him that I wasn't born yesterday, but then he knew that. As much as I wanted to see and talk to Terry I tossed the note to one side and went on with my other mail or rather tried to wade through uninteresting notes, invitations, bills and a tiresome letter from one of my grand-nieces in which she told me about Junior's hives and baby Ethel's adenoids. Why do young mothers think other people are interested in the diseases of their children? For that matter, why do people insist in telling you all about their operations? I've never had one so perhaps I'm just a little jealous, but I know there are lots more interesting topics of conversation. But to get back to baby Ethel and her adenoids.

I sometimes wish I had had a child, with or without the benefit of clergy. Motherhood, if it doesn't make a fool out of a woman gives her a maturity and fulness that I don't possess, although on the other hand one of the sweetest and most motherly women I have ever known was an old maid about whose private life I never had the slightest suspicion.

I skipped through to the end of that letter, not at all interested in the invitation which it contained. Imagine having children under your feet during a hot spell if you aren't forced to do it and anyhow, how could I be intrigued by anything while Terry's note continued to challenge me, face up where I had tossed it? It was as if Terry himself were in the room lavishing his personality upon my resisting consciousness. Why on earth had he written it? What had happened to him? Where had he been?

Terry's dark eyes seemed to dance before me on the page. I fancied I could see his tantalizing smile, the arched bow of his lips and his gleaming white teeth. As a matter of fact, he seemed to be teasing me. Now that, I know, is absurd, sheer nonsense and yet I definitely felt Terry pleading with me to follow the instructions in the note.

I reached for the letter and re-read it. Of course, I didn't believe a word of it. How could I? It was too preposterous, too much like the engaging rogue who had written it.

Would you have believed a note which read?

Dear Ethel:
Come out to Roslyn Thursday afternoon for my
murder. It will give you material for a new book.
Yours,
TERRY

What did he mean? Why Roslyn of all places? How could I solve the murder there? Did he mean a third attempt on his life? Did he write it to give me a jolt? He knows I hate heat and won't, if I can help it, stir out of my own house for anything short of a murder. I was furious with him but there was only one way to get the answers to my own questions and that was to go out to Roslyn.

For the second time in my life I was embroiled in murder, intrigue and horror because a young man who inherited a vast fortune and a thriving business preferred the white lights of Broadway to the abysmal canyons of downtown New York where the offices of the Lassimon Chemical Works were located. If history repeats itself more or less, it is because people are so much alike. Not that Terry was anything like Charlie Doane. Two men couldn't be more exactly opposite than they. Their only similarity was the fact that, born to wealth, they were neither of them interested in the family business and the making of money in that way. Although Terry at the moment was in a financial jam, he was not generally a fool about his money. How or when he finds time to take care of his affairs has always been a mystery to me.

He was like that from a child. He had his finger in several pies at the same time. You see I watched him grow up if you can call his activities growing up. Evelyn Lassimon, his mother, was a nice enough girl in her way, a bit on the colorless side, and his father wasn't what you'd call exciting unless you're one of those people who like to spend hours at the Aquarium. Knowing his background makes Terry so hard to understand. I don't know what happened when he was born unless nature took a little thoughtful time at the moment of his conception and decided that there were enough dull Lassimons in the world and planned then and there a revolutionary move. I'm sure nature was to blame. Anyhow Terry was either a throwback or a pitch forward but he wasn't true to the run of the mill.

I rang for Agnes and told her to lay out my things, to pack our bags and have Malcolm and the car ready at twelve.

"How about luncheon?" she asked.

I told her it was much too hot for me to eat, that she and Malcolm could have cook prepare an early snack for them before we started. I caught her grinning as she turned away. Agnes is a minx and knows far too much about me. She knew very well that we'd stop somewhere along the road and eat frankfurters much to Malcolm's disgust.

Malcolm would have made some woman an excellent but overbearing husband. Imagine being married to a man who wouldn't let you eat hot-dogs or ham- burgers because he didn't think them quite nice. He once suggested, in a roundabout way, that I was too old for such food. What nonsense! You're only as old as you feel and sometimes the way I feel frightens me. I've always enjoyed good food and hope I always will. When I can't eat I'll be ready to die, but until that time comes I'm not going to do myself up in lavender and old lace to grow old and querulous before my time. Seventy-five is no age. Imagine sitting in a corner and getting dotty waiting for your hour to strike. Life has too much to offer if you keep going and take what comes without complaint. Of course one thing in my favor is the fact that I am and always have been disgustingly healthy and in spite of my frail body, as strong as an ox.

I tried once again to contact Terry by telephone. They knew nothing about him at Roslyn. I called Sidney Kenfield. He said he had heard from Terry and was going out to Roslyn later in the day. No, he didn't expect Terry at the office. He didn't know where he was. Then I called Terry's apartment and his Japanese houseboy professed to know nothing about him. There is no servant who can be less informative than an Oriental. They are really intelligent servants but they do give excellent imitations of sheer stupidity over the telephone. I left word at each place I called that Terry was to get in touch with me the moment he arrived. The recovery of the diaries, about which he knew nothing, might possibly change his plans. I felt he should know about it.

As the hours dragged by without a word from him I began to despair and then grew angry all over again. I was unreasonable in my anger but it did me no good. If he wanted to do things in the dark as he had been doing, throwing me a crumb of information here and a morsel there I determined I'd let him go on in his own sweet way. I hate crumbs of any kind.

I spent as much of the balance of the morning as I could in the tub trying to keep cool. Then I began to get ready. I carefully packed the diaries myself. Before I dressed, I took Terry's note out of my desk and sitting at the dressing-table, I read it again, trying to fathom exactly what it meant. I was just as puzzled as I had been when I received it.

I took a long time over my toilet. I don't try to look like a Hollywood flapper, but because I happen to be old, I see no reason for looking like something out of the Ark. Modern cosmetics and beauty aids being what they are, any woman of any age can help her appearance.

The note lay on the dressing-table and mocked me, every word of it. Agnes came and stood beside me. She's an inquisitive wench, never misses a chance to peer over my shoulder in a seemingly innocent way. I put the note into its envelope and thought I slipped it under my bag. Once or twice as I fought perspiration—ladies do perspire in spite of Emily Post and others—I half decided not to go, but that was only a game I was playing with myself. Wild horses, heat, wind, snow or rain couldn't have kept me away from Roslyn. I scented more excitement, possibly danger. You see I didn't believe the note, but then you wouldn't have believed anything as preposterous as that either. Whatever it was that Terry had planned, he was going to be surprised to learn that I had recovered the diaries. I was full of anticipation, just a curious old woman rather badly ridden by the heat, a little off normal and as curious as a half-dozen cats.

CHAPTER 17

We left the house promptly at twelve. By the time we reached the Queensborough Bridge, I was reaching for my third handkerchief. It was then that I realized that Terry's note, neatly folded, was in my purse. I didn't even remember putting it there. I must have done it automatically after I realized that Agnes was trying to read it. Now don't ask me why I kept the fool thing. I should have had more sense, but then hindsight is always so much better than foresight anytime, anywhere. I should have taken it out when we were in the middle of the bridge, torn it into little bits and scattered it to the winds, but I didn't. I couldn't possibly know the complications that would follow. I suppose the reason I kept it in the first place and didn't destroy it in the second was the fact that I wanted to wave it at Terry and ask dramatically,

"What does this mean?"

There are two kinds of fools in this world. Those who write foolish incriminating letters and those who keep them after they have been written. No matter what my motive was I should have destroyed the thing, but I didn't. I wasn't normal. If I were I would have gone to a nice cool movie and forgotten all about the whole business. Ifs, ands and buts have no bearing now on what happened. I did keep it and I did go out to Terry's house.

When we were out on Long Island, Agnes and I had hot-dogs at a cute little roadside stand on Northern Boulevard near Great Neck. We ate them with relish.

Say what you will, they simply do not taste the same when prepared at home and, Malcolm or no Malcolm, when I want them I eat them. Malcolm got out of the car and stood in the shade of the building while we munched our lunch. When Agnes asked him if he wanted one he gave her a withering look. When we were ready for the second one, I called him just to see his nose tilt a little higher.

When he carried them out to us he handled them as if they were poison. I'll bet my cook has a time with him about his food. He's such an old fuss-budget. He poked one into the front seat at Agnes and was thrusting mine through the window at me when I stopped him and told him to open the door.

As he opened the door, I made him wait while I rummaged in my hand-bag for a loose dollar bill. My purse is no exception to the general feminine receptacle.

It is a glory hole into which I tuck things because I think I want to keep them or feel I'll need them.

Several scraps of paper, a powder-puff and other doubtful treasures fell to the floor. Malcolm, the frankfurter weaving in the air, tried to pick them up for me with his free hand without much success. As he leaned forward a thin trickle of mustard oozed out of the roll, ran across the edge of the paper napkin and started for the floor. I just moved my foot in time to miss the mustard. I took the frankfurter from Malcolm, gave him the old paper napkin and told him to open the other door so that there would be some circulation of air while we were standing still. I don't know anything that can get as hot as an automobile that is standing in the sun. The heat soon became unbearable. I suggested we move on.

With the sun broiling down on us and the inside of the car at oven temperature, there was no reason why I should have shivered as Malcolm swung the car between the gates of Tomnahurick. That's the name of Terry's estate at Roslyn. It's an unusual name. It means, the Hill of the Fairies. You probably remember something about it. At the time of Bainbridge's murder the papers were full of the name. They even printed a picture of the original hill just outside of Inverness.

Terry bought the estate after the Bainbridge case was cleared up. Mary Bainbridge had married Arthur Martinson by then and had no further use for it. She was probably glad to get away from the house, anyhow, because the poor dear had never been happy there.

How could any woman be happy with a man like Bainbridge? He deserved his end if ever a man did, but for a time it looked as if Mary would be convicted of his murder. I think she would have had a much more difficult time if it hadn't been for one of her maids, who committed suicide in the lily pond. Well, that's another story, an old one, with which you are probably familiar anyhow. At any rate, I did shiver as we entered the drive. It may have been a premonition, excessive heat or woman's intuition, I don't know. Certainly the ghost of that poor girl who died in the lily pool had nothing to do with it and I had no idea of the things which were to come.

As a matter of fact, I was in a mood to do battle with Terry and leave at once if his explanation of the note failed to satisfy me.

As we circled into the estate and began the long climb up the grade, I caught a glimpse of the house at the top of the hill. Heat waves shimmered from the roof and the long glass-enclosed porch seemed rather broodingly uninviting. At other times I'd always thought the house was rather lovely, commanding as it did a view of Roslyn Harbor, which view, however, is no particular prize now that the sand companies have moved in and gouged out the hillsides destroying what was once sheer loveliness. Those great gaping holes with their puffs of smoke as steam cranes bit into the bowels of the earth angered me. Why must man in his greed destroy the few lovely things that nature has given us?

As we neared the top of the hill the view of Long Island Sound beyond Seacliff was a delight. There were a few sailboats out there luffing along in the fitful breeze. I made up my mind then that if I stayed I would insist upon a sail on the Sound. Terry had a luxurious yacht which lay just off his pier most of the time, with steam up, ready to sail at a moment's notice. I looked down at the water and there, sure enough, was the yacht, a thin trickle of smoke coming from its forward stack.

The driveway sweeps in a broad circle as it approaches the house. I looked over toward the lily pond and thought again about that poor girl, Annie Sims, who had died there. Life gave her more than her share of heartache and abuse plus an incurable disease, but she died gloriously that Mary Bainbridge might live and be free. Martinson told me himself that Annie's death kept Mary's name clean. If the girl had told what she knew, the police would have been able to unearth the whole sordid story. As it was, even a smart District Attorney couldn't make a piece of paper talk. Annie knew what she was doing. She left the note and then quitted a world which had been anything but kind to her. Hers was a glorious soul. Greater love hath no man. It took courage to do what she did and yet she was a social outcast.

When Malcolm stopped the car with something of a flourish and opened the door for me, I lost no time getting into the cool shade of the hall out of the glaring sun. I wasn't expected so early, but that didn't rumple Hubert's habitual calm. He was a perfect butler. I don't think murder would cause him to blink an eyelid; as a matter of fact, it didn't, but I'm getting ahead of the story.

"Don't disturb my bags," I warned Hubert. "I'm not at all sure I'm staying."

"Mrs. Lassimon is expecting you; in fact, Miss Thomas, I have a feeling she's rather depending on you," Hubert said graciously.

"Oh, you do, do you? Why?" I asked.

"I couldn't say," he replied stolidly.

"Where is Mr. Lassimon?" I demanded.

"He didn't say. He telephoned from town," he answered. "He instructed me to send the yacht in for him and the other guests late this afternoon. Perhaps you'd like to go in for the sail," he suggested.

"I just came from town," I barked, annoyed anew at Terry. "It's only two degrees cooler than Hell this minute. I wouldn't go back there for all the Terrys in the world."

Agnes snickered, but Hubert didn't flex a muscle. Malcolm was waiting just inside the door. "Put the car up," I ordered and then said to Hubert. "Have my things taken up. I'm staying."

I was hurt by Terry's thoughtlessness. Why hadn't he told me about the yacht, since it was going in for guests? It would have been the easiest way and the most comfortable for me. The answer was simple enough. He didn't want me on board on the way out.

Why? Well, I'd fool him. But why didn't he want me on the boat between New York and Roslyn? I couldn't imagine the answer but I knew he generally had a reason for whatever he did. I came very near making a bad mistake in the heat of my resentment.

The moment I admitted to myself that his actions were prompted by reason I began to think more clearly and felt rather proud of myself for being right.

In my suite Hubert said, "I'll draw the curtains if you care to take a nap."

He meant well but that suggestion irritated me. Just because I'm old, people seem to think I have to spend most of my time taking catnaps just to keep up with the rest of the world.

"Never mind the blinds," I said. "Send me a limeade."

I selected a cane-bottom chair and sat down. I can't abide overstuffed furniture in hot weather. As Hubert turned toward the door, I asked, "Who's coming?"

"I couldn't say. Mrs. Lassimon didn't seem quite sure. Anything else, miss?"

"Please tell Mrs. Lassimon I've arrived."

"Thank you, Miss Thomas."

He was a perfect servant for Terry, or for any one, as a matter of fact.

While unpacking, Agnes became quite talkative.

"Do you know they say this house is haunted?" she informed me.

"Who says so?" I demanded.

"The servants. They say that the girl is seen walking in the garden near the lily pond on stormy nights, while Bainbridge walks about in the house." She paused, a handful of lingerie suspended in midair, shoulder-straps dangling. "Have you ever seen a ghost, Miss Thomas?"

"No, and don't be filling your head with a lot of nonsense," I advised as I sent her down to the servants' hall because I wanted to be alone. I took the diaries from the bag and crammed them into the flue of the fireplace. As I worked I thought of the things Agnes had said about the ghost. If Bainbridge's wraith wanted to use that flue he would have some difficulty.

I don't believe in ghosts, as I've never seen one, and yet although I've never seen electricity I believe in it.

The longer I live the more certain I am that there are things never dreamed of in our philosophy. If I had been told when I was twenty that men would fly through the air faster than birds I would have scoffed at the idea. Before the War, as late as that, I wouldn't have believed that by pressing a button in my own home I would be able to hear the divine and thrilling voice of Lily Pons coming to me over the air. I refused to believe in radios when they first came out and now they blare at you from every open window and from almost every automobile you pass on the highways. Agnes' remark stayed with me. Could it be that Bainbridge did haunt the place and . . . No, that was silly, and yet I've always believed that houses have definite personality. Some of them seem to radiate happiness while others harbor only unhappiness, strife and tragedy. If ever a house had been badly named, Tomnahurick was it. Hill of the Fairies, indeed! Hill of the Devil was more like it when Bainbridge was its owner.

A tap on the door made me jump. My mind was too full of the thoughts of ghosts. In the open door Althea stood facing me.

"Come in, come in," I cried.

"I'm so glad you've come," she said. "Tell me what has happened."

"I don't know. I haven't heard from him since you left me nearly a week ago," I replied.

"Neither have I," she said. "It's been terrible waiting like this."

I leaned forward and whispered, "I have the diaries."

"You have!" Her face brightened at once. "Where are they?"

"In a safe place, don't worry."

"Did you read them?"

"Yes."

"Do you believe it? You knew my mother—do you think the story is true?"

"I don't know, but I'd say it was unimportant. Herbert Madison loved you both. That's all you need worry about."

"I suppose so," she agreed after a long pause.

It must be a shock to realize after long years that the man you thought was your father had nothing to do with your birth and that your real father is just an unknown man out in the world somewhere. Animals have the right idea. Maternity and paternity never bother them after a very short time while their young are growing. Once their offspring grow up they go out into the world to shift for themselves and that's all there is to it. Family ties are one of the responsibilities we assumed with civilization.

"Don't brood about it, dear," I advised. I felt sorry for her.

"You can't help thinking," she replied.

"No, you can't," I agreed. "That's the devil of it. You'll have to be philosophical. You've nothing to worry about now."

"But I'm a nobody, a bastard," she cried, "and all these years I've been so vain and proud." She laughed nervously. "It's funny, isn't it?"

"Stop it!" I cried. "This is no time for hysterics. I don't know what Terry has planned for this party, but we must be on our toes. We've got to see him through."

"I'm to go in on the yacht. Will you join me?" she asked, getting up.

"I'll think about it," I answered.

There was a discreet tap on the door. I supposed it was Agnes, but it was Hubert, flawlessly correct as usual, announcing without the slightest sign of pertubabation, "The police are here, Miss Thomas, asking for you."

"What do they want of me?" I demanded.

"He didn't say, miss. It's a motorcycle officer. He asked to see you."

For a moment I thought that perhaps we had been speeding on the way out, but discarded that, as we would have been given a ticket on the road. What on earth could a Long Island policeman want with me?

Had there been trouble at my house in town? Had there been a fire? Had Terry been arrested? You know how thoughts will race through your head. My mind was full of such conjectures as I followed Hubert down to the library on the main floor. I knew perfectly well that if there had been trouble at home some of the servants would have telephoned.

I had a glimpse of black boots, doe-colored breeches, a trim waist, and a light tan shirt, moist over the broad shoulders. As I entered the room the man was facing the window. In that one quick glance I knew that he was built as a man should be. He was a perfect physical specimen. He turned to face me. I liked the look of his steady gray eyes and the general softening of his face as he smiled most engagingly. I don't know what he expected but I'm sure he didn't expect anything like me.

"I'm Miss Thomas," I said. "What has happened?"

"Nothing yet, I hope," he replied. With that he put his hand into his trouser pocket and drew out a folded envelope and handed it to me saying, "I'm Saxon of the Nassau County police."

I took the envelope. I didn't have to open it to know what it was. It was Terry's note, but how under the sun had it come into Saxon's possession? As I opened it reluctantly, trying hard to appear calm and matter-of-fact I felt him studying me quizzically.

"I found it at a hot-dog stand," he explained. "I hope I'm not too late for the party." His grin was more grim than humorous.

I knew I'd have to do some fast thinking and tall fabricating to fool such an alert young man, but that didn't worry me, as I've had lots of practice. What I needed was time. The note mocked me anew as it rested in my fingers. If I knew what Terry meant!

I had to say something to satisfy the young man and protect Terry at the same time.

CHAPTER 18

The man facing me represented the Law and had to be answered in such a way as to be satisfied and yet be told nothing. What could I tell him, anyhow? How could I explain the contents of the note when I had no idea, myself, what it meant? He was patient about waiting. There was an amused glint in his eyes. He was a fine-looking lad, sure of himself and full of unpretentious confidence . . . not the type that is engendered by a uniform. It was an inherent quality that goes with a good head and the ability to think clearly and see things in a flash. He'd be a good man to have at your elbow in any emergency, a fine friend and a relentless enemy.

I've always been a creature of impulse and at that moment a plan was born which proved to be a good one. He looked perfectly grand in his uniform and I was wondering how he would look in dinner clothes, when he stirred uncomfortably. I do believe I flushed a bit self-consciously as he turned his eyes away from mine. I blushed because of his discomfort. I've seen young men squirm when lascivious old women eye them too pointedly and too long. Heaven knows what he thought of me, as I stood there wondering how, in the light of the note I held in my hand, I might use him.

He broke the silence by asking without looking at me, "Have you thought of a good answer?"

I pretended to be startled and said, "Er . . . no. To be truthful I was wondering why Terry invited you to the party."

"What party?" he asked, taking the bait very nicely, but I wasn't too sure that I had fooled him.

"Here, this party," I replied, tapping the note with a finger. "Did you get an invitation too?"

"You wouldn't try to kid me, would you, Miss Thomas?" he asked. "Because if you did I might not think it funny. I'm just an ordinary policeman."

"Extraordinary," I replied with a smile.

"Now, I know you're kidding, but thanks for the compliment, just the same. I haven't been invited here to a party or anything else and you know it as well as I do. You're stalling," he accused bluntly. "I'm here in the line of duty. I want an explanation of that note. I went to a great deal of trouble to locate you. I called your house in New York. They told me you were here. Now suppose you tell me all about it." He became very businesslike and impersonal. The smile faded from his lips and eyes, giving way to a determined set of chin and jaw.

"But you knew there was going to be a party here. You said so when I entered the room," I insisted. "There was no harm in my asking you, was there? And there is nothing illogical about your being a guest. Mr. Lassimon has many friends."

"We'll forget that. I'm not a friend of Mr. Lassimon's. When I mentioned party to you I was speaking figuratively. We're quite apt to call murders, parties," he explained.

"A rather gruesome thought," I said. "You don't talk like a policeman at all, or perhaps my sources of information have been wrong."

"Most of us are educated, if that's what you mean, and since the depression you'll find plenty of college men on the force. It's a good job, you know, decent work, fair hours and a chance to maintain your self-respect and eat regularly. But who or what I am can have nothing to do with the note."

"Of course not," I agreed, "but it was sweet of you to humor a fanciful old lady by explaining. This is an invitation to a party." I waved the note at him. "You came in and asked me if you were late for the party. Being an old woman I supposed you were being literal."

"It's a peculiar invitation, unique in party invitations, I should say. You don't mind my being skeptical, I hope."

"Not at all, but if you knew Mr. Lassimon, you'd understand. You've heard of Mr. Lassimon, haven't you?"

"Nassau County's bad boy, they call him," he answered. "Yes, I've heard of him and given him tickets for speeding."

"Then you know what a joker he is."

"Joker?"

"Yes. I wrote a book about the Doane store murders."

"But I don't see what that . . ."

"Don't interrupt," I broke into his speech. "Let me explain. After my book was published all my friends began teasing me by calling me Mrs. Hawkshaw. They say that since that time nothing short of murder interests me any more. Mr. Lassimon was having his little joke by wording my invitation as you see it."

"All right, I'll take that," he said after a moment's consideration, "but I hope for your sake and mine that you're telling the truth." He made no effort to conceal the threat which his words implied.

"What do you mean?" I tried my best to seem innocent.

"In the light of that note, it would be your hard luck if there happened to be a murder here tonight. You and Mr. Lassimon would have to do a lot of difficult explaining and even then I don't believe you'd be able to keep yourselves out of jail. Do you get what I mean?"

I certainly did and said so. "As a matter of fact," I continued, "I'm rather a bit ahead of you. I know exactly how you must feel and I must admit I'm glad to disappoint you. On your way here you probably decided that you were going to be the first one to unearth a nasty plot in high society. Well, you're wrong. You don't suppose a woman of my experience would lose a note like that if it meant anything, do you?"

He gave me a careful scrutiny and said, "No, I don't believe you would. You're no fool and yet," he ended thoughtfully, "you might be careless."

The shot went home, but I think I concealed my slight reaction. "Thank you, Saxon," I said.

"That's all right, Miss Thomas, sorry to have bothered you." He moved toward the door, turned and asked, "What's the name of your book?"

I told him.

"I'll get a copy at the library and read it. It'll be fun now that I've met the author."

"Don't do that," I said.

"Why not?"

"If you'll give me your address, I'll send you an autographed copy."

"Would you?" He came back genuinely pleased.

"It will be a pleasure." I moved to the desk and wrote down the address he gave me.

"Was it a hard job?" he asked.

"What?"

"Writing the book. I've always thought I'd like to try my hand at it but I never get to it."

"That's a human failing. There's at least one good story in every person but putting it down on paper takes a lot of time. I don't know anything about writing. I had a story to tell about my experiences and wrote it. I really can't give you any advice and since it was only a mystery story, I doubt that I'm even considered an author. Some people are very upity-upity about mysteries, forgetting in their literary snobbishness that some of the greatest minds in the world turn to mystery stories for entertainment and relaxation."

"I'm not snobbish about them but they annoy me," he answered, "because they always make the cops so dumb. Detective work is no cinch. It's a hard, heartbreaking job; first searching for clues and then running them to earth, sorting, sifting, discarding, constantly hunting for the one thing that will spell guilt. I'll let you know what I think of yours as soon as I read it. It won't be for a couple of weeks, though, so don't think I'm unappreciative."

"If I hear from you at all, I'll be delighted," I assured him.

"I start on my vacation tomorrow and won't get the book until I return. On my way up here I decided to forget vacation because I believed I was on the trail of something hot. I'd like a good break once." At that moment he seemed like a wistful little boy.

"What do you call a break?" I asked.

"Getting in on the ground floor of something big. I'm sick of handing out tickets to people for speeding They always get them fixed, anyhow, because they have a pull. As long as I'm on the force, I want to go on up. It's not a bad life. You're out in the open a lot and there's just enough danger to make it interesting."

I don't know why I did what I did. Perhaps it was because I didn't feel comfortable about Terry and the note. Perhaps it was because I liked the young man, but then, goodness knows, I like them all if they're halfway decent and show any signs of intelligence. I certainly know that I wanted him for a friend rather than an enemy. Anyhow, Terry was in a jam and wouldn't protect himself, being that type of reckless fool. I felt certain that the house party would be composed of people who were mentioned in and had something to fear from the diaries.

Isn't it odd the way things come to you? Right then and there at that moment, I knew what had puzzled me when I stood in front of the safe in Terry's office. There hadn't been even the smallest bit of torn paper on the floor; therefore the person who took the diaries knew what they were and how they were wrapped. Terry! Had he staged a fake robbery as part of his plan? Had he sent me down there on a fool's errand just to corroborate his story? The more I thought of it the more certain I became that I was right. Terry! Where was he the night I paid the ransom money? He needed money. Oh, no! I didn't want to believe that. Terry wouldn't have had any reason to do a thing like that. He knew I'd give him the money.

My thoughts raced as I went on talking to Saxon. "This vacation," I asked, "does it mean a great deal to you?"

"Just a chance to rest and relax," he replied.

"How would you like to spend part of your vacation here?"

"What's the idea?"

"A little private detective work for me. There's a person coming to this party that I don't trust. I won't tell you my reason but I'd like to have the man watched while he is here. If you want to take on the job it might lead to something."

"A spy job, eh?"

"More or less," I agreed.

"Has it anything to do with that?" He pointed to the note which I held in my hand.

"No, and I don't want you here in an official capacity. I want you to come as a guest."

"I'm afraid my social manners have become a bit rusty since I've been on the police force," he objected.

"Nonsense! There's nothing the matter with your manners. All you have to do is meet people, be agreeable and keep your eyes open."

"But I've never had any experience in real society." His quick glance about the finely appointed room conveyed more than words exactly what he meant.

"Fiddlesticks! Human nature is pretty much alike no matter where you find it. You'll probably think us an artificial lot and you'll soon get accustomed to the trappings with which we surround ourselves. It'll only be for a short time. Will you do it?" I urged.

I knew the idea appealed to him. He seemed to be mulling it over in his mind. "I don't know," he said, which I took to be an admission of weakening.

"Just consider it a lark," I suggested. I wanted him. I knew I'd feel much more comfortable if he was in the house.

"But it might give me a taste for the social life," he said with a grin, "and then after two weeks, I'd be a discontented cop."

"You don't look like a discontented person and I'm sure our kind of life won't appeal to you. We're rather dull," I admitted.

He laughed. "You're honest, at any rate. I'll have to get my dinner coat out of the moth-balls."

It was my turn to laugh.

"And what am I supposed to do?" he asked.

"I'll give you instructions when you come."

"It's a bargain," he agreed. He'd been a long time making up his mind and I wasn't altogether sure I had fooled him. He had been weighing things back and forth as we talked, I could see that.

"What time will you arrive?" I asked.

"I'm not off duty until six. I could get here about nine or nine-thirty. Will that be all right?"

"That will be fine. If I'm not here when you arrive I'll leave instructions for you. You will be introduced as the son of an old friend of mine. You arrived from the West unexpectedly and I brought you out here. Have you ever been West?"

"I went to Ann Arbor and I've been in Chicago. What are we going to do about his nibs, solemn face?" he asked.

"You mean Hubert? I'll take care of him. You know Ann Arbor very well, don't you?" I asked. He nodded. "If we need to do any explaining, we'll say that you were a town boy who attended the home university. Remember all that and under no circumstances must you tell a soul that you're connected with the police."

"Okay. Don't let this make you forget the book you promised me," he flung back over his shoulder as he went out the door.

As I went into the hall Hubert informed me that the yacht would leave at four o'clock for its run to the city. I told him about Saxon and cautioned him to keep my secret.

"Will Mr. Lassimon know?" he queried.

"I'd rather he didn't."

"And Mrs. Lassimon?" he asked.

"I'll tell her."

"Very good, miss."

"You won't fail me, will you, Hubert?"

"No, ma'am. I feel relieved," he answered. "It keeps me pretty busy sometimes watching the guests and the silver."

"This won't be that kind of a party, at least I don't think so," I assured him.

He hesitated a moment then said, "I'm worried about Mr. Lassimon, Miss Thomas. He hasn't been himself for some time. Is he in trouble?"

"Nothing to worry about, Hubert. Just keep your eyes open tonight and tomorrow."

"For anything in particular?" he asked.

"For everything."

As I started back to my room I felt the note crinkle in my belt where I had tucked it. I began thinking about Terry again. Why hadn't he told me about the yacht going into town? Why didn't he want me aboard? I'd meet all the people, anyhow, so that couldn't be the reason. I had a sudden flash of intuition and turned back to Hubert and asked, "Does Mr. Lassimon have a car in town?"

Hubert rang the garage. My guess was right. Terry's car was in town and had not been returned. Why not, if Terry planned to return on the yacht? The answer seemed simple enough once I had figured it out. He was going to drive home. He wouldn't come on the yacht at all. I stopped at Althea's room, told her about Saxon's inclusion as a guest. She seemed pleased at that and disappointed when I told her I had decided against the boat trip. I was following a hunch as I had done so many times before in my life. If I was right, it would give me a chance to talk to Terry alone before the other guests arrived.

At four o'clock I stood at my window and rather regretfully watched the boat steam slowly through the channel beyond Bar Beach and out into the deeper waters of Hempstead Harbor. It looked cool out there. I put on a negligee and rang Hubert, instructing him to let me know the moment Terry arrived. "He ought to be here most any moment now," I said with assurance.

Hubert seemed a bit surprised and reminded me that the yacht had just left.

I rang off and picked up a copy of "Cold Comfort Farm," a book which always amuses me. I didn't read very long, however, because I began to feel drowsy and quite suddenly I found myself craving sleep. It was like the overwhelming urge to sleep that sometimes comes to me when I'm in the theater, a deep heavy cloak of oblivion that envelopes me and will not be denied. I know of no sleep so gratifying.

CHAPTER 19

At least once a week I definitely say to myself that I'll never again make a definite statement about anything, not even a statement. Only an hour before I had scolded Hubert for even suggesting that I take a nap and at that time I went on to say that I didn't sleep in the daytime. I've always said it and yet an hour later and five minutes after I started to read, there I was sound asleep.

Why is it that some unknown force so often makes us do the things we say we never do or never will do? Is there some perverse spirit lurking just beyond our consciousness who likes to make fools of us? I sometimes think that we are receptive to and become possessed of a spirit when our vitality is low. How else can we explain some of the odd experiences that come to us?

Perverse spirit or just ordinary exhaustion, I don't know which it was, but I slept soundly until nearly seven, when I was awakened by Agnes asking me if I'd like some dinner. Of course I wanted dinner and said so as I tried to scatter the fog of heavy sleep which still hovered over me.

I asked for Terry at once and was taken aback to learn that he had not arrived as I expected he would. My calculations had been all wrong. I would have staked my reputation as a good guesser on the chance of Terry coming home by car instead of by yacht. My vanity took its whipping as philosophically as was possible at the moment. If we have sense enough to appreciate it and the ability to see ourselves as we really are, it does us good once in a while to be wrong. Well, I always say we can't be right all the time. It's like taking a finesse in bridge— if it works every other try, we're doing pretty well.

I had been so positive that he would come home alone to have a talk with me that I had to rearrange all my ideas. Why didn't he want me on the yacht? There was so much for me to tell him and with a house full of people there'd be very little opportunity. With a superhuman effort at self-control I pushed the intricacies of our problem out of my head and decided to enjoy my dinner.

Hubert served me on a side porch which commands a view of the harbor. As the long twilight began to fade great sheets of heat lightning flashed across the sky. I knew that somewhere a storm was in progress and hoped that if we didn't get the storm itself we might derive some benefit from it. I don't understand this talk of high and low pressure areas and all that, but whatever it was that was keeping New York gripped in unendurable heat, I certainly hoped would change.

As the lights spotted the town below me and dotted the darkening gray of the harbor water I knew a few minutes of peace and contentment. But it didn't last. Rolling toward us from the north came a great dark ominous cloud which piled itself high into the heavens. The flashes of lightning changed to forked streaks of fire darting angrily across the sky. The heavy breathless stillness of the early evening was shattered by a great rush of wind that came upon us suddenly as a dry storm. The rain didn't come until later. The trees which a moment before had been graven images etched against the sky were transformed quickly into thrashing demons, their arms twirling and smashing in the wind trying to reach the house and clutch me. Leaves raced across the lawn crackling in the wind with ghostlike echoes. The rose trees bent their heads toward the ground. The lily pads in the pool were whipped up and tossed about to settle back hopefully in the short lulls of wind fury. Hubert, like a mothering hen, ushered me inside the house and would have drawn the blinds if I had not stopped him. I love to watch a storm. They say lightning never strikes twice in the same place but we know that isn't true. I know of one church spire over in Huntington which has been hit innumerable times. I wonder why the God of wrath strikes at churches so often.

Far off down the harbor, I could see the lights of a sizable boat. I asked for a pair of glasses and watched Terry's yacht race up toward the sand-bar which protects the inner harbor. The outer bay was a sea of white-caps. The wind swept down from the north across the Sound and into the open mouth of Hempstead Harbor carrying long rolling waves with it. The *Thetis* rolled and pitched like a drunken sailor. At that moment I was rather glad to be just where I was.

As she approached the narrow channel, I knew that her speed had been diminished. She came over the bar without any difficulty and seemed to settle down in the quieter waters of the inner harbor as she steamed toward the landing. They would be at the house in a few minutes and I was dying with curiosity to see what strange assortment of people Terry would bring with him. I knew that Kenfield would be in the party, but I wanted to see the others. I would be there to greet them. I hoped to catch a guilty look of surprise on the face of the person who left me to die in that garage.

I was waiting in the front hall when a station-wagon arrived from the pier with the first load. Archie Van Nuys, spluttering and asking for brandy, was the first one to enter the hall. He was followed by Kenfield, Althea and Daisy Williams. At the sight of Daisy I knew immediately what Terry had been doing. He had collected the entire group of people to whom Mortimer had written before he was killed. Daisy began chattering the moment she spied me.

I can't abide Daisy Williams, never could. She looks like a worn-out soubrette, all frayed at the edges. Daisy was one of those women who never had an idea in her life that amounted to anything until she convinced old Roger Williams that he couldn't live without her. It hadn't taken Roger long to realize that he couldn't live with her. I always suspected that he was glad to die and get away from her. It must have been a blessed relief to him to die, even at her hands.

Under her aimless chatter I rather fancied a note of fear as her eyes swept the long hall before she followed a waiting maid.

I glanced quickly from Daisy to Archie, who was too concerned with himself to reveal anything except the fact that he was damp, uncomfortable and craved brandy.

"Hello, Ethel," he wheezed. "I'll probably catch pneumonia."

He puffed away in the wake of a footman who was leading him toward brandy. Kenfield, with the same idea in mind, joined him.

"You look tired," I said to Althea.

"I am. Such a party! I'm glad you stayed at home. I've never sat through such a terrible dinner. Every one suspicious of every one else and all of them doubly suspicious of Terry. It was frightful. Who is Tom Andrews?"

"A man about town with a rather unsavory reputation. Why?" I asked.

"During dinner he openly accused Terry of stealing the diaries to get money for himself."

I remembered my own recent and rather sudden suspicion of Terry. "Did they squabble?" I asked, knowing Terry's hot temper.

"Not then but later when Andrews suggested that Mortimer's death happened at a most opportune time for Terry."

"So Terry lost control of himself, eh?"

"Yes, when Andrews intimated that Terry was protecting me, who probably had the most to lose."

"What happened?"

"Mr. Kenfield and Dick Bolertho separated them before Terry choked him to death."

"Charming party, wasn't it?"

"That wasn't all. Andrews fell overboard just as we were going under Hellgate Bridge and insists that some one pushed him."

"Why did you fish him out?" I asked.

"Terry did it. It was a quick rescue. He's really very versatile, isn't he?" she answered.

I looked at her quickly. "You've no idea," I said.

Our conversation was interrupted by a blinding flash of lightning and a terrific clap of thunder which seemed to jar the entire house. A gust of wind slammed the doors and billowed the awning on the terrace as the second station-wagon pulled up to the steps and the balance of the party scampered in just ahead of a great sheet of rain which swept across the front of the house shutting out the entire world.

Althea went to her room. I waited as Dick Bolertho and Florence Gunner ran in, followed quickly by Tom Andrews. Terry and his cousin Philip Lassimon were the last of the party.

"Hello, Ethel!" Terry called gladly. "What brought you down here?"

"The heat," I replied.

"I'm glad to see you," he said. He came forward and pecked at my cheek.

"I didn't think you'd mind a self-invited guest. I wanted to get away from the heat. I didn't know you were planning a party." I carried on the little deception which he had started.

"You know all these people," he stated rather than asked.

I nodded in reply. I must say that with the exception of Bolertho none of them seemed particularly glad to see me. They were not exactly a cheerful group. As the last of them were ushered to their rooms I said to Terry, "I want to talk to you."

"Give me a few minutes for a shower," he grinned and bounced up the stairs.

I went into the library and sat at the window watching the storm. The wind sloshed the rain against the house with increasing fury as the lightning tore through the sky and the thunder rolled overhead. I watched the rose garden and the lily pond. If the ghost of

Annie Sims walked on stormy nights I wanted to see it. I strained my eyes against the pane but could see nothing because of the heavy sweep of the rain.

Except for Saxon, my guest, the party was complete. I found myself thinking about the strangely assorted group. No wonder they were ill at ease and edgy coming out on the boat. The fury of the storm dwindled to sporadic flashes of light and low distant rumblings of thunder. Surely Terry had had time enough for his shower.

The house seemed very stuffy as I went upstairs. Naturally it would be, with all windows closed because of the rain. I went down the corridor and tapped on the door of Terry's suite. When he called, "Come in," I took him at his word and in I went. He was in a pair of shorts.

"It's you," he said as he reached for a bathrobe with an utter lack of concern which pleased me. I hate people who are foolishly prudish about their bodies. Mind you, I'm not holding a brief for nudism, I'm still old-fashioned enough to feel that too much exposure, like anything else done to excess, is too much.

"Be comfortable," I said. "Remember I saw you an hour after you were born."

He took me at my word and let the robe fall back on the chair saying, "I keep forgetting that I have no secrets from you."

"At the moment," I reminded him, "you have too many."

"We'll get to that, but how about a drink first?" he suggested.

"Scotch and soda," I answered and watched him as he opened a small bar equipped with a freezing unit and all the things necessary for mixing drinks. He had a beautiful body, carefully proportioned and properly shaped, with a marvelous bronzed skin, the result of constant sun bathing. I've seen men on the beaches, gorillas and hairy apes, round-bellied, skinny-legged caricatures, short stubby men, long lanky, bowlegged creatures and just the ordinary run of the mill and would say, offhand, that Terry is probably one of the few men who look halfway decent in their shorts. Living intimately with a man must be quite an ordeal for a sensitive woman, what with their hairy chests, scrawny legs, knobby knees and all.

Terry moved slowly. His face was haggard and worn. He was tired, but that was not to be wondered at after a day in the city and such a day as it was.

"I knew you wouldn't fail me," he said with genuine feeling as he handed me a cool tinkling highball.

"I very nearly did," I replied. I put my glass down and took out the note and waved it at him. I missed, however, some of the dramatic effect I had planned. "What does this nonsense mean?" I demanded.

"It's not nonsense, but let's drink first because it's a long story. Here's to you." He took a generous draught and said, "It's been rather warm today, don't you think?"

"Yes, and if you so much as mention humidity, I'll leave you flat," I warned.

"Don't excite yourself," he cautioned. "You know we always have the humidity with us." There was a twinkle in his eyes and for a moment he seemed like his old self. I ignored his remark.

"You're standing the heat awfully well, looking as bouncy as ever, only," he cocked his head to one side and pretended to study me for a moment, "I don't like the glint in your eye. Where do you get your pep?"

"Never mind my pep nor the glint in my eye. Just why did you write me this ridiculous note? Why have you been so thoughtless for the past week? Why have you left me dangling in midair for days wondering, worrying about you? Why . . ."

"Hold everything," he laughed, interrupting my flow of questions. "There hasn't been much to tell you up to now."

I didn't like the fatalistic sound of those last three words but ignored them as I went on, "Do you realize that I very nearly went in on the yacht?"

"That would have been stupid of you. I never dreamed that you . . . Why you know that normally I'd do everything in the world for your comfort. I depended on your .. ."

"Don't depend on a woman's judgment too much, or anything else that you think's predictable about a woman, particularly if you make her angry," I cut in. Why have you been so silent? Why so cryptic in your note?"

He seemed genuinely amazed at my outburst.

"Why I . . . I thought you'd understand, and besides I wanted you to have something to occupy your mind on a hot day like this."

"Then you succeeded admirably. Now why not tell me what's on your mind." I wanted to say "if any," but didn't because I've grown awfully tired of that type of wisecrack. Instead I insisted, "What's all this balderdash about another murder? I've already had a brush with the police about that note."

"Ethel! You didn't call the police?"

I wanted him to be startled, but I didn't think he'd consider me such a fool. While I explained to him rather rapidly what I meant I realized anew how very tired he was. If I hadn't been so anxious to get at the bottom of the whole business, I'd have suggested he take a nap.

"Are you sure the policeman believed you?" he asked anxiously.

"I think so, yes."

"You had me worried for a moment." He sighed with relief. "It was a tight spot for you, but then you've been in tighter spots than that."

"True enough," I replied, "but I've always known what I was doing. Come now, tell me about that note. Did it mean anything or didn't it?"

"Yes and no."

"Don't hedge so. Either tell me or not. I can't stand this shillyshallying."

"I think I'm next on the list."

"What list?"

"I follow Mortimer."

"Rubbish."

"I hope so. I don't want to die now."

"You're tired and you're morbid," I considered the number of drinks he had taken and added, "and a little tight."

"Wrong again," he grinned as he poured another Scotch. "Drink hasn't touched me."

I've heard people say that before, particularly men who insist on driving after a cocktail party. If they want to risk their necks, that's their business but I certainly don't think they have any right to risk the lives of other people, going through stop-lights, taking more than their share of the road and traveling at high speeds. I do believe if I were a judge, I'd give men, and women too, life, if I convicted them on the charge of drunken driving. I never ride with a drunk. I prefer the reckless sober sanity of a taxi driver with their faculties working on all four cylinders. That at least is thrilling.

"It's a deep-seated conviction," he assured me, "that has been growing on me for days. Sleep, drink nor anything else can get it out of my mind. I'm numbered." His hand wavered as he put the glass down on the table before us.

"Numbed, you mean and dumb," I retorted. "Don't sit there like that, resigned, self-hypnotized by an idea!" I scolded.

"I'm not giving up. If I have to take it, it will be on the chin with head up."

"If you drink any more you won't be able to move your head or keep your chin up," I reminded him.

"I'm not a quitter, Ethel and I'm not drunk. I may be a little numbed for the moment, but God! you've never seen such a ghastly party as that mob coming out on the boat.

I hope I never have to sit through such a dinner. Here! I'll stop drinking. You're right. I've a lot to do and I want to do it tonight."

"Who pushed Andrews overboard?" I demanded.

"Who told you?"

"Althea, of course."

"She did? That's funny. She was the only person on deck when he went over. At least, she was the one who shouted, 'Man overboard.' He thinks she did it."

"Didn't you check on Andrews' story?" I asked.

"Yes. We all claimed we were below deck. All but Althea. She said she came round the after deckhouse just as Andrews went through the rail. He was tight and probably fell through."

"Why should she push him over and then save him?" I asked.

"Because from the rear he might have been mistaken for me." He paused. "I don't want to think she had anything to do with it," he ended quickly.

So that was why he had been drinking. I've been in and out of love with all sorts of men but I never remotely thought I loved one I believed was guilty of attempted murder.

"Do you still suspect her?" I asked.

"I don't want to, but why must she appear each time something terrible happens?"

"Coincidence," I replied. "Put your mind at rest. She's as innocent as you are."

"Did she say anything about me?" he asked hopefully.

"Nothing you'd be particularly interested in hearing," I replied.

He sighed. "It'll soon be over now. She can have her freedom."

"Don't you believe, 'A bird in hand . . .'" I began.

"Not Althea. Our getting married was an unnecessary mistake. I should have known better. It has served no purpose except to make me realize how dull life will be without her."

"What have you been doing to keep her? Nothing. You ran off, told her nothing. You must remember she's vitally interested in this affair."

"I've been trying to help her. You don't suppose I'd bring this ill-assorted group of people to my house for any other reason, do you?"

"Now that they are here, what are you going to do with them?"

"We were to have a meeting here tonight to decide on a method of recovering the diaries. You've done that for us. Althea told me the good news. We'll write Finis to the episode a little later by having a nice bonfire. Tell me how you got them and how much it cost."

I told him about the recovery of the diaries and my adventure in the garage.

After he had properly scolded me for my foolhardiness he asked eagerly, "Where are they?"

"Hidden in a safe place. What are your plans now?"

"The first thing to do is to see that you get your money back. I'll arrange that when we're all together. I want to see Althea and warn her not to mention the diaries until we have our meeting."

"I'll tell her," I offered.

"I want to talk to her." He bounced off his chair. I'd never watched a man dress before. My, it's so much simpler than all the things a woman has to do! They have an easy time of it in more ways than one, but I'm glad I'm a woman, just the same.

Before he was completely dressed, Hubert tapped on the door to tell me that Saxon had arrived. I didn't take time then to tell Terry about Saxon. He was anxious to talk to Althea, anyhow, and probably wouldn't have heard or understood me.

Saxon was waiting for me in the library. He greeted me with a self-conscious smile. He was just as fine-looking in ordinary clothes as he had been in his uniform, a little less strikingly elemental, if you know what I mean. I was pleased with him. Hubert served us a drink.

Saxon had a small boy's eagerness as he faced me, a highball in his hand. I felt comforted to have him there, but it was a doubtful comfort, as I didn't know what to do with him just then. To carry on the ruse I had started I had to tell him something. I described Andrews carefully and asked Saxon to watch him every minute. Why I picked on Andrews I don't know.

"Where are they all?" he asked.

"In their rooms. I rather expect them to be coming down soon. They're to have, I believe, a private meeting. You and I may not be included, sort of a board of directors conference," I suggested.

"I'll be on the job, all right," he assured me.

At that moment I thought I heard a measured heavy tread somewhere over our heads. Bainbridge! For a moment I froze solid and then laughed a little hysterically.

"What's the matter?" he asked. "For a moment you looked terrified."

"I thought I heard a ghost," I answered.

"You're a great kidder, aren't you?"

There had to be conversation between us. I told him the story of the supposed ghosts in the house. It was a perfect night for them to appear. There was a storm outside and something devilish brewing within. As I talked I moved to the window and peered out. There was a flash of light. I know perfectly well that I didn't see a ghost, but there was something there on the lawn not far from the lily pond, something white and wavering that danced for a second and sent a rod of ice down my spine. I gasped. In the next flash of light the thing whatever it was had vanished. It certainly gave me a bad turn.

I swallowed the balance of my drink and excusing myself told Saxon to make himself comfortable while I was gone. He sensed that something had upset me and suggested that he help. If I had taken him with me things would have been easier for us, but I couldn't know that. I promised him I'd be back immediately. That apparition on the lawn had given me such a start! Queer things can and do happen, things we can't explain in the light of modern philosophy. I was sure it was a warning. I must find Terry. I didn't want to believe that his life was in danger and yet . . .

I was up the stairs and down the corridor in what sports writers call "nothing flat." I rapped on the door of Terry's room and turned the knob. As the door swung open, my heart stood still. In the semi-darkness I saw Terry stretched out on his bed seemingly lifeless. I gasped and moved forward. The next moment I went headlong toward the floor flat on my face. I had been tripped from behind. Even in the commotion of my fall I heard a rustling movement near the door and then a sharp bang as it closed. I scrambled to my feet conscious of an aching ankle. Whoever had been at the door had used a trick I've often seen operated by schoolboys. They had put out a foot over which I had stumbled and in my fall, I missed any chance of seeing the person who had stood flat against the wall just inside the room. I limped back to the door, fumbled for the knob and wrenched the door open.

The corridor was deserted. With my eyes still on the hall my hand felt along the inside wall and pressed the light switch in the room. At that moment a door opened and Althea came into the corridor. I called to her. She came slowly. I then raced to Terry's bed, ankle forgotten.

He was unconscious. There wasn't even the slightest sign of a wound. He gave a gasping breath. I shook him. His eyes opened in a puzzled curious stare. "Are you hurt?" I asked.

"No, sleepy. I must have dozed off." He swung his legs over the edge of the bed and rubbed his head with both hands. He certainly must have a clear conscience or something. The person in his room, my fall, the lights going on and off would be enough to wake the dead, yet he had slept through it all.

"What happened?" It was Althea's voice that thoroughly roused him and brought him wide awake.

"What's up?" he finally asked.

I told him about my entrance into the room and the events that had followed immediately. I can't imagine what my arrival interrupted, but I certainly believed that I had saved his life and I think he believed it too.

"How awful!" Althea said.

I turned to her. "Have you two had an understanding?" I demanded.

"Not exactly," she replied.

"Then it's time you did. You're both working toward the same end and I can see no reason why you don't work together." I turned to Terry accusingly. "I thought you were going to talk to her."

"I don't talk to people when I'm taking a shower," she said.

"Neither do I," I sputtered; "running water makes such a racket. You're not taking a shower now. Unless you're working against us, you'd better put your cards on the table. We need help."

With that I left them.

CHAPTER 20

Now you know, and I know, that we don't believe in ghosts, but I couldn't get the thought of that sudden apparition on the lawn out of my mind. I had no reason to think that Terry's life was in jeopardy. I had every reason to believe he was talking to Althea, and yet I knew instinctively that he was in danger. His morbid fear when I first talked to him that evening may have had something to do with my premonition, I don't know, but it is just possible that he transmitted some of his fears to me which may account for my actions.

I have tried to be rational about it and until the day I die I'll say I don't believe in ghosts but, secretly, I'll always believe that whatever it was I glimpsed by the pool was a warning to me of Terry's peril. If I had talked to Saxon just a few minutes longer I'm positive Terry would have been added to the list of victims of the unknown person who was so intensely interested in the diaries.

I wanted to discover, if I could, the identity of that person. I crossed the hall and tried the door directly opposite Terry's. It opened. I knocked first, then entered. The room was empty and smelled faintly of stale tobacco. On the dressing-table I found a military brush with the initials P.L. on its back. Philip Lassimon's room and very convenient to Terry's door, but that was not proof.

Althea's suite joined Terry's at the end of the hall. I knew where she was at the moment though I wasn't sure where she had been. I had heard a distinct rustling noise as I fell face forward. Had it been a woman? Men's garments don't rustle as a general rule, but a dressing-gown might make a similar noise.

I peered into two more rooms, Kenfield's and Archie's, but found nothing that would help me in my investigation. Tom Andrews' room was at the end of the hall. I tapped on his door. There was no answer. I waited a moment for decency's sake and rapped again, louder than before. There was still no response. The door opened as I pressed against it. I glanced into the room. A light from the dressing-room filtered through the semi-darkness. I could see the outlines of the furniture very clearly. I gave the door a shove and called before I entered.

As I became accustomed to the half-light I realized that Andrews was stretched across the bed. I called again, but he didn't answer. I moved forward and stifled an impulse to scream. Andrews' shirt front was covered with blood.

If I had started my investigation immediately after I fell instead of stopping to talk to Terry and Althea the final murder would undoubtedly have been prevented I can't blame myself, however, because any one would have done what I did then. How was I to know that the person in Terry's room had been seen as he was leaving? My one interest at the time was to protect Terry from the danger which threatened him.

How many times in the course of our lives do we find ourselves saying, "If I had only done this, or that, things would have been different." I have made mistakes, we all have, and those mistakes often change the entire course of our lives. Some mistakes are accidents, some are just sheer stupidity or carelessness. My slowness to act had cost a life, but how was I to know that?

I stood aghast at what I saw. This new move of the murderer would make things very difficult for Terry. Oh, how I wished I had destroyed that silly note of his! What could I say to Saxon in explanation? How could I make him believe me? Would I be forced to tell about those diaries before we had a chance to trap the murderer? Terry really had no alibi from the time I left him until I returned to his room. I was working on the assumption that Andrews had been killed after my entrance into Terry's room, but what did I have to offer as proof?

Nothing! The police would quickly believe when they learned about the note that Terry had killed Andrews. All those people waiting for the next move from Terry couldn't and wouldn't help him if they could. There was no reason why they should. They certainly wouldn't mention the diaries. They would want to keep their secrets hidden. They might even deny any knowledge of the diaries. I didn't want to mention them unless it would be absolutely necessary and yet I knew that the moment the body was discovered something would have to be done at once.

There was only one ray of hope in the whole situation. The murderer did not know that I had seen the body. He would be fearfully uneasy and worried. Why hadn't he killed me as I entered Terry's room? I knew the answer as I thought about it. In the first place he was surprised by my sudden entrance. His first impulse was to hide, which he did flat against the wall. As I opened the door he was between the wall and the door itself. If the knife which had killed Andrews was in his hand at the moment he wouldn't have been able to stab me without doing it very awkwardly. He couldn't have done the trick quickly enough to keep me from screaming. He had decided to take no chances. The room was in darkness. As I passed him he tripped me from behind and made his escape from the room. Andrews evidently had seen him, that would explain Andrews' death.

If the murderer was planning to bring about the discovery of Andrews' death he was not considering me in his plans. He couldn't know I had seen the body. Perhaps I would be able to trap him. Whoever it might be, he or she would be very uneasy until this new murder was disclosed. I could imagine myself in the role of the murderer waiting, wondering when the body would be discovered. I would watch them all. My observations might catch the criminal.

My first problem, however, was to get out of the room unobserved. I tiptoed to the door. I was neither horrified nor made uneasy by the grim figure stretched out on the bed. His just deserts had caught up with him at last, although I was positive he died for a very innocent reason. He must have seen the person who had escaped from Terry's room immediately after my entrance and fall. It's a trifling reason for sudden death, isn't it, but the murderer had to protect himself. He knew that once I discovered who it was that had been in Terry's room I would have the answer to the whole problem.

I peered into the hall. Then cautiously I slipped out and pulled the door tight shut behind me. I should have had more sense, but at the moment was so intent on getting away that I never once thought of myself nor the incriminating evidence that might possibly be used against me. Had I been more thoughtful at that moment, more aware of my own danger, things might have been different, but that is getting ahead of my story.

I wanted to acquaint Terry with this new development. He was not in his room. I rang Hubert on the house phone and asked him to locate Terry at once. I smoked one cigarette after another until he arrived.

He bounced into the room. His mood had changed. He was gay and chirpy, which made me feel certain that his interview with Althea had been satisfactory. When a man's heart sings through his eyes, a woman is usually the reason.

"What's up?" he asked. "The fun is about to begin."

"It's all over," I replied gloomily. Then I told him about Tom Andrews.

"We'll have to call the police immediately, I suppose," he said hopelessly.

"Not for a little while," I prompted. "We must wait until the body is discovered. Unless I'm mistaken, the murderer will see to it that they find the body. I want you to be surprised at the news and I want you to call the police yourself. Remember that," I cautioned. "Watch every guest. The person who brings about the disclosure of Andrews' death should be the murderer. Keep your eyes and ears open. It is a forlorn hope, but it's all we have at the moment."

"And while we wait, we'll have the jitters, you and I," he added.

"Not necessarily. Before we go down, I want to tell you a few things about your guests." I gave him a hasty summary of the reasons for their interest in the diaries.

"Nice people," he said when I had finished my recital.

"Lovely group for a house party," I agreed. "Tell me, why is Kenfield here?"

"He's a good man to have around in a pinch. He's a fast thinker."

"Have you told him anything at all?" I asked, wondering how much information Kenfield had acquired.

"Not a thing. I just brought him along, in case."

"I have an 'in case,' too," I said and told him about Saxon.

"Your Saxon man's going to love this murder, Ethel. He'll never believe that you didn't deliberately make a fool out of him. I'm glad I'm not in your boots." He actually chuckled as he thought of my pending discomfort.

"Don't forget," I reminded him, "that you're the one who wrote the note about a murder which was Saxon's original reason for coming here at all."

"Gosh!" he cried.

"Not so funny now, is it?" I asked.

"Can't you send him away, Ethel?"

"And make things look twice as black for us when the murder is discovered? Oh, no! He stays and I hope he's going to be on our side. We're going to need lots of help, you and I."

Terry was deep in thought. His absorption made me feel shut out and alone as I waited for him to say or do something. Finally he looked up and said, "I think your plan is wrong."

"Which plan?" I asked.

"About waiting for a move from the murderer. He's clever, or she is," he added.

"Then what do you suggest?"

"Put yourself in the place of the murderer. He has tried to think of every emergency. He has out-thought and out-smarted us at every turn. He's determined to get me one way or another, isn't he?" he asked.

When I agreed to that, he went on. "Let's go down now and have it over and done. I promised them that the diaries would be destroyed once they came into my possession. It isn't fair to have them all suffer because of one person. The diaries must be destroyed before the police arrive. Where are they?"

He was surprised when I told him of my hiding-place. I knew he was right. The books had to be destroyed to protect the innocent. We were interested in only one person, the triple murderer, the man who seemed determined to get Terry out of the way along with his other victims.

The package was a bit sooty when I pulled it down from its hiding-place and dusted it off. Terry stood by highly amused at me as I tucked it under my arm and followed him down the long hall.

There were three people in the house who couldn't be included in our little conference. Andrews, for the best reason in the world; Saxon and Kenfield were the others. I found Saxon with Florence Gunner, who had appropriated him and, true to type, Saxon seemed to enjoy her absorption in him. Men are gullible creatures, aren't they? Have you ever had an opportunity to watch a Southern girl artfully working on a man?

As I asked Saxon to keep his eyes and ears open for anything that might happen immediately after our meeting, I glanced across the room where Terry was talking to Sidney Kenfield.

The group moved solemnly into the library. Daisy Williams did her best to appear gay and unconcerned. Florence Gunner entered with an air of resignation. The men eyed me rather skeptically. Philip Lassimon in his gloomy way demanded, "What are you doing here?"

"Ethel Thomas has done more for all of you than you'll ever know," Terry stated defensively.

"Don't bother, Terry," I cut in, stopping him. "What I've done doesn't matter. Just tell them that I, too, am in the diaries."

Several eyebrows lifted as a result of my statement.

"Let's get on with the business," Archie wheezed out his suggestion.

"Yes," Philip agreed. "How are we going to get the diaries?"

"We have them," Terry said quietly.

There was a general sigh of amazed relief. Then several voices expressed the same thought. "But you said . . ."

"I didn't know that they had been recovered until I returned here tonight," Terry explained. "Ethel, at the risk of her life, and for the sum of two hundred thousand dollars, recovered the books while I was contacting you." Terry went on to explain my part of the transaction. He ended by saying, "Each of you owe Ethel approximately thirty-four thousand dollars."

"Thirty-four?" Archie asked. "I estimated it to be a little over twenty-eight thousand. There's seven of us. Where's Andrews?"

"I'm coming to that—" Terry made a dramatic pause, "after Ethel is paid for recovering the diaries."

"But Andrews should pay his share!" Daisy objected. "And since Ethel is mentioned in the diaries, that would make eight of us and our portion would be twenty-five thousand each."

There were several assenting voices to her suggestion. There they were, facing possible annihilation, yet they took time to haggle over a few thousand dollars. Terry started to object, but I stopped him by saying, "I'll pay my share, Terry. Let's not argue about it."

"And what about Andrews?" Dick Bolertho asked.

"He should pay his share," Florence Gunner suggested.

"He can't. He's dead," Terry stated flatly.

I must admit that every one of them seemed genuinely shocked and surprised at the news. I tried to catch all their expressions with a quick photographic glance.

"Dead?" Bolertho repeated. "What happened?"

"Some one in this room knows the answer to that question," Terry answered. "One of you here is a murderer for the third time," he accused. "One of you must confess before the diaries are destroyed."

You've heard the expression about all hell being let loose. Well, that's just a mild way of describing the excitement, accusations and recriminations that made the air blue for a few minutes.

"What low game are you playing?" Philip shouted.

Althea crossed to Terry and stood beside him. She was grand as she stood there defending him. They were a beautiful couple facing those angry, frightened people. Althea's cool steady voice cut across the excited babble and brought order out of vocal chaos.

"Don't be ridiculous, Mr. Lassimon," she began and in her voice there seemed to be a patient quality which adults use to quiet children and put them in their place. "Terry has been working hard for our individual benefit."

Terry's face broke into a smile as she called him by name. He was as pleased as Punch. Althea went on:

"I hate to think of the things that could have happened to all of us if Van Wyck had taken those diaries to a less scrupulous person. We each of us know our secret and our reasons for wanting to keep that secret. I have a great deal at stake and I rather imagine each of you is no less interested than I. I don't care what you've done—that's your business, not mine—and I'm quite sure because of his disinterested actions, Terry feels the same way. I know and you must know that our secrets are safe with him. We can do no good now at this crucial moment to fling accusations at a person who has been working for our interests. I happen to know that because he, through no fault of his own, happened to have our secrets in his possession his life is, and has been, in danger."

"He didn't have to read them!" Daisy said accusingly.

"He didn't read them, I did. He doesn't know what's in them," I cried.

"I do know!" Terry shouted. He turned and stormed at me, "I won't have you shielding me, Ethel. Do you think I'm a baby?"

"Why should she run things, anyhow?" Philip demanded.

"By what right do you tell us that the diaries won't be destroyed unless one of us confesses to a murder?" Florence Gunner demanded.

"Because one of us is a murderer," I answered.

"I suppose your skirts are quite clean," Archie taunted, aiming his remark at me.

"The thing she did can stand the light of investigation better than your secret, or yours, or yours," Terry flung the words at them vehemently.

"They're all lies," Daisy cried, "terrible, terrible lies."

"Stop it!" I cried. "Stop this wrangling!"

They quieted down long enough for Bolertho to ask, "Have you any suggestions to make, Miss Thomas?"

"Yes." I eyed them all for a moment before I went on. The idea came quickly, out of the blue. "I own the diaries now and unless the murderer confesses, I'll turn the books over to the police, a thing Terry should have done weeks ago."

There was a new outburst of protestation at that, but I went on. I've had some experience in out-talking and even out-shouting people at times. I hate to act like a fishwife, but I can play the role if necessary.

"You have your choice," I cried over the babble of their voices. "You're damned if you do and you're damned if you don't. Each of you has something to hide in the past. One of you has a more recent secret. Unless you confess to this latest crime, I shall see to it that the past catches up with you."

"You devil!" Philip Lassimon cried and sprang toward me. He would have choked me if Bolertho and Terry hadn't stopped him.

Terry was amazed at the turn things had taken. So was I, for that matter, but I was enjoying it. I had no idea of forcing such an impasse when I entered the room. Events had really taken the situation in hand. Philip's intended attack on me sobered them all.

"Well?" Florence Gunner asked. "What's the payoff? Let's have it."

"A signed confession," I answered.

"And the means of exit?" she asked. "Aren't you going to furnish a gun?"

"A gun?" I repeated. That question shocked me. I hadn't realized in the swift turn of events that by forcing a confession, we would also make it necessary for the murderer to commit suicide.

"Or poison," Florence continued calmly. "You don't think the murderer will face a trial, do you?"

"That decision rests with the guilty person," Terry said. "I'll give you ten minutes to think it over. Unless I have the confession at the end of that time, I'll call the police. I can't delay calling them any longer than that." He opened the door.

After a long moment of frightened silence, they filed past us, a silent, tortured group, their faces showing how much each one had to fear.

"I wish you luck," Florence Gunner said as she passed me. The girl's casualness bothered me. There was something cold and horrible about the way she was taking it.

"You've no right to do this!" Daisy sobbed, her face a sight to behold, all lined by tears and runny makeup.

Althea was the last to leave. "I didn't know you intended doing this," she said as she followed Daisy.

"Neither did I," Terry replied.

"It's the only way," she said and hurried out.

"Well," Terry said when we were alone, "you think of the damnedest things!"

"But will it work?" I asked.

Before he could answer a terrible scream shrilled through the house. I didn't look at Terry for a moment, I couldn't. There was an end to our plan. I didn't need to be told that the body had been found. Through the open door I saw Saxon and Kenfield dashing up the stairs behind Hubert. The others scampered behind them.

"The fire!" I cried. "Quick! Light it for me! I'll stay here and burn the diaries. Only one person must pay. You join the others. Close the door behind you!"

He ignited the kindling while I hurriedly unwrapped the diaries.

"Do a good job of it," he cautioned as he closed the door behind him. I knew he was thinking of Althea.

I bent the books back and broke the binding. Then I separated the pages as best I could. As soon as the logs began to flicker I dropped page after page on the flames. I spread the books over the logs. The fat was in the fire in more ways than one. Terry and I had something to worry about now. Terry had written that note about a murder. I had deliberately hoodwinked a policeman. I crouched before that fire like an old witch. The heat was terrific. I poked at the books with an iron, twisting them in the flames so they would burn more quickly. I paused for a moment to open the windows. While I was on my feet, I fixed myself a stiff drink of brandy and then returned to the fire. The brandy fortified me. I needed it.

The logs were crackling nicely, their undersides glowing brightly. One by one I lifted the charred books with a pair of tongs and poked them under the red logs where the heat from the burning wood and falling embers would finish them. I was dying to know about the things happening upstairs, but I didn't move.

I never believe in hunting trouble. It has a way of finding you unaided. I moved over to the edge of the table and watched the fire, satisfied that the books had been charred beyond all possible chance of being read. That job, at least, had been done efficiently. I was on my second brandy when Saxon came into the room.

He was full of purpose. He passed me as if I had been an image. He went directly to the telephone. I jumped to put a restraining hand on his arm. "Please, not yet," I begged. "Give me a minute!"

He squared around to face me. His hand slid away from the receiver. "I don't get you, I don't get you at all," he said.

There was a hurt note in his voice. I had expected accusations, a tirade, almost anything but that.

"You wanted a chance to be in on the ground floor of something big, didn't you?" I demanded. I had sudden inspiration and carried the fight right into his own territory.

"But you . . ."

"Didn't I tell you to watch that man, didn't I?" I demanded. "And what did you do? You permitted some one to kill him right under your nose."

That speech was a mistake. I knew it the moment I had uttered the words, so I hurried to make amends. "It's Andrews, isn't it?" I asked.

"So you knew Lassimon was going to kill him?" he said.

"No, no, no!" I cried in desperation. "He didn't."

"Then who did? He invited you down here to a murder, didn't he? If you knew the man was going to be killed, why didn't you tell me? You wouldn't pull my leg! Oh, no!" he said bitterly. "You've just made a fool of me, that's all, and I let you do it, let you take me in!"

The poor lad's pride was hurt and I felt sorry for hun.

"Listen," I urged. "There's so much more to this than meets the eye. I can't tell the story now, but it's bound to come out later. Please believe me. I wasn't trying to fool you, nor was I trying to pull your leg. I asked you to come here because I felt certain that this might happen, only I didn't expect him to be killed. I thought an attempt would be made on the life of Terry Lassimon. You must believe me. I wanted to know that there was some one in the house I could trust and rely upon. You seemed like an answer to a prayer. Believe me, Jim Saxon, Terry Lassimon didn't kill anybody. If you go into this case blindly believing that note, you're going to miss the chance you told me you wanted."

"Then who did kill that man upstairs?" he demanded.

"I was on the point of making that discovery just a few minutes ago."

"How?" he demanded.

"Because of information I happened to possess."

"You should have called the police," he accused and moved toward the telephone.

"Wait a minute, please," I begged. "We'll have that confession. You'll get credit for solving three murders, baffling murders. Isn't that what you wanted?"

"That's no excuse for not calling the authorities immediately," he countered.

"But if you take time for preliminary investigation, fingerprints and that sort of thing before you call them? That will do no harm, will it?"

"You don't want me to tell about that note," he accused.

"I don't care a fig about the note. I want to catch the murderer. Just give me a few minutes." I begged, waiting anxiously.

"I'll give you ten minutes while I do some preliminary investigating," he agreed reluctantly.

CHAPTER 21

`The discovery of the body, the necessity of burning the diaries and my talk with Saxon had made me forget for the moment the confession I had tried to force from one member of the party. When I returned to the living-room they were all there with the exception of Kenfield, who seemed to have hit it off with Saxon and was upstairs with him looking for clues.

Daisy sidled up to me to say beseechingly, "You don't believe it, Ethel? You've known me all my life, sure you don't think that I ..."

"I'm not thinking, Daisy," I replied loudly enough for them all to hear. "This has passed beyond one person's thought. I know Terry's life has been in danger, still is. Some one tried to kill him tonight after he arrived home. None of us are safe until the murderer confesses. There is no other way out!" I knew I was being very emphatic, I meant to be.

Dick Bolertho joined us. "I couldn't help overhearing you," he said. "I'm sure we all heard you. Don't you think you're being a little hard on those of us who may be innocent?"

There was real pain in his eyes as he looked at me. I wanted to tell him that he had nothing to worry about, but I couldn't do it and be fair to the others. For all I knew, he might be the murderer. Just because I didn't want to believe him guilty didn't make him innocent.

Terry was the only one who knew that the diaries had been destroyed. If the others knew, we'd never get the confession. Why didn't the murderer confess? Did he feel confident that he could out-bluff me? Did he know me well enough to feel sure that I couldn't make six people suffer because of one man's crime?

Florence Gunner had been pacing up and down in front of the long couch near the fireplace. She paused before me and asked, "How do you like playing God?"

I was startled. I hadn't thought of myself in that light. I must have seemed like a terrible despot to them. "I don't like it, but there's nothing else I can do," I replied.

She studied me for a moment as if weighing me, shook her head and said as she turned away, "And I always thought you were such a good egg."

I didn't blame the girl for what she said, but the remark hurt, just the same.

Philip Lassimon, his face gaunt and haggard, demanded, "Are you going to go through with this plan of yours?"

I nodded.

"You'll really turn the diaries over to the police?" he insisted.

"Yes."

"Do you realize what you are doing?" he cried.

"Yes, Philip. Did you realize what you were doing when you sold ..." I didn't finish the question.

"Don't say it!" he screamed and leaped forward, his hand again stretched toward my throat.

"Stop these theatrical, hysterical displays!" Althea cried.

"Then stop her!" Archie wheezed at Terry as he pointed at me. "You can! You should! The diaries were your responsibility. You're the one who brought us down here. You . . ." He was choked by a shortness of breath and began coughing.

"I can't stop Ethel and I can't stop the police who will be here any minute and I wouldn't if I could," Terry flung at all of them. "Three times one of you has tried to kill me. I'm not made of the stuff that turns the other cheek."

"By what right do either of you stand in judgment?" Daisy demanded. "You're lives haven't been too pure, have they?"

"My life has been my own business," Terry replied promptly. "What I've done has never brought harm to any one but myself."

"Then why in the name of God start now?" Philip cried. "Have you no pity in your souls, either of you?"

Imagine Philip crying for pity and mercy. Had he no conscience? How could he forget the procession of wretched humans his greed had sent to a living death?

"The case is out of our hands," Terry answered and turned away.

The group prowled about the great living-room like Kilkenny cats watching each other accusingly. Kenfield came down the stairs and was all agog with excitement. He asked me all sorts of questions in an effort to get some information out of me. I tried to ignore the questions, but he pursued me about the room. I was as nervous as a filly about to run her first race, but I must admit I had an advantage over a filly. I could and did take several nips of brandy to steady my nerves.

"Who could have killed him?" Kenfield asked

"I don't know," I snapped. "That's what we're trying to discover."

"How about Terry? Does this put him into more of a jam? Can't we do something for him? You're supposed to be good at this sort of thing. Haven't you any ideas?"

"Yes, plenty of ideas but they're not working. My mind is as blank as a dead telephone line."

"There must be something I can do," he urged.

"There is," I answered caustically. "Keep out of it as long as you can."

"But it's so exciting! Murder right over our heads! Did you ever hear such a blood-curdling scream as that maid gave?" he asked, relishing the memory. "It gave me the shivers."

"And you're giving me the jitters. For heaven's sake, shut up and give me a chance to think!"

He looked terribly hurt as he turned away. His annoying questions did, however, start me on a new train of thought. I crossed the room and rang for Hubert. When he arrived I asked him to bring in the servants but particularly the one who had screamed.

He was back in a few minutes with all the staff grouped behind him. I noticed Agnes' eager face peering over the shoulder of a good-looking houseman. Trust her to pick the best-looking one of the lot. Hubert was leading one girl by the arm. Her eyes were red with weeping. He gave her a slight shove forward.

"Are you the girl who found the body?" I asked.

"Yes, ma'am," she half sobbed.

"Now, don't cry. It's all over. Tell me about it," I suggested gently.

The girl, still upset and confused, faltered through her story.

"I was turning down the beds for the night," she explained. "I knocked on his door but there was no answer. I went into the room. I didn't turn on the switch as I entered because there was a light burning in the dressing-room. I crossed to the bed and snapped on the bedside lamp which we always do. Then I turned to take off the cover and there he was. I thought he was asleep. I was going to come back later, when I saw the blood all over his shirt. It made me sick with horror and then I screamed."

Her last words were barely more than a whisper. I was disappointed in her story. I had hoped to learn that some one of the guests had sent her on her errand of discovery.

I told the girl to sit down and asked some general questions of the group.

From Hubert I learned something that I had not known before. Jackson, one of the housemen, had been delegated to act as valet to Andrews. It was Jackson's testimony that really started things going.

"Did you notice anything unusual about Mr. Andrews' actions on his arrival?" I asked.

"Yes, ma'am," Jackson replied. "He was very nervous and upset, ma'am, if you know what I mean."

I had a good idea because Jackson himself was about as nervous a man as I had ever seen. I smiled at him reassuringly as I asked, "What was the matter with him?"

"He was all wet," he answered.

I heard a titter and scowled at Agnes. She's just the type who would think that remark funny.

Jackson hastened on to explain. "He'd fallen off the yacht. He gave me some clothes to dry."

"I know about that," I said. "Was there anything else?"

"Well, he was annoyed when Mrs. Lassimon came to his room," he answered hesitantly.

I glanced at Althea, but she didn't blink an eye. I dismissed Jackson for the moment and turned to Althea. "What time did you visit Andrews?" I asked.

"I've no idea," she answered. "It was shortly after we arrived home."

I had hoped to establish an alibi for Terry, but Althea was not being very helpful.

"What happened in his room?" I asked.

"Nothing." She seemed surprised at the question. "I wanted to be sure he was comfortable after his mishap."

"How long were you there?" I continued.

"I say, Ethel . . ." Terry began a protest.

"Quiet!" I barked at him.

Althea smiled as she answered my question. "I don't know. A minute or two, no longer."

I glanced at Jackson expecting corroboration, but he said, "I don't know, ma'am. I didn't stay. Mr. Andrews said he'd ring if he wanted anything."

I was so determined to establish an alibi for Terry that I didn't notice Saxon when he entered the room. I turned to Jackson and asked, "What time was it when you left Mrs. Lassimon in the room with Mr. Andrews?"

"It was some time after eight," he replied, "but I don't know exactly."

Saxon's voice surprised me as he asked, "Then as far as we know, Mrs. Lassimon, you were the last person to see Andrews alive?"

"Probably," she admitted.

"She was not," Terry spoke up. "I talked with Andrews after that. I saw him about eight-thirty or a little later. Miss Thomas can vouch for that."

Valiant Terry! He was shouldering the blame to take the onus of suspicion from Althea.

"Can you vouch for that?" Saxon turned to me.

"Yes. I had been talking to Mr. Lassimon in his room," I answered. "It was a few minutes before nine when he left me saying he would look in on Andrews." That was a lie. Terry left me to have a talk with Althea, but if he wanted to play the role of Galahad it was none of my business.

"Why are you so positive of the time?" Saxon insisted.

"Because I was expecting you about nine," I replied. "Hubert announced your arrival shortly after that. I remember glancing at the clock. Punctuality is one of my hobbies. It was three minutes of nine when I left my room and came downstairs to greet you." I had to tell a direct lie to help Terry shield Althea.

"What has he to do with all this?" Philip growled at Saxon."

"He happens to be a member of the Nassau County police force," I announced.

They were startled. Philip changed color. Daisy clutched at her heart. Florence shrugged as she exchanged glances with Dick. She seemed to say, "The jig is up."

Saxon turned to Terry. "Did you talk to Andrews?"

"Yes," Terry replied.

"How long were you with him?"

"I don't know. I didn't notice."

"For the moment we'll assume that you're innocent, Mr. Lassimon. Did you see any one as you left Mr.

Andrews' room? Have you an alibi that will prove Andrews was alive when you left him?"

I glanced anxiously toward Terry. He was getting himself into very deep water in his effort to help Althea.

"No," Terry answered. "I've no alibi, nothing but my word."

Saxon turned to me. "Will you get me a piece of smooth flat silver," he asked.

I nodded to Hubert, who withdrew.

Saxon went on to explain. "I have some fingerprints that I took upstairs." He turned to me. "You've had more than your ten minutes."

Before I could reply Hubert returned with a flat serving-tray. Saxon took it gingerly and asked for a napkin. "I'm going to try an experiment," he explained. "Will you come up when I ask you and place your fingers on this tray?"

It seemed a silly business as we trooped by leaving our fingerprints on that smooth surface. Four or five of us had submitted to the test. Each time, after a moment's close scrutiny, Saxon had erased the marks and nodded for the next person.

As Philip turned away from the silver tray, Saxon stopped him. "You were in Andrews' room," he accused. "What were you doing there?"

Philip gulped in amazement before he spoke. "I went up with him upon our arrival. He was pretty shaky due to his accident."

That wasn't exactly the truth and I was on the point of saying so when Jackson spoke up and said, "Beg pardon, sir. I took Mr. Andrews to his room and this gentleman was not with us."

"It was before you came," Philip said impatiently.

"But I carried his bags upstairs, sir," Jackson insisted, "and was with him for at least a half-hour putting his things away and taking care of him generally."

Philip had snagged himself. It doesn't pay to lie to the police. They have a way of finding you out.

Saxon made no point of Jackson's unsolicited information at the moment. He had a system and a definite plan of action, I could tell that from the way he worked. Had he called the police?

Saxon's next question addressed to all of us was a surprise. "What," he asked, "did Andrews have that interested you so much?"

There was no answer, but Saxon waited patiently for a second or two before he broke the heavy silence.

"I see I'll have to be more specific," he said. "Miss Thomas, why did you go to Andrews' room?"

"Because I wanted to talk to him," I answered.

"Was your conversation satisfactory?"

"Quite," I replied.

"And he was alive and well when you left him?"

"Yes," I answered.

"Ummm," Saxon mused as he pulled his lower lip between his thumb and index-finger. Finally he said, "It would be ridiculous to arrest all of you, and yet..."

"Why don't you prove our alibis?" Philip demanded. "Why don't you get at the truth? They knew Andrews was dead long before the body was discovered," he cried, pointing an accusing finger at Terry and myself. He was wound up and raced on. "They had us all in the library pretending that they were trying to solve the murder. Why didn't they tell you? Why don't you make them tell you what they know?"

"Would you like that, Philip?" Terry asked threateningly.

Philip's anger died quickly.

"I'll ask the questions, Mr. Lassimon," Saxon advised Philip.

"Then why don't you?" Daisy cried. "Why keep us here like this? You've no right to put us on the rack. It isn't fair! She knows more about this death than she is telling."

Saxon took his cue from Daisy and turned to me. "Is that why your fingerprints are the last on the inside knob of the door leading to Andrews' room?" I had been a careless fool. Why had I touched the knob of that door and in so doing spoiled what might have been a good clue? Had I been less intent on getting out of the room unobserved, I might have been more careful, but heavens, a person can't think of everything. I wasn't thinking about myself. I was too engrossed thinking about trapping the murderer and in my absorption had probably destroyed valuable evidence.

"I can explain that," I said to Saxon as he waited for me to make a reply.

"Suppose you do," he suggested.

"I'd rather do it in private," I suggested. I knew we had reached a point where a showdown was absolutely necessary.

"I think you ought to say what you have to say here before all of us!" Dick Bolertho cried.

"If you want me to talk, I'll do it in my own way or not at all," I flared as I faced Saxon.

"As you wish," he acceded with a nod. "Where would you like to go?"

"The library will do," I replied. "I've things to tell you, you'll find extremely interesting." I purposely turned and included them all in that speech.

Saxon stepped aside for me to lead the way. He had nice manners, that boy. Their eyes were turned on me and their faces were sick with fear and dread.

"May these others have the freedom of the house for a few minutes?" I requested.

"Certainly," he replied, "as long as they make no attempt to leave the premises."

I addressed the agonized group watching us so intently. "Your ten minutes were up a long time ago. You still have a chance. I'll try to give you five minutes. You can't hope for more. What one of you must do, you can't do here in this room in a group. Why not separate? You'll probably want some privacy, anyhow."

I turned and marched toward the library door. Would I be able to keep Saxon engaged for five minutes? Would the arrival of the police, if he had called them, spoil our chance of getting a confession? As Saxon closed the door behind us, I saw the group breaking up. They were taking my advice.

CHAPTER 22

Saxon's steady and somewhat quizzical gaze was disconcerting as I faced him. Florence's question still rang in my ears. I was playing God. She was right. I didn't enjoy the role and had no sense of righteousness in spite of the fact that I firmly believed that there was nothing else to be done. It was the only way out for all of them. The murderer must confess.

My second ultimatum gave one of those people in that other room five more minutes of life. No matter how much the murderer deserved to die—and I would gladly have seen him dead at any time through the whole puzzling affair—when I stood there knowing that I had ordered a man to take his own life, I was overcome by a feeling of revulsion and horror. I couldn't imagine the murderer confessing and facing the possibility of a trial for the murders any more than I could fancy the real murderer being willing to have his secret exposed to face the shame and disgrace that must necessarily follow such an event. Had I been in the shoes of any one of them I would have welcomed the chance of suicide. Would he confess or, being a coward as he undoubtedly was, would he decide to take his chances? I had to give the guilty person a full five minutes if possible, but could I dally that long with Saxon? Time can fly so rapidly at some times and drag on so mercilessly at others. Would I be able to do it? I didn't want to tell Saxon all the things I knew. I could see no reason for that and yet . . .

"What did you mean about five more minutes?" Saxon asked.

"In a minute," I evaded and sank into a chair. "Give me a cigarette."

He handed me the package and took one himself. He held the match for me, lit his own and stood watching the flame reflectively for a moment. At least, I thought that was what he was doing, but I was wrong, because he asked, "What did you burn in the fireplace?"

The grate was a charred mass of glowing embers. The diaries were completely destroyed. "Some one must have thrown a cigarette in there," I suggested.

"Would that explain the soot mark on your arm?" he asked, proving he was a keen and careful observer of little things.

"No. I burned some papers that were mine," I admitted.

"Which won't help your case any," he said.

"I'm not worried about my case," I retorted.

"Did you know you left your handkerchief behind in Andrews' room?"

Instinctively my hand went to the pocket of my skirt. Our instincts nearly always betray us. I was so sure that I could confound him with a handkerchief that I was overly surprised to find the pocket empty. One of the many reasons for that pocket is to have a decent receptacle for my handkerchief.

"You still baffle me," he said forlornly.

"Do sit down, please," I begged. "I'm so upset and nervous I can't be normal."

I glanced at my watch. One long minute had dragged by.

He didn't sit down but facing me demanded, "Did you kill Andrews?"

"Certainly not," I cried.

"But you knew he was dead. You were in there after he died and yet just a few minutes ago you lied to me."

"Yes," I agreed.

"Why didn't you tell me the truth?"

Another half-minute crept toward oblivion before I answered, "Because I'm a silly old woman. Crime detection has gone to my head. I think I'm smarter than the police, that's why. One of the guests in this house killed Andrews and because I was instrumental in solving the Doane murders I thought I could force a confession this time, but I failed."

"How could you hope to do that?"

I looked at my watch again. Two and a half minutes were gone. I had been speaking slowly, dragging out my words and had barely used up a minute. It's surprising how much one can say in a minute. If most of us were aware of what we can say in so short a time, many of us would think twice before we speak at all. I wanted that five minutes to end. Wanted it desperately. I knew, however, that I couldn't trifle with Saxon much longer. He wouldn't let me waste his time. He was being respectfully patient with me. We were no longer friends. That sense of fellowship and accord which had been ours earlier in the day had been lost in the yawning chasm of doubt and mistrust which had opened between us. It was my fault. He undoubtedly felt I had betrayed him—made him appear ridiculous. I felt obligated to restore his self-respect—to save his face, as the Chinese so aptly express it. I wanted Saxon's confidence and friendship. I had to tell him something that would interest him and keep him satisfied. I must fill those remaining minutes to his satisfaction. I tossed my cigarette into the fireplace.

"Do you remember how abruptly I left you just after your arrival here tonight?" I asked.

As his cigarette followed mine to scatter crumbling paper dust, he nodded in agreement.

"You'll probably laugh at me when I tell you that I knew Terry Lassimon was in danger at that moment," I began.

"Why should I laugh? I've no idea what you knew," he said.

Three and a quarter minutes had gone. I rose and crossed the room. I opened the door into the hall. "Do you mind?" I asked. "It's so hot and stuffy in here."

"Tell me about Lassimon's danger," Saxon pulled my attention back to him.

I recounted my hurried trip up the stairs, my entrance and sudden fall in Terry's room and then my search of the adjacent bedrooms.

"Why did you suspect any one in those nearby rooms?" Saxon asked.

"Because I looked into the corridor as soon as I had regained my feet and scattered senses."

"And saw no one?"

"Not a soul."

"It's too bad you didn't look into the rooms immediately," he said. "I can understand why you didn't, however. Did you have any particular suspect in mind?"

"No," I answered and looked at my watch. The five minutes were nearly gone. I took a deep breath. I'd have to start explaining or face a murder charge. Somewhere in the house a clock started to strike. I listened attentively counting the strokes. As the last echoing cadence of the chimes died away there came the muffled report of a gun! It sounded like the distant cracking of a whip. A snapping sound symbolical of the life that had been snuffed out.

"Was that a shot?" Saxon asked.

"I think so," I replied softly, completely unnerved. Now that it was over, reaction set in immediately. I wanted to know who it was and yet didn't possess the energy to move.

"Was that what you were waiting for?" Saxon asked.

I nodded and asked, "Aren't you going to investigate it?"

"Who is it?" he demanded.

"I don't know exactly," I replied.

"You're a deep one," he threw at me as he left the room. I followed. He paused to help me up the stairs.

We found Philip Lassimon in the middle of his room, a revolver on the floor beside him. Saxon bent over the body.

So it was Philip. I wasn't surprised. Philip had been in New York all the time. He knew Terry's habits. He knew the old Lassimon apartment house. He had lived there when he was a bachelor. He was terrified; couldn't face exposure and disgrace. He had tried to protect himself and had failed. But why had he been so persistent about getting Terry out of the way? While Saxon knelt by the body, I began a search for the confession which I was certain he had left behind him. I must be honest. I had no regrets about Philip. He wouldn't have killed himself unless Mortimer's statement about him was true.

I went to the desk thinking that would be the obvious place to find what I sought. The desk was bare. I ran to the bedside table expecting to find it propped against the lamp-base. It was not there. I crossed to the dresser thinking to find something tucked into the edge of the mirror. Nothing! I couldn't believe my eyes. Behind me a voice asked, "What's happened?" I didn't turn but called over my shoulder, 'Terry, there's no confession! I've looked everywhere!"

"Terry's downstairs," another voice announced.

I was sure I had heard Terry's voice there behind me, but I had been wrong. Florence Gunner, Archie Van Nuys and Kenfield were peering in through the open door.

Why had Philip died without leaving a confession? It didn't make sense. Had he meant to be diabolically nasty even in death? I couldn't believe that. No man facing the unknown could do such a thing. He had been through too much torture himself to leave those others helpless behind him. Then what was the answer? Philip had died a coward's death. He didn't have nerve enough to face possible exposure. He had taken the only means of escape known to him. He had killed himself because he was afraid to face the future. Oh, what a fool I had been! The murderer was a much better psychologist than I. He probably knew that such a thing would happen and, sure of himself, he had sat there waiting for the death of a man so that he would be clear of guilt for all time. Philip's suicide in the face of all that had transpired was a confession of guilt. The murderer knew that and hoped that I, too, would believe it.

For just one hesitant moment I doubted my convictions. Would a man in Philip's position leave a confession that would bring shame to his family? I believed my reasoning right. If Philip had been the murderer, he would have left such a confession which would have kept his other secret for all time. No, Philip had not killed Mortimer nor any of the others. There was only one thing for me to do and it had to be done immediately. I knew there could be no more requests for time. I could expect no further consideration from Saxon. He would summon the police immediately. What I had to do must be done before the police arrived.

As I moved to the door I heard Saxon say, "He's dead."

"I'll be downstairs if you want me," I called back as I crowded past the little group at the door.

"How about the diaries?" Florence asked.

"You've nothing to worry about now. I burned them an hour ago," I assured her. "Tell the others."

"You devil!" she breathed. She meant it as a compliment, though, because I could sense the relief in her voice.

"Does this mean the mystery is over?" Kenfield asked.

"Yes. It's over," I said and hurried away.

At the foot of the stairs I called Terry and quickly told him what had happened.

"Phil!" he exclaimed as I went into the library and called the police headquarters in New York City. I asked for Peter Conklin. They told me he was off duty. I insisted that they locate him at once and have him telephone me at the Roslyn number. "He'll be interested. It's about the Van Wyck murder," I said as I hung up.

"What are you doing?" Terry asked, coming up behind me.

"I'm not sure exactly, but I think I now have all the pieces to our puzzle," I replied. "I'm waiting for a call from Peter Conklin."

"You're great," he said.

"Don't be too sure about that. Pour me a drink and leave me. I want to think."

Why is it that when you are close to a situation you sometimes fail to think clearly or logically? Is finding the solution of a crime like happiness? Is it on our doorstep all the time?

A straw had shown me how the wind blew. It came suddenly in a quick flash of understanding. How blind I had been all through the whole horrible adventure! How stupid! I had been so puzzled and bewildered and yet now it was like a jig-saw puzzle. The pieces were fitting into their proper places. The answer was before me at last. There was just one thing I must know and Peter could tell me that.

Peter called me in a few minutes.

"Peter," I cried, "I think I have the murderer of Van Wyck and Fergus. You must do something for me quickly. Will you?"

He agreed at once. Terry returned and heard my request.

"And what will that give you?" he asked as I rang off.

"The murderer," I replied.

"But Philip . . ." he objected, "surely you are convinced that he . . ."

"Committed suicide because he couldn't face the possibility of exposure," I replied.

"You're tired, Ethel, worn out by the things that have happened in the past few days. Don't be unreasonable. Philip was our man."

"Philip Lassimon was a coward. He couldn't face the music. He hasn't killed any one," I snapped and went into the hall.

In the far corner of the living-room Daisy sat sobbing as though her heart would break. Whether they were tears of gladness or grief I didn't know and didn't care. I had to find some way to keep clear of Saxon until I heard from Peter and the tests he was making.

Dick Bolertho coming in from the terrace was an answer to my prayer. He came toward me asking, "Did anything happen?"

Between us there was a small rug. I knew the floors were very slippery. As Dick stepped on the rug I gave it a vicious tug with the heel of my shoe and Dick went hurtling to the floor, a most surprised and startled young man. I fell with him, taking great pains to fall on him so that I wouldn't be hurt. As he tried to slide out from under me, I rolled over on the floor. Terry was at my side in an instant and lifted me to my feet.

"Air," I breathed, "I must have air."

"Easy, darling," he whispered. "Don't cave in just when the end is in sight. Come to my room."

I let my legs sag under me and would have fallen again but for his steadying arm. As he lifted me, I let my head fall over his shoulder and whispered into his ear. "I can't talk to Saxon or any one until I hear from Peter."

He started up the stairs. With my head hanging over Terry's shoulder I could see nothing, but I heard Saxon say, "I want to talk to Miss Thomas."

"She's had a bad fall," Terry explained and hurried up the steps.

Althea joined us, asking solicitously, "Is she badly hurt?"

Terry grunted a reply as he jounced me along the hall to his room. He dropped me on the bed.

"Have you called a doctor?" Althea asked anxiously.

"She's just bluffing, stalling for time," he answered. Then I knew it was safe to open my eyes.

"I want to appear to be disabled for a half-hour. Will you help me?" I asked Althea.

"Of course."

Terry had been mixing a drink which I had to refuse. He leaned against the little bar, took a sip from his glass, sighed, and said, "Well, it's all over now, according to Ethel."

I looked at him quickly. He gave me the impression that he regretted the end of the mystery.

"Then it was Philip?" Althea asked.

Terry nodded in my direction, but I didn't reply. I was too busy thinking about the story I'd have to tell Saxon in a few minutes. Through my thoughts I heard Terry's voice saying, "Your worries are over, the diaries are burned. You're free now."

I heard Althea sigh. "It's nice to know the danger is past."

"Will you go to Reno or would you rather I gave you grounds for a divorce here in New York?" he asked. "Our local divorce laws are a bit messy, but I won't mind. I have a reputation anyhow, you know."

"You're very anxious to be rid of me, it seems," she said.

"I—er—" he fumbled for words.

"There are complications," she went on. "I'm Church of England, High Church. We don't approve of divorce. I must think about it."

I glanced across the room at her. Her eyes were smiling at the boy-man who looked puzzled and baffled at the glass in his hand.

"But that's old-fashioned," he finally protested. "We couldn't go on being married just because your church doesn't approve of divorce." He took a step toward her. "I won't go on being married to you and live in mockery. I've loved you, Althea, from the first moment I saw you."

"Even when you doubted me?" I heard her ask as I rolled over on my side.

"More than ever," he replied.

As I pulled a cover over my head I heard him ask, "Do you think that you . . .?"

CHAPTER 23

I didn't see Saxon again until the Nassau County police arrived, swarms of them, taking complete possession of the house. He came to my room with a man by the name of Croft who was in charge. He was a tall, lank chap with a gaunt face made forbidding by the heavy gray shadows under his eyes. He looked like a dyspeptic. A man with a sour stomach can be very unpleasant if he is too far from an available supply of bicarbonate of soda.

When he spoke I was surprised at the quality of his voice. It was soft and rather gentle, not at all the complaining whine I had expected.

"Saxon tells me," he began, "that you know more about the things which have been happening here than any of the others. Is that true?"

"Yes," I agreed.

"Then suppose you tell us what you know. It will complete the rapid survey of the case which Saxon has given me."

"I think all the people concerned should hear what I have to say," I answered. "If you don't mind, I'd like to talk to you and the others downstairs."

He readily agreed to that and withdrew politely, showing a nice consideration for a woman's privacy. After they had gone, I didn't dally unnecessarily long. I knew that I would hear from Peter within the next ten or fifteen minutes.

The living-room, when I went down, seemed an entirely different place. Just a few minutes before it had been a room freighted with fear and anxiety. The warm air, smoke-laden and stale, had been ominous, but now the last rumbling echoes of the storm were rolling away somewhere to the south of us. Hubert had opened the windows. A cool, sweet, earth-tinged breeze ruffled the curtains. Daisy had stopped her sniffling. Archie was contentedly sipping brandy from an inhaler. Bolertho was talking to Florence Gunner, who listened attentively, almost possessively, to the things he whispered.

"Miss Thomas has something to tell us. She thinks you'll all be interested," Croft announced.

They moved forward to make an interested semicircle in front of me.

"I must go back a week or more so that you'll understand the things that have happened tonight," I explained to Croft.

He nodded approval.

I told them about the first attempt on Terry's life when he called on me that early morning. Croft didn't seem to consider that part of the story very important.

"You must bear with me," I said. "The first attempt showed us, although we were too blind to see it at the time, that the murderer had very definite knowledge of Terry Lassimon's activities."

I then went on to tell them about the cocktail party for Altliea and the arrivals of Fergus and Philip Lassimon. I included all the important details. When I told them about the evidences of murder in Terry's flat there were several gasps of surprise.

"Why," Croft demanded, "didn't you call the police?"

"You ought to know the answer to that," I replied and went on to tell them about the finding of the body in my car and our terrible time trying to dispose of it. There was a hysterical giggle from Daisy as I told them of our consternation the next morning when we realized that the body had not been found.

I spoke directly to Croft. "You must realize our terror. The murderer was determined to involve Terry in the murder of Fergus."

He nodded in understanding.

Terry and Althea were sitting on the couch beside Kenfield. I knew as I glanced in Althea's direction that there would be no divorce. Her face was radiantly happy as Terry took her hand and held it tenderly.

"About those diaries?" Croft asked. "Where are they now?"

"Where they should be," I answered, "burned, gone forever."

"You had no right to do that," he protested.

"They cost me two hundred thousand dollars and I very nearly lost my life getting them," I snapped. "Who had a better right?"

That, of course, made it necessary for me to tell them about the theft of the diaries from the office safe just before Mortimer's murder.

Hubert interrupted us to say that I was wanted on the telephone.

"It is important," I explained to Croft. "Do you mind?"

As I left the room, I took Saxon by the arm and walked with him toward the library. Of course it was Peter. He had done all the things I had requested. He had been very thorough in his searching and checking. A time element had been involved. He had checked by police-car, taxi and elevated railroad train.

As I thanked him, he laughed and said that once again he was in my debt. He added, "I have a dragnet out for him now. He can't get away."

He grumbled when I told him that credit for the capture of the murderer and the solution of the crime would go to James Saxon of the Nassau County police force. He had the good grace to say, "Well, under the circumstances there is nothing that either of us can do about it."

As I turned from the telephone Saxon demanded, "Who was that and why did you tell him that I'd make the capture and arrest?"

"Because you will," I replied and whispered the name of the murderer into his ear. "Wait until I have built up the case against him," I warned. "He's smart."

"But I've had nothing to do with it!" he denied.

"You gave me a free hand and the necessary time to get at the facts," I reminded him. "That's a lot and, besides, you're a policeman and want promotion. Take credit when you can get it. Now don't be silly." I steered him toward the library door.

As I reentered the living-room I felt like a prima donna taking a curtain call.

"Go on," Croft urged.

"As I told you before," I took up the thread of the story, "the diaries had been taken from the safe. The front door of the office had been jimmied. Not being experienced in the art of housebreaking I missed an important clue. The door had been jimmied from the inside, but I didn't know it at the time. There was another bit of evidence in that office that I missed completely. The thief had not opened the package to inspect it. There should have been torn pieces of wrapping-paper on the floor and little bits of red sealing-wax left there by the thief as he hurriedly ripped the parcel open to make sure that he had the right books. The thief knew the package. It was not necessary for him to inspect it.

"Before I left the publishing office, Terry Lassimon telephoned to tell me that he was being held by the police at Mortimer Van Wyck's. I went uptown immediately. While I was there a second attempt was made on the life of Terry. As you know, one of the servants was hit by the bullet. When we eventually found the staircase leading to the room I missed another clue which I should have noticed. Just before that, Althea unconsciously gave me a hint which I missed.

"After Van Wyck's murder, Terry left town. While he was away I advertised for the stolen diaries. Again in the excitement of the hunt I missed a clue which you will undoubtedly say was an obvious one."

"But where is all this leading us?" Croft demanded.

"To the man who committed three murders," I replied.

"But I ... we thought Philip Lassimon . . ." Archie blustered.

"Philip Lassimon was not the murderer. Unfortunately for him it was not until after he had killed himself that I suddenly realized the truth."

"What do you mean?" Terry asked.

"Sidney Kenfield is your murderer," I accused, turning to Croft.

Sidney jumped to his feet. "She's stark raving mad!" he cried. "Terry, surely you're not going to let her . . ."

Saxon's hand went down on Sidney's shoulder with the precision and finality of a guillotine blade.

"This is a serious accusation, Miss Thomas," Croft reminded me. "Are you sure?"

"The one person in New York who could have known about those diaries and had access to them was Kenfield," I answered. "He knew their value. The firm was badly in need of money. Terry was worried and tried to borrow two hundred thousand dollars from me. I don't know when Kenfield conceived the plan, but it must have been the night Terry called on me.

"To cover the theft of the diaries from the office, Kenfield jimmied the front door, but he did it from the inside. Kenfield knew what was in that package, he didn't have to look. When he came into the office that next morning his shoulder and sleeve were covered with white dust. I tried to brush it off, but it was very sticky and tenacious dust due to the dampness of his clothes.

"Later Detective Peter Conklin and Terry were covered with the same kind of dust which they gathered by rubbing their shoulders against the wall of that small narrow staircase leading to Mortimer's roof."

"It's utterly ridiculous!" Kenfield cried. "She's gone crazy thinking she's a detective!"

I ignored the remark. "There was some connection between Kenfield and Fergus. What, I do not know. He saw Fergus that day at my house. He was the first person to speak to him. He either sent Fergus to Terry's apartment or knew he would go there. Kenfield knew the apartment, knew about the service elevator, knew how to hide the body. He probably followed us all that evening as we tried to rid ourselves

of the corpse."

"I won't listen to this!" Kenfield cried, rising again.

Saxon forced him into his chair. "I'm afraid you'll have to," he said.

"Go on," Croft instructed.

"The telephone call I just received was from Peter Conklin. He told me that a man could make the trip from Van Wyck's to Terry's office in from ten to twenty minutes, depending upon his means of locomotion. Kenfield had time to get from Van Wyck's to the office before I left. He had plenty of time to go back there to the house next door and shoot at Terry from the roof."

"Why would I want to kill Terry?" Kenfield asked.

"I can't imagine," I replied and went on: "When Althea was being questioned about the murder she told Peter that she heard voices in Van Wyck's room. She said she thought it was Terry, but she knew Terry to be downstairs." I turned to Croft. "Kenfield has imitated Terry in every way possible. It has always annoyed me before."

"Rubbish!" Kenfield snorted.

"When I advertised for the diaries I asked Kenfield to help me. He was most kind. The clue that I missed was the letter the thief sent to me. He told me to be in the drugstore at the corner of my street at a specified time. How did the thief know that I was the person advertising for the diaries? It might have been any one of a thousand people, but the answer came direct to me giving me specific instructions. Kenfield was the only person in the world who knew I was advertising for those diaries. I paid him two hundred thousand dollars and he tried to kill me.

"Tonight on the way out here, Andrews was pushed overboard. Why? He was dressed in clothes almost identical with those that Terry was wearing. For some strange distorted reason Kenfield wanted Terry out of the way. Why, I can't imagine."

Terry turned to Sidney. "You can clear this up, old man, surely you can."

"How can I extricate myself from a frame-up of lies and double-crossing!" Sidney snarled. "You're in league with her to cover yourself and save your own hide. You're just making me the goat! You're the one who needed the money! You're the one who was trying to borrow from old money-bags."

"But, Sidney . . ." Terry began a protest.

"Don't talk to me!" Sidney cried and turned his eyes away from Terry.

Terry was hurt, I could see that. He's not a person who gives his friendship lightly.

Croft ended the discussion between the two men. "Assuming for the moment that Miss Thomas is right in her deductions, is there any reason for Kenfield to desire your death?"

It was a direct question and Terry gave a direct answer.

"Perhaps it was because we had agreed that in the event of the death of either of us the publishing business would revert to the living partner," Terry said.

"That's your motive there, all right," Saxon said, "but why kill those other men?"

"He is the only one who can answer that question," I replied. "He may have been in cahoots with them, but that is something we'll probably never know."

"I'll sue you for this!" Kenfield threatened.

"What made you sure Kenfield was your man?" Croft asked.

"Tonight while Saxon and I were in Philip Lassimon's room and I was so frantically looking for a confession I believed I'd find, I thought I heard Terry's voice at tlie door. If you remember," I turned to Saxon, "I called to Terry by name and Kenfield answered telling me that Terry was downstairs. It came to me suddenly then. The one additional proof I needed was to be sure that Kenfield could have made the trips between the office and Van Wyck's. Peter Conklin has verified that possibility."

"But why did he kill Andrews?" Saxon demanded.

"Kenfield was in Terry's room tonight when I surprised him. He tripped me and made his escape. Andrews must have seen him leaving the room so precipitously. There can be no other explanation for the necessity of getting Andrews out of the way. If you had been smarter," I turned to Kenfield, "you'd have saved yourself an extra murder."

Kenfield turned to Croft. "Are you going to take a rattle-brained old woman's theories as gospel truth? She'll make a fool out of you. She's an egomaniac. She has led you and this man around by the nose since you came here tonight. Ask him!" He wheeled, pointing toward Saxon.

Croft considered those accusations for a moment. He smiled as he said, "You do have a way of managing things, Miss Thomas."

"I had a very definite plan tonight to trap the murderer of Andrews, but unfortunately the untimely discovery of the body spoiled my plot."

"Which was?" Croft invited me to give further details.

"I knew the murderer would want Andrews' body discovered. Terry would be implicated at once and would have a difficult time proving his innocence."

"And your little plan was ruined?"

"Wait a minute," Saxon broke into the talk. "I'm not so sure her plan miscarried."

"What do you mean, Saxon?" Croft asked.

"When they were having their meeting, Kenfield and I were out here. He rang for drinks. When the butler served us, Kenfield yawned and said he would turn in. The butler asked him to wait a few minutes until the rooms were prepared for the night. As Hubert left, he promised to send a maid upstairs immediately."

"I guess that does it, Kenfield," Croft said.

"You haven't one single item of proof!" Kenfield sneered.

Purposely I had saved the most damaging piece of information for the very end.

"But we have proof," I said emphatically.

"What proof have you? You're just guessing!"

"The New York police don't guess. They searched your apartment. They found several packages of bills. Peter Conklin is getting in touch with the bank now for the serial numbers. He'll check on them and call me back," I explained to Croft.

"It's a frame-up! She's tight! She doesn't know what she's saying!" Sidney cried.

"I may be a rattle-brained old woman, Sidney, but I hope I'm not as dumb as you seem to think I am, and what's more, I'm not tight. You're cornered and you know it. We'll have word in a few minutes that will finish the case."

He sagged into his chair. I would have had more sympathy for him if he hadn't accused me of being tight. As I think back on that night now, I should have been tipsy. I suppose the strain and excitement counterbalanced the effects of the drinks I did take.

"We'll have to hold you, Kenfield, until we have checked with the New York police," Croft said.

"You won't have to check," I said. "Peter Conklin promised to call back. Why don't you search his things here? By the time you're through, we should hear from Peter."

All the fight seemed to have left Sidney. He was a dejected figure sitting under the careful gaze of Saxon.

"Keep your eye on him," Croft instructed two of his men and turned to the stairs. "Come along, Saxon."

"And now how about a drink?" Terry suggested.

Daisy came trotting over to me. "Ethel, you're positively wonderful! I'd no idea! Goodness, I'm glad you burned those diaries! You didn't believe them, did you?" she asked anxiously.

I patted her hand. "I didn't even read them, my dear."

"But you said . . ." she began.

"Yes, I know. When I told you we had read them, we were trying to force one of you to confess to a crime you had not committed."

"Then how did you know who we were?" Bolertho asked.

"That was simple. Terry found carbons of the letters Mortimer had written to you. He took them from Mortimer's desk so that none-of you would be implicated in the murder at the moment."

"That was thoughtful of Terry," Daisy gushed.

"No," Terry denied. "It was a matter of self-defense. Remember, I thought one of you was gunning for me."

"Telephone, Miss Thomas," Hubert announced. "Mr. Conklin."

"Call Croft," I cried as I went toward the library.

They all followed behind me and listened eagerly to my one-sided conversation with Peter. When Croft arrived, he held a package of bills in his hand. How stupid of Kenfield to have brought any of that money with him! I turned the telephone over to Croft. He sat at the table and called serial numbers to Peter, who was checking against a list he had received from the bank.

There were one or two things I wanted to know and decided to take that particular time to get the information from Kenfield if he would talk to me. Unnoticed, I slipped from the library and went to the living-room where Sidney brooded under the watchful eyes of two policemen.

"May I speak to your prisoner?" I asked.

"I don't know, ma'am. You'd better ask Croft."

"I did," I answered glibly. There was no point in getting involved in a lot of red tape and nonsense; besides Croft was busy at the moment.

"He might try to get away," the policeman suggested.

"Where could he go? Don't be silly. Guard the doors if you'll feel more comfortable."

They threw a glance toward the windows, saw they were well screened, then moved across to the doors leading to the hall and the library. The room was enormous. I was glad they had gone, as I didn't want them listening to our conversation anyhow.

I nodded to the officers who had taken up their posts and pulled a chair close to Sidney, who turned a bitter pair of eyes toward me. "What do you want?" he growled.

"Some information. I'm curious about one or two points," I replied, my voice lowered so that the officers couldn't hear me.

"Well, you won't get it from me," he retorted and closed up like a clam.

"Don't be such a bad sport," I said. "You played a brilliant game and lost. You played for high stakes— played cleverly. Why can't you take your defeat with the same reckless bravado?"

"It's easy enough for you to talk, you're not facing the chair."

I couldn't be philosophical about that remark. There was nothing I could say. I waited a moment and meant it when I said, "I'm sorry, Sidney."

"I'd have gotten away with it if it hadn't been for you. Why were you so interested? What are all those people to you, anyhow, that you should have gone to so much trouble risking your life? They're not worth it, any of them."

"I was working for Terry, you know that," I replied.

"He was born under a lucky star. I should have known better," he reflected.

That gave me an opening. "Why did you do it?" I asked. "You had so much to lose."

"Because it seemed so easy, that's why. Van Wyck came to me, told me about the diaries and promised me a cut in the blackmail money he would receive from his frightened victims when they believed the books were to be published. We had no idea of publishing the books but we did want Terry to say that he would publish them.

Mortimer couldn't frighten his victims unless they believed the books were to be published."

"You should have refused to be a part of such a scheme," I said.

"The business was in a bad way; Terry was on the verge of going broke. We needed money and I thought Mortimer's plan would be an easy way to get it. I knew Terry wouldn't listen to Mortimer's scheme, so I planned with Mortimer to get Terry interested in a casual legitimate way. I knew Terry's habits. I told Mortimer where to go and what to do to interest Terry. Mortimer haunted Terry's favorite cafes and clubs until they met and had a talk about publishing. Terry took the bait. The plan worked nicely up to that point.

"We thought everything was all set when Terry promised to read the diaries. He spoiled our plans by leaving them in the safe, unread for weeks. Mortimer became impatient, insisted that I get some action from Terry. I couldn't do that without revealing my knowledge of the books. Mortimer began threatening me."

"I don't see that it was necessary for Terry to have read the books. Once Terry had taken them, Mortimer could have told his victims that they were to be published," I objected.

"That's true, but Mortimer felt the people would be more terrified if they knew some one else knew their secret.

"If Terry had read the books at once none of this would have happened," he said with regret.

"Why?" I asked.

"During the time we waited I had a chance to think. I was tempted when I realized that I could get the books into my possession and have all the money instead of taking a cut from Mortimer.

"When I realized that Terry was looking over the books I decided to act at once. With Terry out of the way I could take the books. Mortimer would be in no position to say anything. I prowled about the office that night. I wanted to kill Terry but was afraid to do it there. I followed him. Each time an opportunity presented itself something prevented my doing it. I was warned and should have given up my plan, but I couldn't then."

"You could have taken the books from the safe. You didn't have to do murder," I said.

"I wanted the business for myself. Terry told you that in the event of the death of either of us the business would revert to the other."

It was a bald confession. I said nothing.

"That night when I realized that he was taking the books to your house I became frantic. I thought that was the end of them. I fired that shot and missed him. I had hoped that in falling he would drop the briefcase and I could get it.

"When Mortimer realized that Terry would keep the books he became furious. He threatened to expose me to Terry. I didn't want that to happen. I had to work quickly. That afternoon at your cocktail party I expanded my plan. I decided to get rid of Mortimer and Fergus, who was in the secret. It seemed so easy.

"I told Fergus to go to Terry's apartment and look for the diaries. I promised to join him there. He was searching when I arrived. I had a gun of my own but I used Terry's to shoot him. At first I intended to leave the body there but changed my mind. I wanted Terry out of the way but I was afraid to kill him because of you. I wanted him to become so involved with the police that I would have a free hand to carry out my plans for getting the diaries and blackmail money. If Terry could be accused of a crime and be electrocuted it was safer for me than killing him.

"I took the body down the service elevator. When I saw your car had arrived I believed I could involve you as well as Terry. I chloroformed your chauffeur and then put the body in the car. I was certain that the evidence left in Terry's apartment plus the body in your car would make the police think that Terry was trying to cover his crime."

"Where did you keep the body until I arrived?"

"In the basement. In a locker used by the janitor. That's where I found the chloroform."

I had wondered about that but had not asked.

"How on earth did you get rid of Fergus' body after we left it at Mortimer's basement door?" I asked.

"That was easy. I drive an open roadster. I lifted him in and drove up to City Island where a friend of mine keeps a small boat. I carried him out on the Sound and dumped him overboard."

"Then, of course, you had to rid yourself of Mortimer," I prompted.

"Yes. I felt certain that Terry would appear at Mortimer's the next day. I knew about that rear stair because Mortimer opened the door to get more circulation of air one day when I was there. The morning of the murder I was concealed in the closet while Terry was in the room. I didn't know that Miss Madison was expected there. She very nearly caught me."

He stopped talking and sat staring straight ahead for several seconds. "I'll get my revenge!" he stated, looking up at me.

"Revenge?" I repeated.

"Yes. I'll tell the world the contents of those diaries."

"You wouldn't do that!" I gasped.

"Why not? They're are bad as I am, all of them. Why should I die for the same sort of crimes they have committed? Why should they go free?"

"But, Sidney," I protested, "some of them must be innocent."

"Let them prove it!" he sneered.

"You can't do it!"

"You are the only person who can stop me," he said, giving me a calculating glance.

"How can I stop you?" I asked, puzzled.

"I don't want to face a trial. I want to get away."

"But where would you go?" I asked.

"Over the border," he replied.

"They'd catch you in Canada. It would be just that much worse when you were caught," I argued.

"For a smart woman you can be dense at times," he sneered. "I mean over the Styx, extinction."

I was in a quandary. How could I give him the means of exit? It would be very simple if I had a vial of poison or one of those rings one reads about in fiction. But I had no such weapons at hand.

"If you don't, I'll give my story to one of the yellow journals," he warned.

"I'm trying to think," I said.

"I've thought of a way," he whispered, "but I need help. You must divert the attention of those two policemen for a minute or so, so that I can get to the front door. The rest will be easy. Will you do it?"

As I pushed my chair back, I nodded. I believed him when he said he would publish the stories. It was so pointless to have all that publicity after our efforts to keep the stories from publication. Philip Lassimon and Andrews were dead, they were the worst of the lot. The others might be innocent of the crimes of which they were accused. I had promised them protection. I had burned the diaries, but I could not foresee this situation.

I left Sidney and spoke to the two officers, "Wouldn't you two boys like a drink?" I asked.

"Not while we're on duty," one of them replied.

"I can get you grape-juice or ginger-ale," I suggested.

"Well . . ." the second one answered.

"Just pull that bell cord," I said, pointing toward the fireplace wall.

One of the officers moved forward. The other chap and I watched him. As he pulled the cord and then turned to face us he cried, "He's gone!" He raced across the room.

I followed the two men to the front door. Outside I heard the roar of a motorcycle engine. You know how that din tears silence into shreds. With a sputter and burst of sound it raced away. Kenfield was on a motorcycle. He took the curve beyond the rose garden at a perilous angle and headed on down the hill.

"He'll break his neck!" one of the police cried as he ran toward a police car to take up pursuit.

I was fascinated watching Kenfield. Had he lied to me? Did he intend to run for it? No. He had spoken the truth. Where the drive makes the second turn to wind down the hill, Kenfield continued straight ahead. The machine dug at the slight bank at the road's edge, hurtled into the air for a moment, seemed to pause in space and then plunged downward out of sight.

"I don't blame him," a voice said behind me. It was the second policeman, who had been as fascinated by the escape as I had been.

"It's a horrible way to die," I said and turned away.

"So's the chair," he flung after me as I turned back into the house.

They were just coming from the library as I entered the living-room. The officer made his report to Croft. The group was stunned by the news but I think we all felt relieved as we realized that the necessity for a trial had been taken from us.

Croft sent some men to find Kenfield and care for him. Then he turned to me. "We have you to thank for the solution of the crime," he said.

"Don't forget Saxon," I reminded him. "If he had been less willing to cooperate, we wouldn't have been so successful."

As Croft turned away Saxon came up behind me and whispered in my ear. "I'm sorry for the things I said to you. I thought . . ."

"You didn't say half that I might have said had the situation been reversed," I laughed.

"I didn't know . . ." He was bent on making an explanation.

"Neither did I," I cut him short. "I wanted a man like you near me because I thought there might be trouble."

Of course he beamed at that. What man wouldn't? Bless their hearts, they like the nice things we say to them no matter how old we may be.

Croft came back, the packet of bills in his hand. "I'll have to take these with me, Miss Thomas."

"Just don't forget that it belongs to me," I reminded him.

With the house cleared of the police, Terry proposed a toast to me. I countered with one to the bride and groom. The guests, relieved, wandered off to their rooms.

We were the last to go up, we three. We paused for a minute, at the door of Terry's suite. He was holding Althea's hand.

"Goodnight, my dears," I said.

They kissed me simultaneously, one on either cheek. Althea's eyes were moist. Terry opened his door.

"Goodnight, darling," he said.

Althea stepped into the room. The door closed behind them. I stumbled along the hall unable to see for the tears which dimmed my eyes. I felt foolish about it, but like most women of my acquaintance I always shed a few tears at a wedding, and after all this really was their wedding night.

THE END

Other Resurrected Press Books in *The Chief Inspector Pointer Mystery* Series

Murder at Bridge

When an afternoon bridge party attended by some of Hamilton's leading citizens ends with the hostess being murdered in her boudoir, Special Investigator Dundee of the District Attorney's office is called in. But one of the attendees is guilty? There are plenty of suspects: the victim's former lover, her current suitor, the retired judge who is being blackmailed, the victim's maid who had been horribly disfigured accidentally by the murdered woman, or any of the women who's husbands had flirted with the victim. Or was she murdered by an outsider whose motive had nothing to do with the town of Hamilton. Find the answer in... **Murder at Bridge**

One Drop of Blood

When Dr. Koenig, head of Mayfield Sanitarium is murdered, the District Attorney's Special Investigator, "Bonnie" Dundee must go undercover to find the killer. Were any of the inmates of the asylum insane enough to have committed the crime? Or, was it one of the staff, motivated by jealousy? And what was is the secret in the murdered man's past. Find the answer in... **One Drop of Blood**

AVAILABLE FROM RESURRECTED PRESS!

THE EDWARDIAN DETECTIVES
LITERARY SLEUTHS OF THE EDWARDIAN ERA

The exploits of the great Victorian Detectives, Poe's C. Auguste Dupin, Gaboriau's Lecoq, and most famously, Arthur Conan Doyle's Sherlock Holmes, are well known. But what of those fictional detectives that came after, those of the Edwardian Age? The period between the death of Queen Victoria and the First World War had been called the Golden Age of the detective short story, but how familiar is the modern reader with the sleuths of this era? And such an extraordinary group they were, including in their numbers an unassuming English priest, a blind man, a master of disguises, a lecturer in medical jurisprudence, a noble woman working for Scotland Yard, and a savant so brilliant he was known as "The Thinking Machine."

To introduce readers to these detectives, Resurrected Press has assembled a collection of stories featuring these and other remarkable sleuths in The Edwardian Detectives.

- The Case of Laker, Absconded by Arthur Morrison
- The Fenchurch Street Mystery by Baroness Orczy
- The Crime of the French Café by Nick Carter
- The Man with Nailed Shoes by R Austin Freeman
- The Blue Cross by G. K. Chesterton
- The Case of the Pocket Diary Found in the Snow by Augusta Groner
- The Ninescore Mystery by Baroness Orczy
- The Riddle of the Ninth Finger by Thomas W. Hanshew
- The Knight's Cross Signal Problem by Ernest Bramah

- The Problem of Cell 13 by Jacques Futrelle
- The Conundrum of the Golf Links by Percy James Brebner
- The Silkworms of Florence by Clifford Ashdown
- The Gateway of the Monster by William Hope Hodgson
- The Affair at the Semiramis Hotel by A. E. W. Mason
- The Affair of the Avalanche Bicycle & Tyre Co., LTD by Arthur Morrison

RESURRECTED PRESS CLASSIC MYSTERY CATALOGUE

Journeys into Mystery
Travel and Mystery in a More Elegant Time

The Edwardian Detectives
Literary Sleuths of the Edwardian Era

Gems of Mystery
Lost Jewels from a More Elegant Age

E. C. Bentley
Trent's Last Case: The Woman in Black

Ernest Bramah
Max Carrados Resurrected:
The Detective Stories of Max Carrados

Agatha Christie
The Secret Adversary
The Mysterious Affair at Styles

Octavus Roy Cohen
Midnight

Freeman Wills Croft
The Ponson Case
The Pit Prop Syndicate

J. S. Fletcher
The Herapath Property
The Rayner-Slade Amalgamation
The Chestermarke Instinct
The Paradise Mystery
Dead Men's Money

The Middle of Things
Ravensdene Court
Scarhaven Keep
The Orange-Yellow Diamond
The Middle Temple Murder
The Tallyrand Maxim
The Borough Treasurer
In the Mayor's Parlour
The Saftey Pin

R. Austin Freeman
*The Mystery of 31 New Inn from the Dr. Thorndyke
Series*
*John Thorndyke's Cases from the Dr. Thorndyke
Series*
The Red Thumb Mark from The Dr. Thorndyke Series
The Eye of Osiris from The Dr. Thorndyke Series
A Silent Witness from the Dr. John Thorndyke Series
The Cat's Eye from the Dr. John Thorndyke Series
*Helen Vardon's Confession: A Dr. John Thorndyke
Story*
As a Thief in the Night: A Dr. John Thorndyke Story
*Mr. Pottermack's Oversight: A Dr. John Thorndyke
Story*
*Dr. Thorndyke Intervenes: A Dr. John Thorndyke
Story*
The Singing Bone: The Adventures of Dr. Thorndyke
The Stoneware Monkey: A Dr. John Thorndyke Story
*The Great Portrait Mystery, and Other Stories: A
Collection of Dr. John Thorndyke and Other Stories*
The Penrose Mystery: A Dr. John Thorndyke Story
The Uttermost Farthing: A Savant's Vendetta

Arthur Griffiths
The Passenger From Calais
The Rome Express

Fergus Hume
The Mystery of a Hansom Cab
The Green Mummy
The Silent House
The Secret Passage

Edgar Jepson
The Loudwater Mystery

A. E. W. Mason
At the Villa Rose

A. A. Milne
The Red House Mystery
Baroness Emma Orczy
The Old Man in the Corner

Edgar Allan Poe
The Detective Stories of Edgar Allan Poe

Arthur J. Rees
The Hampstead Mystery
The Shrieking Pit
The Hand In The Dark
The Moon Rock
The Mystery of the Downs

Mary Roberts Rinehart
Sight Unseen and The Confession

Dorothy L. Sayers
Whose Body?

Sir William Magnay
The Hunt Ball Mystery

Mabel and Paul Thorne
The Sheridan Road Mystery

Louis Tracy
The Strange Case of Mortimer Fenley
The Albert Gate Mystery
The Bartlett Mystery
The Postmaster's Daughter
The House of Peril
The Sandling Case: What Would You Have Done?
Charles Edmonds Walk
The Paternoster Ruby

John R. Watson
The Mystery of the Downs
The Hampstead Mystery

Edgar Wallace
The Daffodil Mystery
The Crimson Circle

Carolyn Wells
Vicky Van
The Man Who Fell Through the Earth
In the Onyx Lobby
Raspberry Jam
The Clue
The Room with the Tassels
The Vanishing of Betty Varian
The Mystery Girl
The White Alley
The Curved Blades
Anybody but Anne
The Bride of a Moment
Faulkner's Folly
The Diamond Pin
The Gold Bag
The Mystery of the Sycamore
The Come Backy

Raoul Whitfield
Death in a Bowl

And much more!
Visit ResurrectedPress.com
for our complete catalogue

About Resurrected Press

A division of Intrepid Ink, LLC, Resurrected Press is dedicated to bringing high quality, vintage books back into publication. See our entire catalogue and find out more at www.ResurrectedPress.com.

About Intrepid Ink, LLC

Intrepid Ink, LLC provides full publishing services to authors of fiction and non-fiction books, eBooks and websites. From editing to formatting, from publishing to marketing, Intrepid Ink gets your creative works into the hands of the people who want to read them. Find out more at www.IntrepidInk.com.

Made in the USA
Las Vegas, NV
03 February 2022

43018731R00154